KU-605-655

THE DEVIL'S CHAIR

Priscilla Masters

severn
House

This first world edition published 2014
in Great Britain and in the USA by
SEVERN HOUSE PUBLISHERS LTD of
19 Cedar Road, Sutton, Surrey, England, SM2 5DA.

Copyright © 2014 by Priscilla Masters.

All rights reserved.
The moral right of the author has been asserted.

British Library Cataloguing in Publication Data

Masters, Priscilla
  The Devil's Chair. – (The Martha Gunn mystery series)
  1. Gunn, Martha (Fictitious character)–Fiction.
  2. Randall, Alex (Fictitious character)–Fiction.
  3. Shrewsbury (England)–Fiction. 4. Missing children–
  Fiction. 5. Detective and mystery stories.
  I. Title II. Series
  823.9'2-dc23

ISBN-13: 978-1-8475-1834-7

Except where actual historical events and characters are being
described for the storyline of this novel, all situations in this
publication are fictitious and any resemblance to living persons
is purely coincidental.

Typeset by Palimpsest Book Production Ltd.,
Falkirk, Stirlingshire, Scotland.

To all my friends and colleagues at the Royal Shrewsbury Hospital – I'm going to miss you. And particularly Ana Ireland, office sharer. Thanks for the book about Church Stretton.

'Happy families are all alike; every unhappy family is unhappy in its own way.'

Leo Tolstoy, *Anna Karenina*

PROLOGUE

O *ver my fireplace hangs a painting. It is a very old work,
painted in the sixteenth century and unsigned. I have mused
about this and come to a conclusion: perhaps it is unsigned
because the artist, competent though he undoubtedly was, was not
quite comfortable with the subject. So why was he painting it, you
may ask. Was someone paying him handsomely for his skill in
portraying such a scene?*

I have often wondered as I have sat in my armchair and looked up.

*It is graphic, painted using dingy oils, on an oak panel. A beech-
wood frame surrounds it, which is probably the original. There are
numerous woodworm holes. The shape of the Devil's Chair, in the
background, though very dark, is easy to recognize, so there is no
doubt of its geographical location. One wonders, in its five-hundred-
year-old story, where it has hung. Not in a school or a church, that
is for certain. Its subject matter and title would preclude it from
most, if not all, public places. So I have come to the conclusion
that my picture has probably lived out its life in a place very much
like its location today. Hanging over a fireplace, in a private home,
where its owner can gloat over its subject matter alone and without
witness.*

*I say the painting is graphic. It is exactly that. There are a variety
of expressions on its subjects' faces. The innocent babies, not
knowing for what purpose they have this attention, are wide-eyed
and curious. The older children, however, are more cognisant. They
look anxious; one in particular looks frightened. He is a small boy
with large, dark eyes and the sallow complexion of an Italian.
Perhaps that is a clue to the painter's origins. I don't know. The
boy's mouth is open as, still running, he looks behind him. Fear
etches a line of worry across his young forehead. A small girl has
tripped over her long skirt and lies sprawling in the mud, her face
pressed down hard into the dirt. And even though her features are
completely hidden – you cannot tell if she is pretty or one of nature's
plain children – one can still interpret her terror because her skinny
little shoulders dig into the dirt as though she is trying to bury*

herself into her own grave. From what are the children running, those that are able, you may ask. The babies and toddlers are frozen, for all but the very youngest child knows that above them, behind them, racing towards them, flies evil. One can read it in the crone's face, intent on her ghastly business. Her eyes are burning coals, her mouth toothless, her body scrawny. She is, in many ways, exactly as we would all imagine her.

Not all who flee are children. There is one old man who looks back in terror, his bony knees seeming to shake on the canvas. Is he one of them? Does she want him too? Why? The answer lies beneath. I have said that the painting is not signed. Who would own to spending such time finding this hideous idea, selecting the right brush, the right strokes, the right colours even? No one would own to this but the title, skilfully brushed in below, proclaims itself without bashfulness in letters which are easy to read.

Harvesting the unbaptized.

ONE

Sunday, 7 April, 2 a.m.
Church Stretton, Shropshire.

She didn't believe the stories. It was all nonsense. Meant to frighten people and keep them away. She glanced in the back of the car. Daisy's eyes were wide open. She was too terrified to cry. She clutched the sodden Jellycat squirrel and kept sucking it, which annoyed Tracy even more. Bloody kid.

The child's dressing gown flopped open. In her haste, Tracy hadn't tied it. And she would have sworn that the little sod had wet her new pyjamas. She turned her attention back to the treacherous road. Shit. She didn't dare look down. Too far to fall. But she was going to do this, she was going to get there. She smiled at herself and peered into the gloom. She was going up there. All the way to the top. And then some.

In the back Daisy sniffed and Tracy took her eyes off the road for a second. 'Oh, shut up,' she said. 'Just put a sock in it, will you?'

She turned around and for a second – just a second – she had a pang of guilt. She shouldn't be doing this.

Then she squared her shoulders. She would see this through. She'd show him. She could leave him behind. She didn't need him. She glanced up. The top was shrouded in mist. She almost laughed at her stupid superstition. Of course the Devil wasn't sitting in his chair. The child's eyes were still wide open and she sucked the soft grubby toy even more noisily. Tracy jabbed her foot down hard on the accelerator. The vehicle wasn't a powerful one. It was a tired old VW which had done more than the mileage necessary to justify its existence. But Tracy had a fondness for it because its registration letter was T. It struggled with the steep hill, whining in protest. Whining like the child. Tracy sucked in a long, deep breath. She simply couldn't stand it. The car whined, the child whined, Neil whined. She checked the rear-view mirror then focused on the scene outside. She'd climbed as high as an eagle's nest. An eyrie, she believed they called it. She spluttered to herself, amused at the joke.

Eerie it bloody well was. She hiccupped with humour and peered through the windscreen again. Eerie. And as black as the grave. The car lurched, complaining. She forced the accelerator down again and continued to peer through the windscreen, trying to penetrate the mist. God, it was empty around here. There was no one. No one but herself, the child, the Devil and his demons. And up here in this godforsaken place one could believe in it all. Tracy gave a snort. Ever since she'd been a kid she'd been threatened with being abandoned up here, on the Long Mynd, food for the Devil and his imps. And now?

Bang.

She stopped dead. Then she looked up, out of the windscreen. What the . . . ?

It wasn't possible. No.

Tracy tried to put the car in reverse but the engine screamed in mechanical protest. And she joined the car in its screaming terror as she felt the wheels slide backwards.

TWO

Saturday, 6 April, 11.50 p.m.
Two hours, ten minutes earlier.

It had been a typical evening, an evening of sour bickering, of veiled threats, and as the evening wore on and their blood alcohol levels slowly crept up, the threats and insults became less veiled and more aggressive. Even the TV remote control was the subject of a war.

'Give me that.'

'No. I don't want to watch football. Let's see a film.'

Neil's mood was as bad as his breath. 'Oh, piss off, Tracy. Give it here.'

He lumbered towards her and she screamed. 'Get away from me, you brute! I bet you wouldn't treat your beloved Lucy like that.'

Neil Mansfield hovered over her, swaying slightly as though on the deck of a ship. 'She isn't my beloved Lucy. She's just . . .'

'A client?' she mocked, her voice high and tight. 'Just like I was,

Neil? You think I don't know what's going on?' She sank back into the sofa, her face thin and hard. Her smile was a mirthless gash in it. 'Some people never learn, do they?'

Mansfield returned to his chair, reached for another lager, drank glumly and lit another foul-tasting cigarette. What else was there to do? From somewhere, maybe way back in his English literature GCSE, he dragged up a quote. 'Happy families are all alike; every unhappy family is unhappy in its own way.'

Bollocks, Mr Tolstoy, he thought, his mouth twisting. All *unhappy* families resemble each other too. There's always rows, Mr Tolstoy. There's always alcohol, Mr T. There's always violence, Leo. And there's usually some poor little kid stuck right in the middle.

THREE

Sunday, 7 April, 6 a.m.

'Which service do you require?' The girl was bored. Saturday nights/Sunday mornings were the worst. Lots of drunks and pranksters, relatives concerned about an elderly mother or father, people panicking with chest pain or breathlessness or sometimes simply the lonely, desperate for someone to talk to so they would dial the magic number. Then there were the teenagers 'missing' – not back when they said they'd be. Sian's lip curled. When were they ever? And so they dialled the number: the number that was always picked up and met with a human response rather than a robotic voice assuring you that you are valued, moving your way up an invisible queue and being subjected to hours of dreadful music.

She waited for the caller to make his or her decision.

'Don't rightly know.'

Man or woman?

The caller continued, 'There's a car gorn orf the Burway. Wrecked. Someone's inside 'urt. A woman.'

Sian's hand immediately pressed fire engine, ambulance and police. *Ring-a-ding-ding.* This would get the lot. She knew the Burway, had watched her father back gingerly into a passing place and almost swallowed her heart as she'd looked down the long, steep drop into Carding Mill Valley below.

'Is the woman still breathing?'

'Aaagh.'

'I need your name and contact details.'

There was no response.

Sian glanced at the caller ID. It was a landline. Good. That would make identifying the caller easier. As she tapped out the details into the computer, she smiled to herself. It never failed to surprise her how many callers were reluctant to reveal their identity. She tried again. 'I need your name, caller.'

Again, no answer. She glanced at her screen. He, or was it a she, was still on the line. She tried once more. 'Is the woman in the car conscious?'

The question provoked a chuckle. 'You'll have to come and see tha-at for yourselves.' Sian gave a deep, exasperated sigh. How could anyone even think this was remotely funny?

Try doing my job, wanker.

She tried again. Her performance would be monitored. 'Is the person alive?'

This time not only was there no answer but the caller had hung up. The screen was now blank.

Great, Sian thought. If this was a hoax she would personally make sure *the caller* paid a ruddy great big fine.

Sunday, 7 April, 11.30 a.m.

Afterwards, Neil would try and grasp the memories but they were hazy, unclear with large black patches preventing continuity, slippery as eels. If he closed his eyes he could see Tracy's drunken fury, her repeated accusations about him and Lucy. Shouting rang in his ears. The smell of alcohol, of stale cigarettes. And then the piercing scream of the child as her mother raised her from the cot. He squeezed his eyes tight shut. He needed to clean his teeth. Another scene: Tracy running up the stairs. *Thump, thump, thump*, anger in every step. The child's screams melting into pathetic crying. And then, abruptly, *silence*.

Then *thump, thump, thump*. She was coming back down the stairs. In her arms was the child, in a pink dressing gown.

He stretched out his arms for her. 'Daisy,' he said softly. 'Daisy.'

But Tracy whirled past him like a banshee, the child struggling, holding her arms out back to him. He thought he heard Tracy say the name of her friend, Wanda.

Another blank patch. Somehow he was outside, in the road, reasoning with her, pleading with her. *You're not fit to drive. At least leave Daisy behind.* And then . . . The car door slammed. The door frame swallowed him up. He fell backwards into the house, still trying to reason with the empty room.

'Don't go,' he said. 'Come back here.'

And then the sofa curled him up into her arms.

He was vaguely aware of the child's fright and felt a fizz of anger. Trace could do what she liked, his angry, fuzzed-up brain insisted. But Daisy, well, that was different. She was just a kid.

It was his last coherent thought. The last thing he remembered hearing was the hollow slamming of a second car door and then an engine revving up too hard.

FOUR

Monday, 8 April, 8.30 a.m.

The day had started with a chilly drizzle that shrouded the approaching spring and mocked the citizens of Shropshire, reminding them that winter was a ghost always chasing behind them and spring was out of arm's reach. They could not have it – yet. The spectre of the ghost was gaining on them however hard they ran.

Maybe this year spring would not come at all; neither would summer. Like Narnia under the grip of the white witch, it would remain forever winter.

Just to rub it in, on the great rounded hump of the Long Mynd it had snowed early on Sunday morning. A light powdering iced its summit, turning it into a huge round cupcake. This, of course, was a great challenge to climbers. The intrepid would have climbed right into the snowline and beyond except that the police had closed down the entire area. Late Saturday night/early Sunday morning it had been the scene of a serious car crash. The driver was in a coma in hospital.

Monday, 8 April, 9 a.m.
The coroner's office, Bayston Hill, Shrewsbury.

Martha could always tell from Jericho's demeanour when he had important information to 'impart'. (Impart being one of his favourite words, usually said with intense emphasis and deliberation). However, this morning was patently *not* one of those mornings, Martha observed as she walked through the door. Jericho obviously had little to *impart* and it was visibly pissing him off. His head jutted forwards, his chin on his chest, his shoulders bowed and his face contorted into a deep and sullen scowl. Martha had seen this before. This was Jericho sulking because he was not 'in the know'.

She smothered a smile as she closed the door softly behind her. Her officer was so easy to read. 'Good morning, Jericho,' she said briskly.

He hardly looked at her. 'Mrs Gunn,' he mumbled and she eyed him. This was a real and very deep sulk.

She waited. Jericho was not great at keeping secrets. He would soon spill the beans. And so he did.

'Car rolled down the Burway late Saturday night, early Sunday morning,' he said, almost accusingly. 'I heard it this morning on Radio Shropshire.'

Oh, this was a disaster. For Jericho to learn of such dramatic news on the local radio station? Oh dear. No wonder he was in such a deep and intractable sulk.

She cast her mind back to Saturday night. It had been a wet, cold spring night, dark before eight, the weather threatening a terrible summer even before it had begun, with whispers of dark events lurking in the future: floods and landslips, disasters that were brewing in the clouds, waiting to drop on an unsuspecting, vulnerable, but ever-optimistic population who dreamed of the balmy season promised in the word *summer.* But the word altered in meaning when you inserted the adjective *British* in front of it. On Saturday night she had been glad to draw the curtains to shut out the mist that tried to roll right into the house and, in spite of the month, she had lit the log burner. Some time during the night there must have been a drop in temperature. By Sunday morning the damp rain had turned into treacherous ice and on higher ground a powdering of snow.

'Little girl's missin',' Jericho continued. 'Seems to have vanished into thin air. They's been lookin' for her all through yesterday. No sign of the child.'

'And the driver?'

'Drunk, they say. *She's* in intensive care,' Jericho deliberated, 'in a coma.'

Martha hid a grimace. Ah . . . so this explained it even clearer. A woman in intensive care was not yet a candidate for the coroner – or for her assistant. Once she had reached the haven of the hospital staff who were trained to pull people back from *the brink*, the chances increased that their driver would survive. And Jericho would feel he had been cheated. She eyed him closely and read resentment in his eyes – and something more. His eyes were not quite meeting hers, and his face had a heaviness about it that wasn't explained by the car wreck followed by a hospital admission. Her curiosity was stirred. She herself knew nothing. After the rigours of the working week she had long ago decided that Sundays were to be a family day and news-free, whether the events were good or bad. So unless there had been a major catastrophe on a Sunday she would remain unaware of it until arriving at an empty office on Monday morning, serenaded on her journey in by Classic FM. She needed, even for one brief and contrived day a week, to see the world as a place of harmony and peace, without grief. It was an old habit, one she had inherited from her mild mannered, chapel-going Welsh father.

Keep Sundays sacred.

So whatever had happened on Saturday night/Sunday morning on the Burway, she knew nothing about it.

But now Jericho would soon *enlighten* her – to the best of his ability.

'She seems to have vanished into thin air,' he said again, his eyes now lifting to hers, still holding a heavy and puzzled grief. 'Daisy, her name is. It were her mum who were driving. Four years old, Mrs Gunn. That's all she was. She were in the car and now she's missing, they say. They can't find 'er anywhere.' He shook his head before continuing. 'People's been lookin' since early yesterday mornin'.' He paused for breath before speaking again, his frown deepening. 'I'd 'ave joined 'em if I'd known.' He shook his head, his grey locks twitching. 'That Burway.' He practically spat the word out. 'Nasty bit of road that. Narrow and treacherous. Made for accidents.'

'Even late at night when there's unlikely to be much traffic up there?'

'Unlikely. Not impossible.' He paused for a moment. 'When it's misty the Devil himself's sittin' up there in his own chair laughin' at us, it is said, and it would have *bin* misty that early Sunday mornin' round about two a.m.' He glanced quickly across at Martha, wondering how far he could push it before she told him off for his superstition. 'Some say it's Him that deliberately rolls in the mist and the wicked weather to 'ide 'imself when he's sittin' in his chair. It's a devilish place, Mrs Gunn.'

She wanted to scold him, to tell him not to be so ridiculous, but she had driven up the Burway towards the Long Mynd late one evening, not long after Martin had died. The twins had been howling in unison, almost as though they had absorbed some of her grief and feelings of hopelessness and panic. How on earth was she going to cope with life in the future? As they had wailed in misery she had known they would not settle. And so she had strapped them into their car seats and taken them up the Burway to sit on the wild and blustery top and try to calm herself with the huge, 360 degree panoramic view, as though sitting on top of the world would help her. But instead of calming her and the twins they had started screaming even louder, a note of terror in their little voices which had made her aware of the raw menace of the place. She had recalled the ancient legends and had driven back down the narrow, winding road in even more panic. She had not stopped until she had reached home and had not relaxed until the twins had stilled and were safe and asleep in their cots, and all the doors were locked and bolted. Checked twice. Three times. And even then she had fancied that something of the chilly evil of the Long Mynd still seeped underneath the door and clung to the air in the house.

So how could she laugh off Jericho's superstition when she knew how easy it was to believe in myth and magic in such an area?

Jericho carried on, determined to say his piece. He stuck his chin out and put his face close to hers, his eyes bouncing superstitiously off the walls as though he was afraid someone was listening in. 'It might belong to the National Trust these days, Mrs Gunn,' he said in a whisper, 'but that don't civilize a place, do it? You get two stroppy drivers what won't give way on the Burway and you tumbles all the way down to Carding Mill Valley and almost certain death. You'd have to be as lucky as the Reverend Carr to survive that.'

The story of the Reverend E. Donald Carr was an interesting one. It was no myth or legend but the honest and true story of a minister who had walked between his two parishes, Ratlinghope and Wolstaton, over the Long Mynd, and was caught up in a vicious snowstorm. Miraculously, some would say, he had survived in spite of snow blindness and losing his shoes, and was found the next morning by children in Carding Mill Valley who were terrified by the sight of a snow-clad man emerging from the mountain. Encouraged by friends, the Reverend Carr had written down his story of the surreal Disney colours of snow blindness and losing both shoes and gloves, using the frozen body of a mountain pony as a landmark and witnessing hares who bobbed in and out of his vision before he plummeted down near-vertical snow walls clutching his Bible. The story had subsequently entered into the folklore of Church Stretton and the Long Mynd.

'But our driver did survive it,' Martha pointed out. 'She's in hospital.'

'Ah,' Jericho conceded, his eyes gleaming with drama and anticipation, 'she's in intensive care. But the real problem, Mrs Gunn, is where is little Daisy?' He paused for effect before continuing. 'The police and the public have been looking for her for more than a day and a night and they haven't found her. Not so much as a hint of her. So where is she?'

'Is it certain she was in the car?'

'The woman's partner says so.'

'She might have been thrown from the vehicle.'

'She'd have to have been thrown a mighty long way for them not to find 'er. Them's searched the area and is still searching,' Jericho said.

'Then they'll find her.'

'Not if—' But even Jericho had the sense not to complete this sentence.

He shrugged and left the room, while Martha crossed to the window. Her view was north, towards the town of Shrewsbury, but in her mind's eye she looked south and saw instead the rounded humps of the Long Mynd rising from the Shropshire plain like whales basking in a flat sea rather than, as legend suggested, piles of earth dropped by an angry giant. Though sometimes it is easier to believe in myth rather than the fact that the Shropshire hills are the result of volcanic activity millions of years ago. Martha stood for a moment, tossing her thoughts around, recalling the night when she had imagined herself and the twins exposed to the malevolence of the place, and shivered when contemplating the fate of the little girl. So far, it was another sinister mystery which could be laid at the foot of the Stretton Hills.

Like Jericho, she wondered what had happened to her. She pictured a small body thrown from the car, finally discovered yards from the crash site, and squeezed her eyes shut. Before the days of compulsory child car seats she had known children thrown up to eight hundred yards from the point of impact. The origin of the 'Child on Board' notices was a tragic crash where the children had not been found until the next day, dead not from the impact but exposure after being thrown over a hedge into a field. In the inquests she had held on children who had not been strapped in she had been torn between sympathy for the parents and anger at their neglect. In such cases she could never point the finger but she had read in their guilty faces that she did not need to. They'd pointed the finger at themselves.

'Daisy,' she muttered to herself, liking the name and mentally preparing herself to meet the little girl in tragic circumstances. She knew the drop from the Burway into Carding Mill Valley. A four-year-old could hardly have survived such trauma if she'd been thrown from the car, nor a second night out on the Long Mynd, undiscovered by increasingly desperate and despondent searchers. But then, even if Daisy had been strapped into her car seat, she still might not have survived the impact.

Her eyes lost their focus and her mind shifted to the driver, the mother, who had made it to hospital, and must have driven up one of the most treacherous roads in the county late at night with a small child – drunk, too, if what Jericho said was true.

She turned away from St Mary's Spire, which rose over Shrewsbury. She had enough problems to deal with on a cold spring Monday morning without fretting about two people whose fate may or may not lie in the coroner's court. So she put the events to the back of her mind and concentrated on the morning's work, but her mind disobediently kept wandering back to the puzzle of the missing child. She was relieved when, at lunchtime, Jericho knocked on the door. Instead of calling him in Martha went to open it herself. Jericho Palfreyman was standing there, scowling and making a futile attempt to block the unmistakable, gangly form of Detective Inspector Alex Randall who was standing behind him, eyebrows raised in mute appeal for an audience. She smothered a smile. 'It's all right, Jericho,' she said, trying to keep her face straight and block the gladness she felt at the detective's presence. 'I was going to stop for lunch now anyway.'

Her officer couldn't resist a soft 'harrumph' of disapproval but he stepped back all the same. A moment later Alex was in the room, his restless form bringing turbulence in his wake. He was frowning and she caught some hesitance in his manner. 'Hello, Martha,' he began, then grinned sideways at the door. He was only too well aware of her assistant's antipathy towards him. He was also aware that it stemmed more from protectionism than any real dislike for him personally. A coroner has many demands on her time. Jericho simply tried to minimize them.

Which was his job.

No sooner had she shut her assistant out than the detective began to apologize. He shuffled awkwardly. 'Bit embarrassing this,' he said, 'consulting you when there is no body.' His hazel eyes flicked up to meet hers. 'I know you have more than enough to do without . . .'

'Ah,' she responded, indicating her computer screen where the latest news headlines were displayed. 'The little girl who was taken by the fairies.'

Randall's grey eyes scanned the screen. 'Told you it was embarrassing,' he said drily, then seemed lost for words.

'Well?' she prompted.

'I'm sorry,' he said. 'I know I really shouldn't be bothering you with . . .' His voice trailed away and he tried again. 'I mean, it's nothing to do with . . .'

She took over. 'I take it this visit is connected with the car that rolled down the Burway early on Sunday morning and the little girl who is currently missing?'

Detective Inspector Alex Randall looked relieved. 'It is,' he said quietly, his mouth still open as though ready to continue.

It was obvious that he needed to unburden himself.

'Then sit,' she invited. She sat down in one of the two armchairs in the bay window, Alex in the other. Somehow the town of Shrewsbury, with its violent and dramatic history seemed a fitting backdrop for his story, witness as it had been to such dramas. 'Fill me in.'

She was fully aware that the detective would be confiding in her facts about the case that were not in the public domain. She was equally aware that he hadn't paid her the insult of asking her to keep these facts quiet.

'OK,' he said, relaxing a little. 'Briefly. We have Tracy Walsh, the thirty-two-year-old partner of forty-year-old Neil Mansfield. They've been together for two years.'

Martha interrupted. 'Neil Mansfield is not Daisy's father, then?'

'No. Tracy had actually been married, briefly, to Daisy's father, an Allistair Donaldson, but the couple split up not long after Daisy was born. Daisy has her mother's surname, which Tracy reverted to on the break-up of her marriage. Donaldson lives near Inverness. He's a fish farmer and has had little to do with his daughter. According to the local Scottish bobby who interviewed him his contact was little more than a tenner at Christmas. Tracy had had a few partners since Allistair but she and Neil met two years ago and have lived together for a little over a year. It is, apparently, a volatile relationship. They live in Church Stretton and are well known for their public drunken arguments. The local police have been called in several times.' He sighed. 'And as is usual in these cases, Piggy in the Middle is little Daisy, four years old, not surprisingly a rather quiet, withdrawn little girl.' He looked up, his eyes soft, knowing she would want his sources. 'Again, according to the neighbours. Anyway . . .' He sighed. 'On Saturday night the couple had yet another drunken argument after a bout of drinking that had started at lunchtime.' His eyes met hers in weary cynicism. 'They were pissed out of their brains. Tracy's blood alcohol level was three hundred milligrams and that was hours after she'd left the house. No alcohol was found in the car so . . .' He left her to draw her own conclusion.

'Crikey. Three hundred milligrams? That's quite a few ciders,' Martha commented.

'Yeah. And somewhere nearing four times the legal driving limit,' Alex said. He continued: 'At sometime around two in the morning Tracy runs upstairs and grabs her daughter, saying she's had enough of Neil and is leaving him – she's going to stay with a friend. She takes the car up the Burway towards the Long Mynd and the rest . . .' He opened his palms. It was as though he had run out of words.

'What about Neil? Why didn't he try to stop her?'

'He says he thinks he did – before he passed out. He pleaded with her to leave Daisy with him.' A shadow crossed Randall's face. 'He says he was *going* to ring the police but . . .' He shrugged, his face bleak. 'It's an awful story,' he said, 'but not exactly uncommon.'

Martha put a hand up as though to ward off his words and the images they conveyed. 'Don't,' she said. Then, 'So where does Neil Mansfield think she was heading?'

'She has a friend, a girl called Wanda. He thought he heard her name being mentioned. Those two are pretty thick. Wanda lives in Ratlinghope. It's possible she was heading for there,' he paused, 'but never made it.'

Martha eyed him. There was something else. She waited, knowing her silence would give him the opportunity to say what was really troubling him.

'There are some puzzling facts,' he continued quietly. 'In fact, the entire event is a series of anomalies.' His eyes met hers. 'I'll start with what we know for certain. The accident was reported somewhere around six on Sunday morning.'

'Yes?'

'The call was made from a local cottage.' He gave a twisted smile. 'Hope Cottage.'

Martha was bemused. 'What's so puzzling about that?'

'The cottage was empty at the time,' Randall continued. 'It belongs to a single woman who works mostly abroad. Her name's Charity Ignatio and she's currently in Dubai. Last night she was at a public dinner in the city. I've spoken to her this morning and she has assured me that when she is away no one goes into her cottage. Not even her cleaner. So . . .' His eyes locked into hers. 'Who made the phone call? Who reported the accident?'

Martha made no comment, so he continued: 'When the local police and air ambulance arrived the car was surrounded by a group of girls doing their Duke of Edinburgh Award. Wisely, they hadn't tried to remove Tracy from the car. She was unconscious at the time with a broken neck, a head injury and various other broken bones.' Alex looked less than sympathetic. 'Daisy,' he said gravely, 'is still missing. There is absolutely no sign of her. The Duke of Edinburgh girls plus members of the general public familiar with the Stretton Hills have helped us look for the little girl but we haven't found her.' He leaned forward, his face strained. 'She's vanished,' he said simply, baffled.

'Could she have survived the accident and wandered off?'

Alex sat back in his seat, watching her from beneath lowered lids. 'Of course, it's possible, Martha,' he said, 'but we've searched every square mile of that immediate area. She's only four years old and would have been in shock. Possibly injured. The people who have helped us search know these hills, the valleys, the streams and the vegetation like the back of their hands. They could walk it blindfold. We've found a soft toy but have yet to identify it as Daisy's.'

'Then is it certain she was in the car in the first place?'

Randall's expression was grave. 'According to Neil.' And she could hear the doubt in his voice.

'Well, Alex,' she said softly, 'you know the old adage: "When you've discounted the impossible, whatever remains . . ."'

'However improbable.' He looked up, a hint of a smile softening his features. 'She *hasn't* been taken by fairies, Martha, as one of the locals, a Mr Faulkener, has suggested.'

'No,' she agreed.

'Or the Devil.'

She shook her head. 'Not him either.'

His eyes were pleading with her for some rational explanation.

'Well,' she said, bound to respond to the detective, 'call me a pedant but it would seem to me that whoever made the phone call has Daisy.' She hesitated, before adding, with concern harshening her voice, 'Who may well be injured. Was the caller a man or a woman?'

'A woman, the call centre girl thinks.'

'Thinks?'

'She thought a woman with a gruff voice but it could have been a man.'

'What *exactly* did the caller say?'

'That there was a car,' he gave an apologetic smile, '*gorn orf* the Burway and that a woman was hurt.'

Martha frowned. 'Someone,' she repeated. 'Not two people or anything suggesting a child was in the car?'

'No. There was no mention of the child.'

'I assume the caller didn't leave a name?'

'Correct. Until we called at the place and found out the facts we just *assumed* the caller was the owner of Hope Cottage. We were busy with the rescue operation so didn't check out Hope Cottage for some hours.'

Randall stopped speaking for a moment. He was frowning and looking out of the window, as though searching in the town for some clue. 'There is something else,' he said reluctantly. 'The tyre tracks.'

'Go on.'

'Tracy drove up the hill, it would appear, at quite a lick. There are fresh tyre marks around one or two of the corners. Obviously, at that time of night, she wouldn't have expected to meet another car. Fact is she probably wasn't in a state to care much. But whatever her mental state she came to an abrupt halt and started reversing madly as though she was panicked about something.'

'Perhaps the drink overwhelmed her so she changed her mind?' Martha suggested gently, 'and thought she'd go home after all.'

'It's possible. The tyre marks veer all over the road so I suppose we can't rely on her acting rationally.'

Martha caught the doubt in his voice. 'But?'

'It was an emergency stop. There was quite a bit of tyre left on the road. She went into a skid then reversed. That's when and why she slipped and fell into the valley.' He made an attempt at levity. 'Reversing on a notoriously dangerous road when drunk as a skunk is never a good idea.'

'No.'

He obviously felt he needed to emphasize this point. 'The marks on the road suggest she made an emergency stop as though something was blocking her way forward.'

'Another car, perhaps?'

'There were no marks of another car. We've put boards out and made appeals on local radio and TV. No one's come forward to say they were on the Burway Sunday morning around two a.m.'

His eyes met hers. 'Anyway,' he said, 'whatever the reason that Tracy Walsh lost control of the car it left the road, rolled over and over down into Carding Mill Valley and finally came to rest on its roof.'

Martha was thoughtful for a moment. Then she started firing questions at him. *Rat-a-tat-tat*. 'The child's safety seat,' she began.

'Yes?'

'Was the buckle open or fastened?'

Randall's eyes gleamed. This was exactly why he had left the scene of the investigation and come here. 'Open.'

'Was there blood on it?'

'No,' he said cautiously, 'but there was blood on the back of the seat in front and some inside the roof of the car. We've taken samples for DNA and will be analysing all the bloodstains.'

'Sorry, Alex.' She apologized in advance of asking: 'There's no chance she's *underneath* the car, is there?' She didn't really think so. Alex Randall was a thorough and intelligent officer but she had to explore all possibilities.

'No,' he said. 'When the fire service cut Tracy out they lifted the vehicle. Daisy wasn't underneath.'

'Toys? Did she have a favourite toy that was always with her?'

'A Jellycat squirrel, according to Neil.' Alex made a face. 'If it's the one we found at the scene it's a horrible brown smelly thing.' His eyes clouded with an apparent stab of a memory.

'They always are,' Martha said, without noticing the detective's wince. She was recalling the twins at three years old. They too had had a soft toy, sucked to bits, grubby and smelly. Baba. They could never sleep without it.

Alex's next words brought her back to the present. 'We found one like it in a bush a hundred yards away from the car, but as I say, we aren't certain it's Daisy's.'

She wanted to say, *If it is, then Daisy cannot be not far away*, but it would have seemed crass. Detective Inspector Alex Randall was a senior officer. He and his team would not have overlooked a child's body. So, after staring at him for a few minutes, she substituted what she had wanted to say with: 'Tell me about Neil Mansfield.'

Randall made a face. 'He's not such a bad bloke. He works as a painter and decorator – quite hard – all hours. People speak well of him.'

'How old is he again?'

'Forty. He's been married before. His marriage broke up when he started an affair with Tracy. He was doing some painting for her.'

'Tell me about *her*.'

'From photographs, she's very attractive. Flirty, blonde, vivacious, fun in a tawdry sort of way. According to people who knew her she was sultry, volatile and fiercely jealous, a heavy drinker.' His face clouded. 'Now she's just a thing, breathing via a machine. Anything but vivacious.'

Martha lifted her eyebrows.

Randall's face changed again. 'She's very smashed up now, Martha. Some of her facial bones are broken. She has multiple injuries. Her face is badly cut and bruised. She's currently on life support and would win no beauty competition.'

'What are her chances of survival?'

For the first time since he'd arrived, Alex grinned, though only for a second. 'You know doctors, Martha. I can't get a straight answer out of them but things don't look good to me.'

'And Neil, has he visited her?'

Again, he felt that her point was significant. He shook his head. 'Not yet. He's waiting at the house in case . . .' He didn't need to finish the sentence.

'Did anyone else see Daisy in the car that night?'

Randall shook his head. 'We have some CCTV footage of the vehicle travelling up the High Street in Stretton. We can just about make out Tracy but we can't tell if Daisy is in the back or not.'

'So it *is* possible that Daisy was never in the car?'

'Possible, yes. Some officers are having a go at enhancing the images, though, well, I'm not too hopeful. But the little toy, Martha, if it is hers . . . Surely that points to her having been in the vehicle? Neil says she was never without it.'

'Well, she is now.'

It was a sobering thought. They were both silent, Martha recalling Sukey's screams when she had mislaid her Baba.

'I take it you've checked the house where the couple lived?'

'Superficially. Yes.'

'And Hope Cottage – have you been inside?'

'It's locked up,' he said. 'We've looked through the windows and shouted through the letterbox but it's almost a mile from the crash scene. The weather's been so cold. I can't see a four-year-old child managing the distance.'

'Your caller might have carried her.' She regarded him with concern.

He added, 'We're getting in touch with the owner to see who has a key and gain access.'

'The cleaner – surely?'

'She's on holiday in Spain,' Randall said heavily. 'We can't get hold of her – at least we haven't yet.'

'Do you know what the Saturday night argument was about?'

DI Randall smothered a smile. He was well used to the coroner's interest in cases; how she would direct the topics, examine events from all angles. Upside down, inside out. Back to front. Front to back. 'Again, according to the neighbours – they lived in a semi with very thin walls –' he explained, 'Tracy suspected Neil of having an affair.'

'I see,' Martha said, unsympathetic. 'History repeating itself, then?'

'We haven't broached the subject with him yet,' Randall said. 'It would seem a tad insensitive with his partner so badly injured and the child missing.'

'It isn't like you to worry about being insensitive,' Martha commented drily.

'He isn't a suspect in a crime. I don't need to pry so deeply into his personal life.'

'But you'll be taking the car in for forensics?'

'It's routine in a near, still possibly fatal, crash. The car might have been faulty.'

'But you don't think so.'

'No.'

Neither spoke the words, *or tampered with.*

Instead Martha continued, 'And Neil didn't pursue Tracy and the little girl?'

Randall opened his notebook. 'He said, and I quote, "We'd both had a fair bit to drink. Tracy ran up the stairs. I didn't know what for. I thought maybe to be sick or go to the loo but she came running back down with little Daisy in her arms. I tried to stop her but off she goes, blasting into the night. It was two in the morning. I'd had a shedful. I was in no fit state to go in hot pursuit. Last thing I remember is crashing out on the sofa. I woke up the next morning with a sore head."'

'I don't suppose for a minute that you checked *his* blood alcohol level?'

'Didn't need to,' Randall said with a smirk. 'I could smell it right across the room. His hands were shaking and his breath was pure booze. But he wasn't driving anyway and he'd admitted having a drink. We had no reason to breathalyse him.'

Martha nodded.

He paraphrased the contents of his notebook. 'He half thought that Tracy would go around the block and then come back, tail between her legs. She'd done it before but as he came round the next morning he realized that she wasn't back. He tried her mobile phone but it went straight through to answer phone. He started ringing round friends and relatives, including Wanda Stefano, the friend Tracy had mentioned. When he got no joy there he rang us. By that time we'd got the call about the car and were already on the scene.'

Martha thought for a moment. 'Apart from the mystery person who phoned, who else was first on the scene?'

'When the squad car got to Carding Mill Valley the car was surrounded by the party of youngsters doing their Duke of Edinburgh Award. They'd camped out the night a little further up the valley. It was about a quarter past six by then.'

'When they got there did they see anyone else?'

'No – they said the place was deserted.'

'Did the D of E girls hear anything in the night?'

'They weren't sure. Most of them said they'd slept really soundly as they'd done a fifteen-mile hike the day before. And their camp site was about half a mile from the crash site.'

'Was Tracy wearing her seat belt?'

'According to our preliminary forensic accident investigators she must have been. If she'd not been wearing one she would have exited the car either through the windscreen or through the side or rear window depending on the roll. The vehicle might even have landed on top of her. She'd have to be very lucky to have survived that.'

'Tell me about Hope Cottage, where the phone call was made.'

'It's a lovely place – Victorian stone and pretty as a picture but you'd need a four-wheel drive to live there. It's reached by a muddy track and must get cut off by heavy snowfall or even heavy rain. The trade-off for the inconvenience is its views across the valley, which are wonderful, and its sheer isolation.'

'Isolation? Carding Mill Valley?' Martha queried. 'You must be joking. Every time I've been there it's been packed.'

'Weekends maybe but in the week and out of season it's quite peaceful.'

'What about the D of E students camping?'

'Well, those too,' Randall conceded.

'I take it none of the students has admitted entering the cottage and making the call?'

'No.'

'Is there any sign that Hope Cottage was broken into?'

'No.'

Martha stood up, stared out of the window and then said softly, 'You must find her, Alex.'

And he stood behind her, close enough for her to sense his nearness. 'I'd like to promise we will,' he said softly, 'but I've learned not to make promises I might not be able to keep.'

And before she had a chance to turn around and face him, he had gone.

FIVE

Monday, 8 April, 2 p.m.

Detective Sergeant Paul Talith parked neatly on the road and tugged open the gate, which not only sagged but badly needed a lick of paint. He and his wife, Diana, had recently moved house and Talith was gaining an interest not only in football, which had always been his abiding passion, but in DIY, so he was particularly noticing things like a gate that needed a paint job and a new hinge.

Tracy and Neil had lived with Daisy in a sixties' semi which also needed a total makeover: it had peeling paintwork and a gutter which had leaked down the walls leaving a long, mossy stain. Talith's interest in home building extended to the garden and he scanned this area too with a critical eye. Unlike others in the row, the front garden was messy. A few optimistic daffodils poked cheerfully through a lawn that was sadly neglected, weedy with bare mud patches and more than its fair share of moss. The path was a series of concrete slabs which lurched drunkenly towards the front door.

Talith pursed his lips in disapproval, lifted a meaty fist and banged hard, making WPC Lara Tinsley almost jump out of her skin. The door opened. With reluctance, it seemed, almost on a ratchet, one stiff inch at a time.

Whatever the misgivings Talith might have had about Neil Mansfield's home-caring skills there was no doubt that his world had been turned upside down by recent events. He was a plump, lazy-looking man of medium height with a beer gut which bulged the size of an eight-month pregnancy. He was tidily dressed in a maroon crew-necked sweater and jeans, and he was wearing slippers. His face was lardy pale, very slightly sweaty and sagging with tiredness and grief. He looked unhealthy – a cardiac risk. Again, this was a knowledge and skill Talith had acquired since the mortgage company had advised him to lose weight and quit smoking. He was trying but it was proving much harder than he'd thought. Cigarettes even invaded his dreams, pushing their way between his lips. He would wake with the scent and taste of tobacco in his mouth, feel his lungs dragging in the forbidden smoke and think of a fry-up for breakfast. Talith took a deep breath in and savoured the evocative scent while Neil Mansfield stared back at them, his eyes hollow and haunted. He looked as though he hadn't slept for a week.

'Have you . . .' he asked with eagerness, his eyes sparking for the briefest of moments as he looked from one to the other, only for the spark to extinguish as quickly as it had risen. Even Talith, who was not known for his sentiment, felt a lump in his throat. He simply shook his head with an apologetic, 'Sorry, mate,' quickly followed by a, 'can we come in?'

Mansfield stood back politely, then led the way into a small square sitting room, garish black and orange wallpaper on one wall, the others, mercifully, painted plain cream. The television was on, but the sound was down and they had the feeling that Mansfield hadn't really been watching it. It had been a distraction, something to mop up his ragged senses and fill the gap of emptiness and silence. On-screen people moved and gesticulated and words below added detail. At a quick glance it looked like *The Jeremy Kyle Show*. The people looked angry and there was a baying audience, their jeers felt even through the silence. Mansfield glanced at it, his head tilted to one side, uncomprehending. He'd just wanted to fill the void. With this? Talith was surprised but looking at Neil Mansfield he realized that nothing on the television was penetrating his consciousness. His eyes looked vacant. Spaced out, lost and unhappy. The room smelt stale, testimony to many past nights of alcohol and cigarettes and little fresh air. There was a pungent scent of some plug-in air freshener but it didn't – not really. In the corner, peeping around the edge of the sofa as though it shouldn't really be there, stood a large plastic toy basket. Both officers saw it and immediately shifted their glances away. No one needed a reminder of the missing child. Mansfield passed a hand across his forehead and sank down on the sofa without inviting the two officers to do the same.

They did anyway, dropping heavily into the saggy brown armchairs.

Next to where Mansfield had been sitting a baby doll in a grubby pink Babygro was lying face down. It looked as though Neil Mansfield had been holding it and dropped it when he'd heard them at the door. He looked down at the doll, then up at the police, and shook his head as though he had suddenly come to his senses. 'But I've already . . .' he protested.

'. . . Given us a statement,' Lara Tinsley filled in smoothly, sympathy oozing out of her flat, plain face. 'We know that, Neil. We just want to go over it with you. Why don't you tell us a bit about you and Tracy first? How long have you two been together?' she asked chattily.

It did the trick. Tinsley was adept at putting people at their ease. Besides, people love to talk about themselves and this wasn't a dangerous subject – surely?

After the briefest of pauses Mansfield started up. 'I met her couple of years ago,' he said, before explaining, 'she needed some work doing.' He looked up, a light warming his pleasant brown eyes. 'Her bathroom needed a lick of paint and some tiling.' He smiled. 'You know how awkward some of these little rooms can be. I went along to sort it. And things . . .' Now there was hesitation in his voice. 'Things sort of went from there.'

'You were married at the time?'

Mansfield nodded, shame-faced, and tried to justify his actions. 'Tracy, well, she's a looker, you know. She just about swept me off my feet. I fell in love with her instantly. Daisy, too. She is such a sweet little thing.' His glance dropped to the baby doll and his face sagged even more.

'And your wife at the time?'

Mansfield gave a rueful smile and they knew his romance had cost him dear. 'Karen?' He sucked in a deep breath. 'Took it bad. In fact, bloody livid, she was. Called Tracy all sorts of names – a whore and . . .' His eyes flickered over them. 'I don't want to say stuff . . .' His face looked sad, '. . . but she *was* really angry. Her and the boys, too.'

Talith felt a prickling of interest. 'And is your wife still angry?'

Mansfield shrugged. 'I don't know. I don't have much to do with her now.'

'And your sons?'

'Them neither.' Both officers knew that his apparent disinterest was no more than bravado. Mansfield paused and dropped the facade. 'Unfortunately.' His eyes looked down at the floor and a look of pain contorted his features. 'I didn't think it'd cost me the boys too,' he said with endearing honesty, 'but they've stuck by their mum and, well, there isn't anything I can do. Not really.'

'How old are they?' Lara Tinsley asked.

'Fifteen and thirteen. I thought as they got older and got into girls themselves that they'd maybe understand that I'd been swept off my feet but . . .' His voice trailed away miserably but neither of the two police felt much sympathy for him. It was a common enough scenario.

Talith continued. 'Tell me about your relationship with Tracy.'

As though he had erased the accident from his memory, Neil Mansfield smiled. It turned him into a handsome man, a charmer, one who would be attractive to females. His eyes were warm and friendly. He sat up straight and unconsciously sucked his stomach in. 'She were sparky,' he said. 'Full of fun. Great to be with.'

'But you had a lot of arguments?'

'Yeah. Trace were very jealous, you see. At first she was worried I'd go back to Karen and the boys. She'd shout and scream and threaten all sorts of things.' His face crumpled into a careworn expression, aging twenty years in an instant. And now you could see what Mansfield would look like when he was an old man. Forlorn. Lost. Someone who had taken the wrong road all his life. He rubbed his forehead with his fingertips as though trying to erase the lines of concern and unhappiness, then he looked up, haunted. 'It were . . .' He peered into the air. Began again. 'It was . . . it was hard.' Again he tried to explain further. 'Harder than I'd thought.'

Now they did feel sorry for him, but they had a job to do.

'And Saturday night?'

'Was pretty typical,' Mansfield admitted. 'Trace was in a bad mood. She'd wanted to go out for a curry but we couldn't get a babysitter. Then she . . .' His honest brown eyes flickered around the room and now looked evasive. 'So we had to stay in. I wanted to watch football. The Shrewsbury match was on Sky Sports.' He licked his lips. 'Then Trace starts up. I'd been doing a job for a girl. A woman,' he quickly corrected.

Talith licked the end of his pencil. He sensed quarry nearby. 'Her name?'

'Lucy.'

Talith looked up expectantly. 'Surname?'

'Stanstead. Lucy Stanstead. She lives over in Norbury and I'd been doing some decorating for her. It was taking a bit of time. Longer than I'd thought. Trace wasn't happy about it.' A hint of mischief softened his features. 'It was another tricky job.'

And now both officers recognized him as a serial flirt, a man who loved women – a man who would probably never manage to stay faithful to just one woman but would flit from one to another without any lasting fidelity.

Lara faced him, feeling the bitter taste of hostility. Why were women drawn to these shallow philanderers? Her own husband had had a brief affair. They had 'patched up' their marriage. But what remained was just that, a patched garment. Not quite the same perfect piece of clothing but a poor consolation with an ugly, obtrusive repair that would fool nobody. Her voice was an oil slick as she asked her next question. 'And was there any truth in Tracy's suspicions?'

The evasive look was back. Lara Tinsley had the feeling that Neil Mansfield was about to lie and badly. Any respect or sympathy she might have had for him gurgled down the plughole.

And perhaps Mansfield sensed it because his answer was guarded. 'Not really,' he tried, biting his lip and avoiding looking at her.

WPC Tinsley gave Talith a quick glance. *Not really? What the hell does that mean?*

Talith raised his eyebrows and asked the next question. 'Is this – this Lucy girl – is she married?'

'Yeah.'

Talith and Lara Tinsley exchanged another glance.

Mansfield filled in, awkwardly, 'Her husband's in the navy. He's away a lot.'

'I see,' Talith said heavily.

And the two police officers thought, *So Tracy was probably right.*

'Go on,' Talith prompted.

Mansfield continued to look uncomfortable. 'Look,' he said. 'I can't remember everything. It's all a bit hazy. See?'

Oh, yes. They see all right.

'Trace got in a really bad mood. She was shouting. I think . . . I think Daisy had wet the bed or something and she started crying. Trace went on up to her. She used to get really cross if Daisy wet the bed and she'd drunk a few glasses of wine by then so she were a bit—'

He looked up. 'A bit tetchy, if you know what I mean.' He gave a cynical snort.

'Trace was already a bit fed up with Daisy because she'd sort of stopped us going out. After a bit Daisy started screaming.'

Shock still froze his face at the memory. 'Then Trace came down. She were shoutin' at me. She said somethin' about goin' out, somethin' about goin' to Wanda's.' He sniffed but made a pathetic attempt at jauntiness. 'It were just the drink talking,' he said.

Lara Tinsley spoke. 'Had she threatened to leave you before?'

Mansfield looked ashamed. 'Every day,' he said. He swallowed before continuing. 'I told her she was too pissed to drive. She told me to mind my own business so I had another cider.'

The officers exchanged glances. *Great idea.*

'Next thing I knew, she were comin' down the stairs holdin' Daisy.' He passed his hand over his forehead again and looked bleak. 'I just thought she were bringin' her down to comfort her but she'd wrapped her up in her dressing gown.'

Talith looked up. 'Daisy was in a dressing gown?'

'Yeah.'

'There's been no mention of that before.' He made a note in his pad. 'What colour was it?' He could guess the answer.

'Pink.'

Talith had been right. Had the situation not been so tragic he would have felt smug, given himself a mental pat on the back for reading it so astutely. As it was he simply felt sick. Where was that small pink dressing gown now? Was it stained with blood? Wrapping up the cold corpse of a four-year-old?

Neil looked mystified by such interest in the colour of a child's garment but after the briefest of puzzled pauses he shrugged, sniffed again and continued on with his blurred version of events.

'I thought Trace was probably going to give Daisy a bit of a cuddle but she walked straight past the door.' His eyes drifted towards the doorway as though he half expected to see mother and child still there, waiting for him to notice them. But the hallway yawned empty. There was just a blank wall. Mansfield shook his head in disappointment and continued with his story. 'Next thing I knew I could hear the car startin' up. I couldn't believe it. I couldn't believe she'd drive. I went outside and shouted at her not to be so stupid but she started screamin' at me to leave her alone.' His eyes were wide and confused now. 'I weren't touching her but I thought the police'd be comin' in a minute if we carried on like that. The neighbours, you know. They've done it before – reported us for public disturbance. The police have warned us a couple of times and they always believe the woman so I didn't argue. I just shut up. I didn't think she'd go anyway. I thought it was all a bluff. And if she did take the car I never thought for a minute she'd be so stupid as to go up the Burway.' He heaved a great, sad sigh. 'But, as we know, she did.' His face crumpled. 'Mad cow.' He blew out an angry breath. 'Anyway, she drove off, little Daisy in the back, probably crying, in the car seat. I went to call the police and then I thought *no*. She was well over the limit. She'd be banned. She'd probably lose her job.'

Talith gave Lara Tinsley a swift glance and picked up on the hostility that was hardening her face. He knew his colleague's story only too well. She had been open and quite public, firstly furious with her husband and his 'fancy woman', then grieving, and lastly suspicious. It had been the suspicion which had remained. Back then he'd witnessed all the emotion which he could see reflected in her face now. He felt he should be the one to continue with the questions.

'Where was she heading?' he asked, pen hovering over the pad, ready to scribble.

'Wanda's, I think,' Mansfield said, dislike sharpening his voice. 'Wanda Stefano. She's a troublemaker. Fed Trace all sorts of lies about me.'

'Like what?' Lara asked with the smoothness of a cappuccino.

'Stuff,' Mansfield said grumpily. 'Not a word of truth in it.'

'What sort of stuff?' asked Talith.

Mansfield shook his head, terrier-like. 'Crap,' he said sharply. 'Crap like I'd made a pass at her.' He looked up, mischief in his eyes. 'I didn't fancy her,' he said simply. 'It was all in her imagination.'

And both Talith and Tinsley made a mental note. *That's another call we have to make.*

'Where does Tracy work?' Tinsley realized this was an angle of Tracy Walsh's life they had not explored.

'At the Long Mynd Hotel. She does a bit of cleaning and sometimes waits in their restaurant.'

Tinsley felt that some response was called for. 'Right.'

After a polite pause Neil continued, his voice changing now to
become self-pitying and indulgent: 'I didn't imagine any of this
would happen, believe me. I just thought that Trace would see some
sense after all. I thought she was just being dramatic, that she was
just tryin' to frighten me and would drive round the block and come
back again, tail between her legs, little Daisy in her arms.' He folded
his arms. 'I thought she was calling my bluff.'

Lara Tinsley looked closely at him. Was there was something
insincere – something not quite right not only about his words but
in the way he was telling the story? As though they worked inde-
pendently of his brain, Mansfield's fingers fumbled across the sofa
and found the doll. They closed around the soft neck, squeezing the
pliable face until the features distorted and the glass eyes bulged.
As if he was short-sighted he moved the doll nearer to his face and
stared at it as though he had never quite focused on it before. An
expression of grief saddened his face but there was anger too as he
breathed in, long and slow, as though he could divine the whereabouts of the child merely by breathing in the air that surrounded
her doll. It was a form of divining that felt almost pagan. He may
not have been her father, but Neil obviously cared very much about
little Daisy.

His eyes also on the doll, Talith spoke. 'Did you in any way
blame Daisy for coming between you and Tracy? For preventing
you having a social life?'

Mansfield screwed up his face. 'No,' he said initially, before
adding, 'it isn't her fault. She is just a little girl.'

Tinsley and Talith exchanged yet another glance.

Talith pressed on. 'Tell me a bit more about your relationship
with little Daisy.' Mansfield didn't answer straight away but, as
though he was invoking the child herself, he caressed the doll in
the crook of the sofa, giving it a sentimental, almost maternal glance
before crossing the room to the mantelpiece and picking up a framed
black and white photograph in an ornate silver frame. A little girl
peeped shyly around a door. Pretty little milk teeth, curly dark hair.
Big, big eyes. It was an artistic photograph.

'A friend took that,' Mansfield said proudly. 'Thought she was
pretty enough to be a model.'

'Do you mind if we keep this?' Tinsley asked. 'We'll let you have it back, of course, when we've taken a copy.'

Mansfield looked reluctant but he handed it over. 'You asked about the relationship between me and little Daisy?' He turned around to face them. 'It's good,' he said, returning to the sofa. 'She's a sweet little thing and it isn't as though I'd come between her and her real dad. He'd gone when she was just a few months old. She's never even known him. He'd never been interested in her. I'm the only dad she's really had.'

He looked suddenly agitated. 'I don't know what to do now,' he appealed. 'Whether to stay here in case Daisy turns up or to go the hospital and see Tracy.'

'I think you should go to the hospital,' Lara Tinsley said gently, not wanting to point out the patently obvious – that if the child was still missing thirty-six hours after a serious car accident in a remote and exposed area which had all but killed her mother, it was kind of unlikely that she'd simply come walking back in here unscathed. Mansfield didn't seem to realize that '*little Daisy*' was probably dead, or at the very least seriously injured. Or she could have been abducted in whatever state by their mystery caller. And what could his or her motive possibly be for concealing a dead, injured or at the very least traumatized child? Hardly benevolent. But Tinsley didn't point any of this out to Neil Mansfield.

'We need a list of the clothes Daisy was wearing,' she said.

Mansfield looked resigned. 'Pyjamas,' he said. 'They're new. Tesco's.'

Tinsley waited, pen poised.

'White with . . .' Mansfield searched his memory. '. . . teddy bears on, I think,' he said. 'Yellow teddy bears.'

'Slippers?'

'I think so,' Mansfield said dubiously.

'Pink as well?'

Mansfield smiled ruefully and nodded.

'Anything else?'

'She was holding her little toy. She's always sucking on it.'

'Do you have a picture of her holding it?'

Mansfield reached for his mobile phone, scrolled through a couple of pictures then passed it across to the two officers. On the screen was a picture of Daisy, tears on her cheek, her mouth full of what looked like a soft toy with a bushy tail. It looked identical to the Jellycat squirrel they'd found near the crash site in Carding Mill Valley.

Tinsley handed the phone back to Mansfield, who was watching her with guarded wariness.

With a quick glance and a nod from Talith, Tinsley affirmed what must have been going through Mansfield's mind. 'Yes,' she said. 'We found one like it near the car. We'll be testing it for Daisy's DNA to ascertain whether it's hers.'

Mansfield nodded, his face a sickly green.

'There is one other thing,' Talith said quickly. 'This is a recording of the nine-nine-nine call made to report the accident. Can you listen to it, please, and tell me whether you recognize the voice.'

'There's a car gorn orf the Burway . . . Wrecked . . . Someone's inside 'urt . . . A woman.'

Neil Mansfield listened intently but his face remained baffled. Slowly he shook his head, mystified.

With a quick glance at her colleague, Lara Tinsley stood up. 'Is there any chance we can take a look around Daisy's room?'

Mansfield jerked his head towards the staircase. 'Be my guest,' he said with cold sarcasm.

The staircase was narrow and carpeted in pale beige which had more than a few wine stains decorating it. Daisy's room was patently the one at the top, on the left, the one with a Barbie doll beckoning them in. It was neatly decorated (presumably by Neil) in lemon wallpaper and a teddy bears' picnic frieze with a small single bed in its centre. The window was open, the bedclothes still thrown back, a damp patch on the bottom sheet bearing testimony to Mansfield's story. Toys and books were scattered around randomly, some clothes – a small pair of jeans, a flowered dress and a cardigan. Shoes but no slippers. On the wall was a poster of a Disney princess and hanging on the back of the door was a Snow White outfit, red and blue bodice, bouffant yellow skirt and plastic crown. It conjured up a picture of a very typical little princess, everyone's beautiful, innocent child. They turned away from it and headed back down the stairs. There was nothing to be gained here; they had what they needed. 'If there is any news of Daisy we'll be in touch, Mr Mansfield. We have your mobile and landline?'

Mansfield nodded, his face haunted. 'What do you think's happened to her?' he asked. Answers, unspoken, floated around the room, insubstantial as bubbles blown from a wand: *Daisy is dead,*

Daisy is not dead. Daisy is hurt. Daisy is OK. Daisy is lost. She will be found. Someone has abducted her. Daisy is frightened but Daisy is alive.

Talith gave it to him straight, with a hand on the man's shoulder. 'The truth is, Neil, we don't know.'

Perhaps the true awfulness of the situation was just beginning to penetrate. Or maybe not. A spasm of revulsion jerked Neil's body. 'I won't ever forgive Tracy for this,' he announced. 'If harm's come to that little girl it's *finished* between us.' His eyes bulged. '*Finished.* She can do what she likes with 'erself. That don't matter. But to put little Daisy through all that . . . It's unforgiveable. Besides, all them rows, all that drinkin'. . . I thought everything'd be great,' he bleated. 'Not like this. It's not how I thought it would be.'

'Nothing ever is,' Tinsley muttered under her breath, the self-pity nauseating both officers equally.

There was nothing to be gained by continuing the conversation. Tinsley and Talith moved towards the door. As they opened it, Lara Tinsley couldn't resist turning to confront him. 'And would you say you're happy now, Mr Mansfield?' she challenged. 'Was it all worth it? Eh?'

Mansfield said nothing, but he shook his head and chewed on his lip so hard a drop of blood appeared, which he licked away as quickly as a frog swallows a fly.

SIX

Monday, 8 April, 3 p.m.

Alex Randall had returned to the Long Mynd and was standing on the Burway, looking down into the crash site and Carding Mill Valley. An icy wind seemed determined to pierce his coat so he held it tighter around him as he studied the area. It was all too was easy to follow the trail of destruction the car had left: broken bushes, deep furrows in soft, muddy turf ending three hundred feet below at the bottom in a large oil slick. The wrecked car, which had been treated by the fire service with as little respect as a tin of baked beans, lay drunkenly on its side. Jagged shards of metal showed where Tracy Walsh had been cut out of her eight-year-old, post-office red VW Polo. Police tape fluttered everywhere, keeping the general public out though they peered from all four sides of the valley, curious. The area was as alive and busy as an ant hill but the Burway was firmly shut and would remain so until they had extracted every single piece of forensic evidence from the area and found the child. Found the child? Randall's face froze.

What was the hope, realistically? That they would come across a small body thrown from a car wreck? A body? It had always been a dim possibility and even that was fading fast. No. That wasn't the answer. In his heart Randall had little hope of finding Daisy Walsh alive and a cold, milky sun did little to lighten the proceedings and give him hope. He observed the scene from the top and felt a heavy misgiving which was almost a dread. He could not erase his image of the child, injured and frightened, crawling in the cold and the dark through the terrain, unseen by the officers, who from this vantage point looked as small as pygmies, combing every bush and tree until they found her. Or some sign of her. A few officers in fisherman's waders paddled up the stream, lifting stones and pulling water weeds out of the way. The general public would be excluded for a little while longer yet. Daisy had now been missing for thirty-six hours and the truth was that however thorough the search was they were unlikely to find a frightened child shivering behind a bush. If Daisy had been in the car the search now was for a body. Randall frowned. Or else she had been abducted from the scene, probably by their mystery caller. His underlying dread was that they would find nothing. Ever. They would never be certain what had happened to the little girl.

The weather was cool but as Randall took a few steps down into the valley the wind dropped and it became muggy. Tonight there would be more thick fog. The Devil's own weather, it was said amongst the locals. The damp folded him into it like a blanket and for a moment it misted out the view so he felt he was alone and the other personnel somewhere else behind a thick screen. It was disorientating. He could not say exactly where he was. He was aware he must be careful not to step over the edge and, like the VW, tumble down into the valley. Then the mist cleared a little so he could look around him. The surrounding colours were muted: soft greens and browns, as gentle as English – or Welsh – country-side. This was, after all, the border between the two countries. In this blanketing fog even the voices of the officers were muted, their shouts softly distant and less staccato.

Randall took a few more steps up the Burway, rounding the corner and climbing the steep slope to where Roddie Hughes, ex-SOCO, now an independent crime scene investigator, was ignoring the damp to kneel on the floor. Dressed in a white forensic suit, he was measuring tyre skids with a woman, presumably a colleague, at his side, filming the proceedings. Roddie specialized in vehicular crime scenes. He stood up and grinned as Randall approached him.

'Afternoon, Alex.'

Randall returned the greeting and focused his attention on the tyre marks. Roddie scratched his head and looked ruefully at the damp knees of his forensic suit. Doubtless underneath he would be wearing a smart city suit and at a guess that too would have damp knees.

'She was doing about fifty,' he observed, looking around him.

Alex grimaced. Fifty might be reasonable on a straight road or a dual carriageway but on this narrow, winding and precipitous road it was breakneck speed.

Roddie continued: 'She wasn't even driving straight on the way up but when she came around this corner she must have had a bit of a shock.' He took three steps backwards. 'Here,' he said, stamping his foot down on a thick spread of rubber. 'It must have been right *here*. Which means . . .' He stepped forward ten, twenty yards and looked down at the road surface, '. . . whatever she saw must have been around here.' His voice tailed off. Neither man could see any sign of activity at this point.

Randall frowned. While there were clear tyre marks where Tracy had slammed on her brakes, there was no corresponding skid beneath Roddie Hughes' feet on the road. 'It can't have involved another car,' he said slowly, 'or we'd see more marks.'

Hughes shrugged. 'Not,' he said, 'if the other car was already stationary.' He hesitated. 'It might have been nothing. She'd been drinking heavily. She might have *thought* she saw something without there being anything really there. It might even have been . . .' His eyes drifted upwards towards the Devil's Chair looming through the mist. Then he looked back at DI Randall. He was watching the detective very intently as he spoke. Alex felt something uncomfortable in his gaze and turned to look at him. 'Oh, surely, Roddie, you can't believe all that . . .' His mouth opened and he was tempted to laugh. 'Not all that Devil stuff, folklore, surely?'

Again, Roddie shrugged. 'She might have *thought* she saw something like that. You have to admit,' he said, looking around him as the mist danced, 'this is an eerie place, particularly at night. Strange, inexplicable things do happen here.'

As he was speaking the woman straightened up and Alex met a pair of very fine grey eyes fringed with long, curling black lashes. She was tall and long-legged, with silky brown hair and a very forthright stare. She gave Hughes a swift, prompting glance and he flushed. 'This is, erm, this is Sophie,' he said with more than a hint of embarrassment. The girl's eyebrows lifted and she watched him with an amused expression. Hughes drew in a deep breath and finished the sentence with resignation. 'My fiancée,' he said.

Randall felt his mouth twitch. Last he'd heard Roddie Hughes had been married to a teacher and had two teenage kids. As he shook the girl's hand and congratulated his colleague, Randall still felt bemused. Did no one stay married for the long haul anymore? The hollow answer returned like an echo, to mock him. *No one except you, Alex.* He felt his mouth tighten primly. Of all life's little ironies, this one dropped a bright red cherry right on top of the cake. As the happy couple busied themselves collecting samples, measuring distances and taking a hundred and one more photographs, stills and movies, DI Alex Randall felt he could have stood there, on that big damp hill for a long, long time, pondering life matters, particularly his own, but he was distracted by a shout. Someone, at the bottom of the valley, was holding something high, like a trophy. Randall quickened his step and slid down the bank. Please God, let it be something that leads us to the child, he prayed. Had he been a Catholic he would likely have crossed himself too. He almost did anyway.

As he got nearer he recognized the officer as PC Gethin Roberts, who was holding something small, sodden, grubby and pink in his hand, rivulets of stream water trickling down his arm on to the grass. It was a child's sodden slipper with wet nylon fur. Roberts looked pleased with himself. They had the Jellycat squirrel and now they had a slipper. Both were signs that the child had been here. Holding it in his gloved hand, Gethin Roberts approached Randall. 'Sir,' he said.

Randall studied it. It looked about a four-year-old's foot size, as far as he was an expert on the size of children's feet.

Don't go there, Alex.

On the front was a worn plastic moulding of a Barbie doll. He took out his phone and connected with DS Talith.

'Are you still with Mansfield?'

'Just left, sir,' Talith replied. 'We're on our way back to Shrewsbury. Not that we learnt anything,' he enlarged grumpily, 'except that Tracy and Neil were a dysfunctional, miserable, drunken couple. And,' he added bitterly, 'it sounds as though Mr Mansfield is up to his old tricks again.'

'You mean . . .?'

'Doing a bit of decorating, if you get what I mean, sir.'

The way Talith had uttered the words Randall *got what he meant* all right.

'We've found something, Talith,' he said. 'A little girl's slipper that looks about the right size for Daisy. I want you to go back,' he instructed. 'We've only found the one – so far. Don't tell him it's turned up. Just ask him what Daisy's slippers were like. This one's pink with a Barbie doll on the front.'

'Righto, sir. Yes, sir.'

'Don't tell him that we've found it,' Randall repeated, although he knew Neil would guess. 'Just ask and then get back to me.'

The sodden slipper was placed in an evidence bag and the team began to search for the other. As they focused on the area along the stream an orange flashing light strobed up the valley. The recovery truck had arrived. Noisily beeping its intention it reversed into position, the driver climbed out and started talking to the officers. The wrecked Polo would now be winched on to the low loader then taken to the police pound – every inch of it scrutinized and analysed to yield its story. Randall watched it gravely. He had his doubts that any evidence from the car would tell him the whereabouts of the little girl. A drunk driver falling off the Burway – Tracy wasn't the first and she wouldn't be the last. He wanted to find Daisy. The rest was no real mystery. In some ways he almost agreed with Abel Faulkener's well-voiced opinion. It really was as though the child had been spirited away by fairies.

He turned away from the scene. Not one person would swallow that explanation.

Talith was none too pleased at having to turn the car around and drive back down the A49 to Church Stretton. He wasn't at all keen on having to visit Mansfield and the shabby home again either but if the child's slipper had been found at least it bore out the claim that Daisy Walsh really had been in the car on the fateful night and something had happened to her. Surely, he reasoned, they would soon find her? He gave Lara Tinsley a swift explanation as he did a U-turn on the A49.

As they pulled back up outside the house Mansfield was just getting into his van. He looked surprised to see them again. Surprised and – again – there was that radiant hope that they were bringing Daisy back to him.

They were going to have to disappoint him for the second time that day.

Mansfield stood, frozen, on the pavement and waited for them to draw near. He was oblivious to an elderly woman pulling a Sholley behind her who muttered crossly at having to detour on to the road, the shopping echoing her disapproval as she dropped off the kerb. She continued chuntering until she was yards past while Mansfield stood rooted to the spot, unconscious of either her presence or her annoyance.

He took a step forward, hands outstretched as though he would lift the invisible child from their arms. 'You've found her?'

Lara Tinsley put a hand on his arm as she shook her head.

'No,' she said gently, then, 'it's best if we go inside, Neil. We won't be long. I just have a simple question.'

Mansfield's hand was shaking as he tried to put the key in the lock. They could see numerous dents and scratches where he and/or Tracy had fumbled to insert the key before. As it finally slipped in he turned around, opened his mouth to speak and closed it again. Instinctively Talith knew that Neil Mansfield was not asking the question that hovered on his lips because he was afraid of the answer they would give: *We've found her body.* They both felt sympathy for him but were mindful of DI Randall's instructions. Mansfield wasn't quite in the clear yet. Who knows. The entire story might still have been fiction.

They waited until they were inside and the front door closed behind them before Talith spoke. 'I'm sorry, Neil,' he said, 'we haven't found her.' Then he asked casually, 'You said that Tracy had put Daisy's dressing gown on?'

Mansfield nodded.

'Did she put the little girl's slippers on too?'

Mansfield's eyes panicked and Talith realized he had jumped to the wrong conclusion. He pressed on quickly. 'Did Tracy put Daisy's slippers on?'

Neil Mansfield seemed unable to answer. He frowned, looking bemused.

'Slippers? I can't remember,' he said. 'You asked that before. Why are you asking again? What's it got to do with . . .'

His thought processes were too slow to work it out for himself.

'Try to remember,' Lara prompted gently.

Mansfield shook his head.

'*Think*,' Talith prompted.

So Mansfield made an effort. He squeezed his eyes tight shut and muttered the word *slippers*. For a moment nothing happened. Then his eyes popped open. 'Yeah,' he said. 'I think she was.'

'What were they like?'

Neil Mansfield gave a snort. 'Fluffy pink things,' he said, almost smiling.

'Any motif?'

'Some Disney thing, I think,' he said. 'A doll or something.' And then it clicked. The colour drained from his face. He looked from one to the other, blinking quickly. 'You've found them, haven't you? Is she – was she—?'

'Wearing them? No.'

Talith would have found it easier if he could have told Mansfield that they had found a child's slipper but Randall had instructed him not to so he was left with an awkward silence which Mansfield interpreted with a bowed head. 'OK,' Talith said eventually. 'Sorry to have held you up. Were you going to the hospital?'

Mansfield nodded. 'In the morning. I'm bloody dreading it,' he confided. 'I don't know what I'm going to say to her.'

Lara resisted making the unhelpful comment that it wouldn't matter much. People on ventilators weren't usually up to scintillating conversation – or violent quarrels for that matter. But Tracy Walsh's alcohol level on a drip would probably be the lowest it had been for years, so maybe it would be worth a try.

They left.

It could be hard to keep the general public out. Back at the Burway a few people must have got through somehow. They must have walked over the hills via the public footpaths either down in the valley to the crash site or to the point where Tracy Walsh's car had first left the road. A few bunches of flowers with attached notes of sympathy had been laid as tributes on the verge.

Randall looked around him. Was he being watched? Had the search been thorough enough? Had they missed her? Walked over the very spot where her body was? The Long Mynd was full of gulleys and undergrowth, the mountains looming up, forbidding. There were small caves and places where trees had fallen, leaving landslips of mud and roots, somewhere where a four-year-old could, it was possible, be imprisoned.

The question was a drumbeat in his mind. Was she here?

The day was still dull, grey and miserable, reflecting his mood. There was hardly a hint now of any sunshine. As he scanned the horizon Alex Randall believed that somewhere, on these mountains, laid the answer. Beneath were ancient mine workings, tin and other minerals. And then the sun came out from behind a cloud so he was only aware of the raw beauty of the place which inspired him to believe that Daisy Walsh was still here. She had never left the Long Mynd. He scanned the horizon and caught sight of the shape of the Devil's Chair through the mist. She might be hurt. She could be dead. She could be injured but she was – still – here. He watched the searchers, some on the heights, others wading through the brook, still more painstakingly searching the entire valley. There was a buzz around the incident room in the National Trust teashop, a concentration of busy people. The low loader, with its orange lights flashing and warning beeps, struggled back down the narrow valley, taking with it the wrecked vehicle. Randall shook his head. He wanted – needed – inspiration.

And then the mist parted and he saw the small white cottage named Hope Cottage. He strolled across to WPC Delia Shaw. 'We need to take a walk,' he said. 'Let's go.'

SEVEN

They slipped on wellington boots, zipped up their oilskins then traipsed the half mile to Charity Ignatio's cottage. It was a modest-looking place, whitewashed, with no more than a patch of steeply sloping hillside as its garden and a tiny patio just big enough for a table and two chairs. It was plain and lacked any sort of inspiration. It looked somehow featureless, anonymous. There was nothing particular to mark it out. No car stood outside. Charity was still in the Middle East, somewhere up country now and not expected back for more than two weeks. They had managed to speak to Shirley, the cleaning woman who had returned from Spain and let them into a small secret. Randall handed Delia Shaw a pair of latex gloves and they pushed open the wicket gate and stepped into the garden, climbed up to the front door. 'Now then,' Randall said, finger on chin. 'We need to gain entry without putting up the Shropshire Police's bill for door bashing.' To his right was the white flowerpot prettily planted with lemon primroses. Randall lifted it up and sure enough exposed a Yale key with a plastic tag on it. He held it up as a trophy. 'Helpful of them to label it "front door",' he observed and sighed. 'Oldest trick in the book. I wonder why people aren't a little bit more imaginative.' He inserted the key in the lock and opened the front door. The house was like the Tardis – much bigger from the inside than it looked on the outside. Open plan, with pale walls and white-painted furniture, it looked quite spacious. Slipping on overshoes they stepped straight into a sitting room, long windows to the front overlooking the hills. *The Silent Hills*, as Malcolm Saville had called them. Randall looked at them through the window. He could have done with the hills being a little less silent. But then when have hills spoken? He creased his face up as he recalled *The Sound of Music*, then realized Shaw was watching him. 'Sir,' she asked uncertainly. He simply smiled. He wasn't going to share this one with her.

They walked through the lounge into an equally spacious and tasteful kitchen, cream units lining the walls, topped by black granite. The floor was grey slate. All was neat and tidy, everything put away except one coffee mug in the sink. Optimistically Randall bagged it up, knowing the chances were that the mug would hold Charity Ignatio's lipstick and DNA, not that of their mystery caller. He moved through to the back door and tried it. It was locked and bolted from the inside. He looked around. There was no sign that the child had ever been here. He could send in the fingerprint and forensic boys but in his heart of hearts he didn't believe that Daisy Walsh had ever been inside Hope Cottage.

WPC Shaw watched his movements without comment.

The two of them explored the rest of the house. The cream carpeted lounge came complete with log burner, shelves of books, mainly on business management, a large flat-screen television and a small sofa with chintzy, loose covers that smelt of fabric conditioner. Upstairs were two bedrooms painted blue, with double beds and built-in wardrobes and a very smart bath/shower room, as sterile, bright and spanking white as an operating theatre. There was no sign of either the missing child or of the intruder who had made the call. It was hard to believe that it had come from here.

Randall looked around. Apart from the solitary coffee mug there was no sign that *anybody* lived here. It was soulless, with no personality stamped on its interior either. It struck Randall that Ms Ignatio led a very tidy and ordered life, most of it away from the cottage. Hope Cottage was merely a pied-à-terre, a place where she dropped in from time to time, not a home. Randall found himself a little curious about this anonymous woman and her tenuous connection with his current case. They trooped downstairs and Randall eyed the phone – a cordless device that plugged into a central line. He hit the redial button and found himself apologizing to the emergency services, which told him something useful. No one had used this phone since their mystery caller.

Their mystery caller who had vanished right back into the silent hills. Well – it was up to him to find him or her.

EIGHT

Tuesday, 9 April, 8 a.m.
The coroner's office, Shrewsbury.

Martha had come in early. She hated uncertainties and the fate of this one little girl was exactly that. Uncertain. Come to think of it, she reflected, the fate of the mother was equally uncertain. Life on intensive care was precarious however competent and dedicated the staff. She sat, chewing on the end of her pencil, trying to work out what had happened and why. But it was impossible. No rational explanation seemed to fit. She kept coming back to the mystery caller and it didn't make sense. What had the caller been doing so early in the morning in such a remote area? Had he or she been there by chance? Why had she or he taken the child? In the end she stopped trying to work it out, gave a deep sigh and bent back over her work, but the questions continued to gnaw at her from the inside out, like a rat inside a cardboard box, trying to escape. At the back of her mind she felt there had to be a reason. A rational explanation, a valid explanation for why all this had happened. Something to replace this void.

She well understood it when people voiced their relief at a body found, a fate known. It was the only way one could have any chance of closure. She made a face. *Closure.* She hated the word. It had become a cliché, overused and undervalued but sometimes it was the only appropriate expression.

But, she mused, Tracy aside, who would have closure in the fate of this one little girl? From what she'd heard so far Daisy's father had little to do with his daughter. What was the phrase Alex had used? A tenner at Christmas?

What about grandparents? Perhaps.

Her job frequently offered up more questions than answers but she always strove towards resolution. She was realistic enough to know that this valued phrase, *closure*, was not always possible, and she had watched with sadness those relatives and loved ones who left the coroner's court with bowed shoulders, deepened frown lines and sheer unhappiness that she suspected would never be resolved. It was these cases that stained her mind and bothered her months, even years later. There were times when a solution she knew to be false was proffered and she was tempted to snatch at it. But underneath she knew that it was better to stick to the truth, even though, like coroners up and down the country, she could be lured into white lies:

No, he/she didn't suffer.

Yes, death was instant.

He/she would have known nothing about it.

Sometimes it was counterproductive to delve into those last terrifying and painful minutes of violent death.

And then there were the other white lies, designed to protect the relatives in their part in the tragedy.

It was inevitable/unavoidable. There was nothing you or anyone else could have done to prevent it. This, too, was not always strictly true. An argument avoided, a drink not poured, an apology or a different action *would* have stopped the event. And she knew it. She usually hoped they did not.

There was no thought or malice behind it. Psychopaths don't have thoughts and they are incapable of feeling malice, so this, at least, was true in some circumstances.

He didn't mean to kill him/her. It was an accident. The wrong place at the wrong time. Or the right place at the right time? And for Martha, the most difficult of all. *I'm sure God didn't plan for your baby to be born with this defect. It was not a punishment to you, his parents.* How do you explain that one, Coroner? With great difficulty.

The trite untruths could spill out like a waterfall tumbling over a cliff edge. So easy, so tempting – and often so untrue. But that last one about God always caught her out. There weren't always *any* explanations to make things easier or kinder and on those occasions she simply felt inadequate.

Martha sighed. Being a redhead with strong Celtic blood, she wanted certainty in black and white. She disliked being manoeuvred into an open verdict. She would look across the coroner's court at the family and read the disappointment – the chagrin and the sadness that her failure to bring closure had left. This was what she was left with – the family, always the family, and the detritus of the dead.

So far, apart from Alex's one visit, she was not involved in the Church Stretton case and it was quite possible that she never would be. If Tracy recovered and the child was found alive she would have no role; no cause to meet any of the players in this particular play. But if Daisy's body was found or Tracy Walsh died in hospital events would move straight into her jurisdiction and she wanted to be prepared to meet them. As a doctor she was well aware that even if Tracy survived there was no guarantee she would make a full recovery. And even if she did recover, it was likely that she would remember nothing of that night. Tracy would have to be very lucky indeed to make a full recovery and from the little Martha knew about the injured woman she would guess that Tracy Walsh was not blessed with good luck. Martha leaned forward in her chair. These were troubling thoughts. She reached out. Jericho had brought in an early edition of the *Shropshire Star*. And, having no real facts to brief the public, the newspaper headlines had fallen into cliché: a *missing* child, a *young* mother *'bravely fighting for life'*. As Martha crossed to the window and watched the sun rise over the town, she gave a wry smile. There were two words trotted out by the press at intervals as regular as an artificial Christmas tree in December. The first was a verb. *'Fighting.'* If only they had seen people in intensive care they would drop the phrase and never use it again. There was no fight, just pod-people, lying still, not moving, dependant on the staff for every single one of their bodily functions, including – and most importantly – breathing.

The other word that made her wince was the adjective '*brave*'. She had forbidden it when applied to Martin because the word was so terribly inappropriate. The correct word was not brave but desperate. As desperate as the man who clings to a life raft after a shipwreck or a cliff face after a slip. People are *desperate* to live. Anyone who knows that to let go is certain death is *desperate* not brave because there is no choice. To let go is to die. To fall into a place none of us is really sure of – not Catholic or Jew, Muslim or Buddhist, and certainly not Christians. None of us really knows what will happen after death because, whatever the fake medium might say, no one has ever come back to tell us – not really. Not convincingly. And the moment of death itself? There is no guarantee that death will be kind or gentle. We do not 'go gentle into that good night' for death is not good but a painful, terrible struggle using every muscle and bone, sinew and fibre in the attempt to survive. To outwit the Grim Reaper and buy five more minutes.

Martha turned away from the window, disturbed now by the memory of Martin's final days. She closed her eyes to blot them out but they were still there, implanted behind her eyelids, his unhappy groans ringing in her ears, not because of a physical pain – which can be easily controlled with Midazolam or opiates – but for the mental torment when he considered the fact that he would not be around for those two beautiful children for very much longer. But the thing she squeezed her eyes most tightly against was his apology for abandoning her. The phrase had cut her like a knife.

'*I'm so sorry.*'

She returned to her desk. There was no point in drowning herself in memories. She had work to do, a future to live. And . . . The thought put a smile on her face. There was Sam and Sukey, a pair of children emerging as very interesting adults.

Sam was signed up for Stoke City now and he loved it, never tiring of saying that it was a football club that was 'going places', even when they had a run of losses. He had a couple of 'really good mates' on the team and got on well with the 'current manager'. He was happier living at home with his mother and sister and had adopted a different attitude to the game. He'd stopped castigating himself when he missed an opportunity or made a bad pass. And when he did well and scored he'd learnt to take that on the chin too, uttering a self-deprecating grunt, coming home, wolfing down his tea and talking about things other than football. Martha smiled. She was pleased with the way he was developing into an adult. And the main thing? He was happy. And that was all that mattered to her.

And Sukey? She had started her training as an actress, found a new poise and had developed a way of listening, a sort of inner calm. She had an air of concentration, a habit of listening much more carefully to what others were saying.

Yes, she was proud of her seventeen-year-old twins.

They never stopped startling her, Martha thought, smiling. She could never have predicted that those two noisy babies would somehow turn into these two wonderful people. Parents love their children, or at least most do, but Martha was realizing how much she liked them too.

She turned away from the window and returned to her desk.

Neil Mansfield was nervous about entering the intensive care unit in spite of the fact that the nurses were kind and quite thoughtful. They'd put him in the relatives' waiting room where a Spanish doctor had come in, sat down and explained to him that Tracy's injuries were severe and that there was every chance that she would not recover. Neil had had a panic attack and started breathing fast. Did they mean she was going to die? Or was he going to be expected to be a carer for a horribly injured, perhaps brain-dead Tracy? Hell. *No!* he screamed inwardly.

All the time the doctor was speaking a nurse in pale blue scrubs was standing in the doorway, a witness to his words. Mansfield looked up at her once or twice. He had the feeling she wanted to say something but was taking her cue from the doctor, her glance bouncing between them, gauging his reaction. At the back of his mind he kept wondering what it was she wanted to say. Her lips even parted twice in readiness for words and she leaned forward but nothing came out so Neil was left wondering. The doctor took no notice of her at all but continued speaking, saying that the next two or three days were critical and that, possibly, some *tough decisions* might need to be made. When he spoke these words both doctor and nurse eyed him very intently and then each other but gave Neil no clue as to what the phrase *tough decisions* meant.

They paused, giving him a cue to ask what they meant by the phrase but Neil said nothing. The truth was he didn't dare ask. He searched one face and then the other but found no clue there either. He only knew that the nurse in scrubs approved of the phrase because her body relaxed. Her arms unfolded and she gave a ghost of a smile in his direction.

He realized that the doctor had said what she had wanted him to say. He asked Neil if he needed anything clarifying then stood up abruptly. The interview was at an end. He clapped a hand on Neil's shoulder. 'Would you like to see her now?'

Mansfield wasn't sure whether he did want to see her or not. He had a conflict of emotions. Part of him wanted to see her just to wring her bloody neck. Silly cow. She'd brought this on herself. Why hadn't she listened to him? Piss drunk, argumentative and then go driving up the Burway? With Daisy? He wanted to shake her awake and ask her himself. Where the hell is Daisy? What have you done with your own daughter? Why did you take her with you? If your intention was to self-destruct why didn't you leave the child in bed, safe and warm and alive? *I would have looked after her, Trace. I'm not even her bloody father but I'd have taken better care of her than you.*

But another part of him was desperate to see her, to get some answers about himself. He was left wondering why he had ever got himself ensnared in this sticky web of infidelity and ultimate destruction. He wanted an explanation of why he had allowed his life to glug down a sinkhole. Lucy Stanstead wasn't going to provide either an explanation or a solution but maybe Tracy would. He trotted behind the doctor until they reached the keypad door that led into the unit. He peeped through the window and felt reluctant to enter. Part of him was very, *very* frightened. What would she look like? They'd said she had facial injuries. Did that mean scars? Would she look like Frankenstein? Would he faint when he saw her? He was frowning as he followed the nurse to one of the beds. He had a feeling that there was something dark behind all this, some grey shadow that blocked out light. There was something he sensed but did not understand. He wasn't sure he ever would do or wanted to. It was like lifting a drain cover. You knew there was something deeply unpleasant, something murky underneath it. And so you hesitate, thinking of all the reasons why it is better *not* to lift it. And yet you know that in the end you *will* put your fingers into the holes and you *will* heave the thing up and similarly you *will* peer down that black, slimy hole. And inhale as you do so. Neil Mansfield knew that one day he would lift the drain cover on the events of the last two days.

The nurse let him approach the bedside alone, watching him with a wary glance. Mansfield looked down at his girlfriend.

He didn't recognize her at first, except for her hair. Long and blonde, with fashionable dark roots, and spread over the pillow like some old painting he'd seen in the art gallery in London in another life – a happier one when Joshy had been doing a project in school on painters and had begged him to take him to a London art gallery. Mansfield squeezed his eyes tight shut against the memory. The regrets were like lemon juice in his eyes, sharply stinging and making him blink. He focused on the person in the bed. Apart from the lovely hair (bleached and streaked by a very competent and expensive hairdresser) nothing else about Tracy was recognizable. There was nothing to tell him that this person really *was* Tracy. Maybe this was all a mistake and *that* was why little Daisy was missing. It was the wrong person, the wrong car. He half turned to ask the nurse whether she was absolutely *sure* this was Tracy Walsh. He scanned the rest of the unit. Surely there had been a mistake? This couldn't be Tracy. Then he saw the name, clearly written on a whiteboard behind the bed in unmistakably large letters, scrawled in thick black felt-tip pen: TRACY WALSH, and underneath her date of birth: 21/4/1980. Correct. The date gave him a jolt. It would soon be her birthday and he hadn't bought her a present. He snorted and glanced back at the *thing* in the bed. Like she was going to notice? What the hell did you buy someone in this situation? A weekend in the Cotswolds? A scary driving experience? Yeah, right.

But the name over the bed had confirmed that it was her. She had a tube sticking out of her mouth which was connected to a machine that rose and fell to make her breathe. It was so rhythmic and precise that Mansfield found himself matching the machine's respirations, breathing in unison with her. In – hold – out. In – hold – out. Their chests rose and fell together, as one.

Tracy was connected to lots of machines. A drip was putting drops of clear fluid into a vein in her arm. *In – hold – out. In – hold – out.*

And so the rhythm grew, like an orchestra when the instruments join in the solo performer. The screen at the side of her bed joined in too with patterns he recognized as displaying her heartbeat.

Mansfield looked up and watched the monitor. He felt hollow in the pit of his stomach, as though half his organs had been replaced with a void. The nurse was still watching him encouragingly. 'Speak to her,' she urged. 'She may well be able to hear you.'

So he spoke, and tried to sound normal. 'Hello, Trace,' he said. He felt stupid talking to this thing in the bed. The doctor was adjusting one of the machines but his dark brown eyes were resting on him, a faint question still unasked. Mansfield felt even more uncomfortable. The doctor was expecting him to do or say something and he didn't have a clue what.

He felt panicked and mumbled something about needing to go to the toilet. The nurse offered to show him the way. She even waited outside until he'd finished, which embarrassed him. He'd hardly needed to go really. He'd had to squeeze out a couple of drops. It had been simply an avoidance tactic and a not very clever one at that. He blushed as he came out. But she didn't. She was a very pale girl – almost looked anaemic, as though she needed a hearty, meaty meal. But surely her colleagues would have picked up on that here in the hospital? She had lovely skin, though – a proper porcelain complexion, but unfortunately her eyes were sloping, which made her look a bit sneaky and sly. He would have liked to ask her about the phrase *tough decisions* but like before he was afraid of the answer, sure it would involve something deeply unpleasant. And so he left the drain cover firmly in place.

For now.

When he returned to the ward a woman in her fifties was visiting, presumably, her son. He was another pod person with thick brown hair. She was crying and a nurse had her arm around her. It distracted the doctor and his nurse so Mansfield was left alone with Tracy. He eyed the machines and wondered which one he would have to disconnect for Tracy to die.

Then the nurse was behind him, writing something down on a huge chart on a slanting board. Mansfield plucked up courage. 'Which machine is Tracy dependant on?'

The nurse's eyes slanted even more. *She almost looks Chinese.* 'All of them,' she said shortly and turned back to her charts.

Mansfield looked at Tracy and reached out his hand to hers.

NINE

R andall scanned the area as he spoke to the forensics team. They were downsizing their search for the little girl and the move was making them all despondent. But Randall knew the search had been thorough. Wherever Daisy Walsh was it wasn't here. Huge as the area was it was empty of features and the entire place had been fingertip scrutinized by hundreds of people, both the general public and officers trained in search and rescue. Sniffer dogs had roamed the area, using some of the little girl's clothes to identify her scent. Yet in the square miles they had covered all they had found was the one sodden slipper which Neil Mansfield had tentatively identified as belonging to the little girl, and the Jellycat squirrel which was definitely hers. And they had DNA from the child's saliva.

Randall frowned, standing still, leaning into a chilly wind. How had Daisy vanished? Into the hillside? Surely, reason argued, she must have been abducted by their mystery caller? But, he unconsciously echoed Martha's thoughts, why? What was behind all this? What dark forces? His mouth tightened. Was it possible Daisy really had been spirited away? A cloud smothered the cold spring sun and the panorama darkened as though to alert him to this possibility. In this remote and spooky place it was hard not to include the supernatural as an explanation. But if their mystery caller really had abducted the child, why had she called at all? The girls on the D of E award would have found the car crash in an hour or two. Had it been their conscience telling them that Tracy might die? Had it then been a vain attempt to save the woman's life? And why, subsequently, had the caller not come forward? Why draw this kind of attention to herself? There was no crime here, simply a car accident and a vanished child. The abduction was the crime. Randall breathed in the purest air then opened his eyes wide. He had thought something significant. *The abduction of the child was the crime.* Had this turned their attention away from the possible encounter of two cars? How important was that? The fact that the caller had chosen to remain hidden only focused suspicion on her. None of it made any sense and it rattled DI Randall. The child had to be hurt. The forensics team had found evidence of blood smeared on the back of the seat in front of the child's seat. At the very least, she would be shocked. She might well be dead. She would almost certainly need medical attention and she should be with her family, people who loved her. That pulled him up short. Who did love her? Presumably Tracy but she was in no fit state to care for her daughter. Apart from her there was only Neil. Again Randall felt that this too was significant. But for the life of him he couldn't see how. He gave quick sigh of puzzlement and frustration.

He and his team had spent hours talking the situation through. He'd always encouraged his officers, however senior or junior, to voice their ideas, assuring them that no one would ridicule them for at least putting forward a theory. But even the most imaginative of his team had failed to come up with any rational explanation.

They had had strong support from both local and national press, front page headlines appealing for any information, but still nothing had turned up. It was a blank, a void, and a tragedy. It was worrying and frustrating, and the news from the hospital was discouraging. Tracy was now suffering 'major organ failure'. Randall was no medic but he could easily work out that this was not good news. It looked as though Tracy and Neil had had their last drunken argument. As Randall stood on the Burway and looked down into Carding Mill Valley, he felt a deep despondency. He could not remember any case even remotely like this, so he had no precedent to turn to. Nothing to give him ideas and hope. Worse, looking at his officers' faces was like staring into a mirror. All he saw was an imperfect reflection of his own confusion. He looked around at the blunt mounds of the secret hills. And reflected that, with their dark tales of folklore and legend, they weren't helping him either.

Needing at least some encouragement he was tempted to visit Martha again but something stopped him. It wasn't only that it wasn't fair to keep burdening her with his police problems. He didn't think she minded that but . . . A vision of her green eyes sparkling with merriment made him smile briefly. He wasn't being fair to her and he didn't only mean police officer to coroner. Oh, no. It was something much deeper than that. And that was a place he could not allow himself to explore. He turned back towards the incident room. Time for a briefing.

For now they were still working from the National Trust rooms in

Carding Mill Valley, but they would only be staying there for one more week. They may as well return to Monkmoor Police Station in Shrewsbury for all the good they were doing out here. The officers were waiting for him, quiet as he entered the room. And that, in itself, was a bad sign. Usually they were raucous and noisy, confident of a satisfactory conclusion. And soon. But as he scanned the whiteboard he realized how very little they had to go on. The wait for more forensic results was always frustrating but Randall had learned to be patient – or at least not to be too impatient. The trouble was that every hour they wasted could be costing a little girl her life. She could be dying as they were waiting for results or a lead or simply just waiting. But forensics would not be hurried, and so far the only results they had were the DNA on the squirrel. The fingerprints on the telephone matched numerous other prints taken from all around Hope Cottage. They had already fingerprinted the cleaning woman and excluded her prints. 'Probably Charity Ignatio's,' he said gloomily, reading the report. 'Doesn't exactly help us.' Whoever the caller had been, like all felons, she – or was it conceivably a he? – appeared to have worn gloves. There were no rogue prints. It was unlikely, though not impossible, that Daisy had been in the cottage at some point, but children tend to touch things with sticky fingers, leaving plenty of prints. There was no sign of her if she had been there. No hair, prints, or anything else that could possibly place the little girl inside Hope Cottage.

They listened yet again to the familiar recording. Even if they could be sure it was definitely a woman that would be something.

'There's a car gorn orf the Burway.' Randall listened hard. The harshness of the voice meant it could be man or a woman. 'Wrecked. Someone's inside 'urt.' Pause. 'A woman.'

But as he continued to listen he felt sure that this *was* a woman, someone in her forties – fifties possibly. The officers listened and PC Gethin Roberts made his comment. 'She almost sounds as if she's putting the accent on,' he said.

Randall pressed the pause button and eyed him quizzically.

'She sounds deliberately gruff,' Roberts persisted, his face slightly pink. 'And, come on, who really speaks like that these days?'

'Point taken, Roberts,' he said kindly. 'So you think if we emphasize the point that this is a *local* woman it could be a red herring?'

Roberts looked dubious and a bit embarrassed.

Gary Coleman cleared his throat. 'Who else but a local person would be around the Stretton Hills at six o'clock in the morning at this time of year, sir?' His fellow officers nodded their agreement. Randall pressed the play button again. The emergency room asked whether the woman was breathing.

'Aaagh.'

'I need your name and contact details.'

The line went dead. The caller had said all she was prepared to say. Randall felt chilled. The caller sounded as though she just didn't care. Worse than that, it could even be a matter of fun to her. A tease. A joke. She was playing them along. Knowing the child was still missing four days later, it felt malicious. Whose hands was she in? Surely this person's? But in the call there had been no mention of Daisy. No, '*I have the little girl*'. No, '*She's safe*'. Why not?

Nothing. No reassurance at all – only this person who seemed to be gaining the higher ground and getting plenty of satisfaction from her position too. Randall winced.

Whose hands was Daisy Walsh in? What would they do to her? Where was she, for goodness' sake?

His officers looked downcast. Randall waited for suggestions but apart from house-to-house interviews, the press and TV and continued meetings with the main people involved, he felt as though he was in a prison yard, watched by vigilant guards and surrounded by four tall walls topped with razor wire and no visible door to the outside. He needed a break. A ladder.

This was shit.

'OK,' he said finally, turned to the whiteboard and drew bullet points as he ran through four key points outlining what they already knew and their next steps. 'We think our caller has Daisy. We think it is a woman of middle age. We think she is local. So we focus a concentrated search of all local people within, say, a ten-mile radius of Church Stretton.'

At least it gave them something to do. He smiled. It felt as though they were getting somewhere and making the point that Daisy was probably within his ten-mile radius, even if it was an arbitrary figure, had the effect of making him feel they were progressing forwards.

But when the officers had filed out, geographical areas allocated like slices of a pie, Randall realized he needed something more.

And so he did something he had never done before. He roped in a forensic linguist attached to Birmingham University, a woman called Claire Tarrow. Randall was convinced: find the mystery caller and they would find Daisy. It was all in the voice. He was haunted by the question: was the child still alive? Was this a race against time? Was there any way by more inspirational policing that they could possibly save her life? Even now? As they floundered in their investigations was the child's life ebbing away? Or were they already too late? Was she dead? Was their mystery caller concealing her body? He quickly moved away. It was the chance that Daisy was still alive and that they would find her that energized him and kept him and his team working longer and longer hours, barely taking a break, in a desperate search for the missing child. And all that time Tracy lay in her hospital bed, unaware of her daughter's fate, certainly unable to help them find her, still in intensive care, intubated and with no sign of improvement. Rather, she seemed to be suffering a slow, apparently inexorable deterioration. Randall had visited her once or twice, even speaking to her, though he believed it was futile to ask if she could help them find her little girl. As he'd expected, there was no response. Not a flicker of an eyelid or a twitch of a muscle, and after ten minutes each time, realizing there was no response, that Tracy was, to all intents and purposes, the living dead, he'd left even more downhearted.

When he'd announced to the officers still hanging around the incident room that he had requested the service of a forensic linguist Randall had initially watched a wave of sympathy ripple around the room. It only rubbed it in how desperate he was. It was called *pulling out all the stops*. But then, one by one, they realized the sense of the move and the sympathy turned into acceptance, then approval.

TEN

Thursday, 11 April, 11.10 a.m.

Next morning Claire Tarrow turned up at Monkmoor Police Station, a neat, small woman in her thirties. Randall suspected she was aware of her height, or rather the lack of it. She wore impossibly high heels which she wasn't very good at balancing on and which only served to draw attention to her smallness – only a little over five feet, at a guess, without the heels. With them she was a respectable five foot five. She wobbled once or twice, losing her balance, and Randall put out an arm to catch her which she acknowledged very prettily with a smile and a flash of her rather nice blue eyes. However, in spite of this, she had a confident manner and an alertness about her which was reassuring. She shook his hand with a grip that would have done credit to a professional boxer and he quickly formed the opinion that she was nobody's fool. As he passed her the papers about the case she slipped on a pair of oversized glasses and the blue eyes were sadly hidden. She picked up the tapes and inserted them into the machine.

She played them through three or four times without comment, making copious notes in the tiniest writing he had ever seen. He squinted across but was unable to decipher a single word.

Finally, she looked up. 'Just fill me in a little more about the little girl . . .' she hesitated, 'and the relationship between her mother and her partner.'

Randall painted as realistic a picture as he could about the home circumstances, describing Neil's flirtatious character, Tracy's drunkenness and the rows between the two, and Claire's face clouded over. 'Not a million miles away from my own home life,' she said.

Randall murmured something sympathetic which Claire batted away as though it really didn't matter. She started asking her questions without delay or further confidences. 'Did you find the child's blood in the car?'

'Some. Not much. Consistent with a minor injury – a scraped knee or a cut finger. And of course we don't know how long it has been in the car. An injury might have been sustained at some other time. It's possible that . . .' His voice trailed away.

Claire Tarrow looked incredulous. 'You're saying you're not even sure she was even *in* the car?'

Alex Randall gave a long, heartfelt sigh. 'We're pretty sure she was,' he said, 'but we have to consider every eventuality.'

'Of course,' she said with heavy politeness. 'So, let's get down to business.' She adjusted her glasses up her nose.

'Naturally, you believe that this woman . . .' she tapped the tape, 'holds the key to the missing child?'

'I'll be honest,' Randall said. 'I haven't got any other ideas. If *she* doesn't know where the child is, who does?'

'You're certain she's nowhere on the hills around the Devil's Chair?'

Randall replied frankly. 'As certain as we can be. It's a huge area. We've searched it as thoroughly as we possibly can. I'm ninety-nine per cent certain she isn't there.' He paused, frowning, but determined to be as honest and open as he could be. 'There are a couple of caves,' he said. 'We have searched them and it's unlikely that a four-year-old would have gone deep into them and not responded to someone calling her name but, I suppose, it's not theoretically impossible. We've had the helicopter up with a heat-seeking device. It isn't impossible she's out there but if she is she's not alive. Or, at least, not able to respond.'

'So.' She removed her glasses, holding them loosely in her fingers. 'You want to know . . .?' The blue eyes looked sharply into his.

'We're not a hundred per cent sure whether it's a man or a woman,' he began.

'A woman. Without a doubt.'

Randall nodded. 'One of our officers wondered whether the caller really is local – or whether they are affecting a local accent to put us off the scent.'

'Well, your officer is wrong,' Claire said, frowning. 'This woman is Shropshire born and bred. The way she uses words is typical of that part of Shropshire. Church Stretton and its surrounds hold a fairly isolated population. There is also a hint of Welsh in her inton-ation, which isn't surprising considering we're practically *in* the country.'

Randall listened.

'And she is a rural person, I'd say,' Claire continued. 'Not a townie and not someone who spends much time in the town. There's very little contamination of her speech with contemporary phrases, so I suggest she's not a great one for TV either. I think she lives an isolated life and has probably never been resident out of the area. She's unlikely to have gone to university. Her sentence construction and vocabulary would suggest perhaps a farmer's wife or country dweller. The *gorn orf* is very telling. As is the fact that she uses the word *wrecked*.' She looked up at him, frowning. 'That's unusual in this day and age. Most people would use the word *crashed*. It's almost as though she belongs in a different time.' She made a wry face. 'I'm not being much help, am I?'

'You can only do what you can do,' Randall said glumly, wondering what he'd really expected from her. 'Any idea of age?'

'Forties, I'd think.' Claire looked thoughtful. 'Is there a mobile signal in Carding Mill Valley?'

'It's patchy. Why?'

'I was just wondering if your caller had a mobile phone.'

Randall listened.

'Everyone does these days,' Claire said, 'even country folk. I wondered why your caller broke into a cottage and used a landline which would lead you straight to Hope Cottage?'

'Mmm.' Randall was impressed. Perhaps it was something they should have paid more attention to. He proffered an explanation. 'It is the nearest house to the crash site so would be the obvious choice.'

Claire persisted with her ideas. 'Did she know it would be empty? Or was she expecting someone to answer to her knock?'

Randall made a mental note to look again at the results of the fingerprints in and around the cottage; in particular, any prints on the front door and knocker. He wasn't particularly hopeful. A person who had left not one fingerprint *inside* the cottage after she'd used the telephone would be unlikely to omit the chance of prints on the front door. But they could hit lucky.

Again, Claire spoke, more musing than questioning this time. 'Was it happenstance that Ms Ignatio was away or did she know that the cottage was frequently empty?'

Randall's ears were cocked. 'You mean she knows the person who lives in Hope Cottage spends a lot of time away?'

Claire nodded. 'Local knowledge. Was it lucky or unlucky that no one was in?'

Randall shrugged.

'And another thing – what was she doing in that area so early in the morning?' She hardly waited for a reply before hurrying on. 'Well, I can only reiterate what I can say with certainty, Inspector. Your lady is a local. Born and bred here and she hasn't lived away. At least, if she has it hasn't affected her local accent. She may be a country person and local but she's not uneducated. If the little girl is with her I agree with the theory you say you're working on. Your caller lives within a ten-mile radius of the Long Mynd.'

Randall felt uplifted until Claire continued, 'That isn't to say that she hasn't taken the little girl somewhere else.'

His spirits dropped right down as he faced the truth. 'In spite of a well-publicized press campaign, she could be anywhere.'

Claire didn't respond to this.

He realized he still wanted to squeeze more from her. 'What about this person's character?'

'There we're in the realms of conjecture,' she said, almost scolding him. 'Accents and intonation, the way we speak and so on is one science. To try and analyse a person's character through their speech is a bit more difficult.' She smiled, softening her words. 'And that,' she said, 'is the realm of the psychiatrist. I wouldn't pick up on personalities – unless, of course, they make threats or say something that makes you realize they're a psycho, a weirdo or troubled in some way.'

'And this woman?'

Claire smiled. 'I don't think she's a weirdo or a psycho or troubled in any way. Quite the reverse, actually. She's stolid and practical.'

'If she's so stolid and practical what's she doing abducting a child from the scene of an accident?'

'You're absolutely sure she did?'

'Too much coincidence,' he said, 'given the circumstances.'

'Probably,' she responded.

Randall persisted. 'Why take the child?'

Claire sighed and answered with reluctance. 'Because she lives in the past.'

'Which means what, exactly . . .?'

'Church Stretton and the Long Mynd is an area steeped in folklore and old traditions,' she said slowly. 'I suspect it's something to do with that.'

Randall didn't even feel like laughing. 'You mean black magic?' He couldn't believe he was having this conversation.

Claire shrugged. 'Black magic, white magic. I don't know, Inspector. I just feel that there is something mystical going on here, don't you?' She opened her eyes wide and smiled. 'It's up to you to find out what.'

Randall nodded. He'd finally run out of questions.

'We'll extend our house-to-house search,' he offered.

Claire Tarrow picked up her bag. 'Sounds like a good idea to me.'

Randall thanked her and asked her to submit her bill to the finance department.

He held out his hand. 'Thank you very much for coming up, Claire.'

'I'm afraid I haven't helped very much.'

'You might have done,' he said cryptically. 'And you don't mind if I ring if there's something else I need to ask?'

'Not at all.' Claire Tarrow lifted her eyebrows.

The room felt empty when she'd gone. Randall sat for a while assimilating the facts she had given him. A middle-aged local woman. Surely it would narrow the search?

ELEVEN

Thursday, 11 April, midday.

'**M**r Mansfield.'
Neil turned around with a guilty start.
The doctor and nurse were both watching him with curious expressions, suspicious but with a heavy dose of sympathy. He couldn't work it out.

'Can we have a word?'

'Yeah. Sure.'

They led him back into the small visitors' room and closed the door. This time the nurse sat by his side, her look of sympathy deepening.

Mansfield looked from one to the other. What the hell was going on? Had they read his mind? Seen him finger one of the plugs on the wall? Had they heard the voice advising him to switch her off?

'I'm Doctor James,' the doctor said, blinking sandy lashes out of sandy eyes. 'This is a little awkward. Basically, Mr Mansfield, we've done some tests.'

Mansfield looked even more quickly from one to the other, his glance bouncing between them. The doctor's words seemed to blur into one another, as though something was blocking his hearing.

'What we're saying is that Tracy is highly unlikely to recover,' the doctor said.

Mansfield was panicking now. Were they saying that he was going to have to care for her, when she was like this? How long was she going to live? Like this . . .

'There's very little brain response,' the doctor said, pressing on. 'And we find that if a patient doesn't recover in the first week or so they are unlikely ever to.'

Mansfield put his head on one side, like a chicken, frowning and trying to understand what it was the doctor was saying.

Whatever it was, he was finding it difficult.

He felt like saying *spit it out, mate* but it seemed a bit cheeky to prompt the medic, so he stayed silent.

'At some point we may think it's best to switch the ventilator off, in which case . . .' The doctor couldn't look at him. 'We will need to consult the next of kin. Umm, you're not actually married?' Mansfield frowned. What were they saying?

'So her next of kin would be . . .'

Suddenly the penny dropped and Mansfield was appalled. 'She has a mum and a sister,' he mumbled. Tracy's mum and her horrible sister who had never forgiven Tracy for being prettier than her.

The nurse spoke now. 'I don't believe they've been in to visit her,' she said. 'There's only been you.'

Mansfield stopped looking at the doctor and focused on the nurse instead. 'It doesn't surprise me,' he said. 'She hasn't spoken to either of them for years.' He paused. He was beginning to realize what it was they were saying.

The doctor spoke again. 'Right, well, it's very difficult in these sorts of cases,' the doctor continued, 'but . . .' Again, he gave Neil a long, calculating look and suddenly with awful and sharp clarity Neil knew exactly what it was that they were finding so hard to say. He knew now what the *tough decision* was.

They were going to turn her off. Because . . . But wait. It wasn't just that. There was something else. He only knew half the story. The doctor was speaking about . . . organ donation. The words became distinct. And now he realized that Tracy, his partner, could be about to be turned into a collection of random spare parts, and that it would be her mother and sister, not him, who would make the decision. This was patently not how it should be. It was not right. He tried to protest.

The doctor was still talking. 'How much do you know about transplants?'

Mansfield stared.

'Or renal dialysis?'

'Nothing.'

But that wasn't quite true. He *did* know something. He'd walked past the dialysis unit on his way into the hospital. He'd seen the sign and all those people hooked up to those huge machines, pipes and tubes everywhere. And they had just been sitting, reading the paper, some on their iPads, some chatting to the nurses, having a cup of tea.

'They have to come in for that three times a week,' the doctor said, as though he'd read his thoughts, seen the images crowding his mind. 'Tracy can help those people.'

The nurse spoke next. 'We have people who are blind because they need corneal transplants.'

Neil was recalling Tracy's eyes. Her pretty, dark eyes. He squeezed his own tight shut.

'And her heart and lungs,' the nurse added.

Neil stared at her. And in ten days' time it would be Tracy's birthday. What a great present. Instead of perfume, clothes, money and dinner out here it was being suggested she donate her liver, her lungs, her spleen, her eyes, her heart and Neil didn't want to think what else.

So they were keeping her alive only to harvest her organs?

Then they rubbed salt into the wound. 'Do you have a number for her mother?'

TWELVE

Sunday, 14 April, 4 p.m.

In spite of a few messages left on both her landline and mobile, it had taken the hospital a few days to track down Tracy's mother, Pat Waterman. The doctor spoke to her, trying to explain what it was they wanted.

'Yeah,' she said. 'OK with me.'

Doctor James pointed out that they would need written consent and Pat appeared irritated. 'You're saying I got to come all the way to Shrewsbury just to sign some form?'

'You may want to say goodbye to your daughter,' the doctor said patiently.

Perhaps Pat Waterman realized then that she should make some effort. 'I can come this afternoon,' she said in a chastened voice. ''Bout four. OK?'

'That should be fine,' the doctor said, already making plans.

Organ harvesting takes place in the morning. It makes it easier to plan for the beneficiaries who have to be lined up, hopeful contestants in a life-and-death tournament. Theatres have to be prepared, patients called in, surgeons, nurses, theatre attendants, anaesthetists. All have to be ready, waiting in the wings in gloves and scrubs.

Monday, 15 April, 8 a.m.

Tracy Walsh finally gave up her struggle – or rather, the doctors did – at eight o'clock in the morning. She was taken to the operating theatre, her organs treated as carefully as though they belonged to an ancient Pharoah of Egypt, and finally, when all that could be done had been done, she was pronounced dead and, as was the custom, the team made a prayer of thanks from the people who would be eternally grateful for the decision.

So Tracy was dead and still there was no sign of her daughter.

It isn't only human organs that have to be harvested early in the morning. Certain herbs and fungi also need to be collected while the dew is still on them. The plants are picked as carefully as the surgeon lifted out Tracy's heart, lungs, corneas and kidneys, and placed in a basket.

Monday, 15 April, 10.30 a.m.

Martha had been kept informed of all the events. In fact, they had needed her permission for the organ donation to go ahead. As always it made her aware of mortality, of generosity, of lives transformed and of the savings to the National Health Service.

Wednesday, 17 April, 11 a.m.

Randall watched the lorries moving in, the computers disconnected and lifted. He scanned the panorama. Moving out felt like he was abandoning the child – giving up hope. He was still worried that they had overlooked something. He felt a terrible pang of guilt as he watched his officers pack up their desks and computers, relinquishing the tea rooms back to the National Trust.

He and Talith were still there when the lorries pulled away and all but their car had gone. It didn't help that one press photographer was recording their retreat. With a long lens and tripod he was taking picture after picture. At least some of them would end up on tomorrow's front page accompanied by dismal and depressing head-lines. Randall could almost have written them himself.

Failing to find missing child, police abandon crash site.

Randall spoke, more to himself than out loud. 'Have we done everything we could have here?'

Talith gave out a deep sigh. 'Have we ever, sir?'

Randall turned to face him. 'What have we missed, Paul?'

'I don't think we've missed anything, sir. At least, nothing tangible.' He too lifted his gaze up from the valley right to the top of the hill. 'The little girl isn't here.'

Friday, 19 April, 9.30 a.m.

In some ways life was easier back at Monkmoor Police Station. For a start they did not have the world and its photographer watching their every move. Comings and goings were not recorded, mobiles and computers worked faster here and their location gave them distance, a certain amount of detachment, from the case. Randall felt he could focus better on the enquiry.

Their morning briefings began to take on a different shape. There was energy and optimism. Areas were marked out, properties ticked off and ideas flowed like quicksilver. Then PC Sean Dart made the suggestion that they speak to Wanda Stefano. He looked embarrassed when DI Randall praised the idea. 'You're right, Sean,' he said. 'We've neglected her. We should at least talk to her and see what she can tell us about that night. If anything.' He grinned at the PC. 'Maybe you'd like to take that on?'

'Yes, sir.'

The team filed out and Randall was ready to start the day. He was contemplating where next to direct the enquiries when the phone rang.

It was Roddie Hughes and he was sounding pleased with himself. 'We've found traces of paint on the bonnet of the car,' he said. 'Fresh black paint and a very small dent. Do you know whether she's had a prang in it recently?'

'We can soon find out,' Randall said tersely. 'Do you think it's important?'

Roddie was silent for a minute and his answer, when it came, was guarded. 'Obviously I can't be certain but I keep visualizing those tyre marks on the Burway, Alex. She was tanking along at fifty miles per hour when all of a sudden she screeches to a halt and, pissed as she was, bangs into reverse. Now – put that into perspective. If she'd had a prang that could explain things. Particularly if the other driver was angry at her speed, maybe even realized how drunk she was.'

'No one's come forward,' Alex said thoughtfully.

'Which means they either haven't heard about the tragedy – highly unlikely considering your press coverage – or they have a reason for not coming forward. At least, Alex, if the dent happened that night it places someone else at the scene.'

Randall was silent for a moment, so Hughes pressed on with his ideas. 'They might feel responsible for what has turned out to be a fatal crash. They might have been drunk themselves at the time and know that at the very least they'd be charged with leaving the scene. It's possible it was a stolen car or a drugs thing. You know what the general public are like, Alex. Maybe it was a married man who had no business being up there. The possibilities are endless but . . .'

'It gives our officers another focus for their enquiry,' Randall said.

'Looking at the point where the two cars collided,' Hughes continued, 'and the height of the paint mark, I'd lay a guess it was a four-by-four. Certainly something quite high off the ground. Actually, thinking about it, a typical drug dealer's car.'

Randall chuckled. 'Right. Thanks.'

'There is one other thing.' Hughes sounded hesitant. 'Sophie and I are getting married in August. We wondered if you and Erica would like to come?'

Randall was so appalled at the prospect that he was speechless.

Hughes hurried on. 'It's only a small affair. Nothing huge. Just a small do at The Walls in Oswestry. About fifty people. We'd love it if you'd come.'

'Leave it with me,' Randall said in a strangled voice. 'I'll speak to her. But . . .'

Hughes chipped in. 'It's on the sixteenth. We chose a Friday because it's cheaper.' He gave a dry cough of a laugh. 'Divorce comes expensive these days.'

When he'd put the phone down, Alex Randall sat, thinking. Take Erica to a wedding? He couldn't think of anything worse. His colleagues would be there. He could just imagine how she'd react to them and them to her. Mental illness is a subtle alienator. And his colleagues would always look at him askance, knowing the secret about his wife that he had tried so hard to keep from them. Sometimes he had great sympathy for Jane Eyre's Mr Rochester. They shared the same impediment. But then he could hardly lock her away. Erica's condition was anything but stable. It depended on her medication at the time. Randall grimaced. Or the phase of the moon at the time. Who knew? Certainly not the psychiatrists. He could not go to the wedding. Not with Erica. He had to think up a suitable excuse. And quickly so it would seem a genuine prior engagement rather than something dreamed up to avoid the 'do'. He liked Roddie Hughes and thought he could have liked Sophie too. He didn't want to offend him. But there was no way he was going to be seen with his wife in public.

He forced his mind back to the case. Hughes was right on all counts. He knew about vehicle collisions and paint marks. If there had been a collision between two cars that night not only would it explain Tracy's sudden stop, the panicked reversal and the subsequent accident, but it also potentially introduced another person into the puzzle of Daisy Walsh's disappearance. There was no explanation why the driver had not come forward, though all of Roddie Hughes' suggestions were possible. But surely the accident and subsequent abduction of a little girl were enough to outweigh a minor prang or a drunken encounter? They must know what had happened – if not on the night then later through the media. The police couldn't have dreamt up more headlines. The driver must have realized that the accident he had witnessed, or possibly caused, had been serious. They must have seen the crazy reversing and the subsequent fall into the valley. But it hadn't been them who had called the police, unless their mystery caller and the driver were the same person, and when the car had tumbled down the bank they had watched from the Burway, seen it roll over and over and then rescued the child, walked to Hope Cottage and made the call. Four hours later? Neil had said that Tracy had left the house a little before 2 a.m. The car had been picked up by the CCTV on Stretton High Street at 1.58 a.m. It was a ten-minute drive from Neil and Tracy's home to the spot where the VW had left the road. That scenario was a possibility but hardly likely. Surely the more usual thing would have been to call from the top of the hill where there was a good mobile signal. And as Claire had said, who is without a mobile phone these days, particularly in a remote country area, late at night? But calling from a mobile number, Randall mused, would have made the caller identifiable. *999 calls have caller ID.*

Was it the *driver* who had Daisy? Was it possible that the driver and the caller really were one and the same person, and they'd deliberately waited to make the call? Or were there two people involved, their caller and the driver? That seemed a more likely scenario, considering the delay of four hours between the crash and the telephone call. Hope Cottage was no more than a ten-minute walk from the crash site.

Concealing a collision which had resulted in such a serious and high-profile accident suggested *something* or more truthfully *someone* malicious and failing to report an accident was the most minor infringement which could certainly conceal something worse. But he was still left with the question: why take the child?

To save her, or because she was a witness?

He summoned Talith.

Sean Dart, meanwhile, was knocking on the door of a tiny farm-worker's cottage in the village of Ratlinghope. The house was small enough to be a doll's house and he was surprised when a normal-sized female answered the door. Wanda Stefano was a pale woman with long, straight hair hanging in thin red rats' tails and a sixties, full Cher fringe. She had an air of weariness about her which instantly infected PC Sean Dart. He couldn't stop himself from yawning.

'Don't let me keep you up,' she said sarcastically, adding, 'Constable,' when she saw his ID.

'Sorry.'

'Let me guess.' Wanda had a lovely husky voice which Sean appreciated. 'You have to be here about poor old Tracy.'

'Yeah. Can I come in?'

She nodded and led the way into a doll-sized sitting room so small there was only enough room for two armchairs and a television. He sat in one and she, adjusting her tight jeans so she could bend her legs, sat in the other.

'What do you want to know?' she asked.

'Anything you can tell us about her.'

'I take you haven't found Daisy?' Her head jerked towards the TV. 'There's been nothing on the telly.'

'No.' It felt like a confession.

'You want to know about Tracy? She was the greediest woman I've ever known. She was proper mercenary. She'd sell her own mother she would if she could get away with it and they promised her thirty pieces of silver.' The woman touched a small gold crucifix around her neck. 'I know you shouldn't speak ill of the dead but she was such a one. In a way.' The dark eyes warmed. 'You almost have to admire her. She wouldn't let anything or anyone stand in her way. If she wanted it she'd have it, Neil being an example. The trouble with Tracy was that if she spotted something better she'd just go for that.'

'The drinking,' PC Dart said tentatively, 'was that much of a problem?'

'More recently,' Wanda said. 'I think she suspected that Neil was up to his old tricks again. She didn't like that. It was OK for her to take him away from his wife and kids but she didn't like it if the same thing was done to her.'

'How do you think she was as a mother?'

Wanda blew out through her lips. 'Not much better or worse than average,' she said.

'And Neil?' Dart was fishing in the dark now.

'I wouldn't trust him as far as I could throw him,' Wanda said dismissively.

'Tracy said she was driving over to yours.'

'It happened if they had a row.'

'She'd drive over the Burway?'

Wanda nodded. 'There was no point trying to tell her anything when she'd had a couple.'

'Did she ring that night and tell you she was coming?'

A wary nod was his answer.

'So what do you think has happened to Daisy?'

Wanda shrugged. 'I don't know,' she said. 'I honestly don't know. I don't like to think. She's such a lovely little girl.' Her face was stricken. 'I just hope she's alive. That's all.'

Stirring, stirring, muttering and mumbling. Bubble, bubble. Work to do. Potions to mix. I start to wonder as I try to straighten my bent back. The message . . . Yes, it wouldn't be long now . . .

Friday, 19 April, 11.20 a.m.

Forty-five minutes later, Talith was back outside the sad, neglected house which spoke of the unhappy people who had lived there. He smothered a grin. If the cottage from where the phone call had been made was called Hope Cottage he would have named Tracy and Neil's place in Church Stretton Hopeless Cottage.

Mansfield opened the door to him. The house smelt cleaner. Someone had been at it with the polish and Mr Muscle. Talith sniffed appreciatively. Nice.

'Mind if I come in?'

Mansfield grinned and held open the door. 'Be my guest.' He seemed jaunty about something.

Talith preambled by saying, 'I'm sorry about Tracy.'

Mansfield looked away. 'Best thing possible,' he murmured. 'Someone benefitted, I think,' he continued. 'They donated some of her organs.' He looked away and his face soured. 'With the permission of her next of kin – her mother and sister.'

Talith was shocked. Not only was Tracy dead but Mansfield was talking as though they'd had a garage sale of her belongings. 'I'm sorry,' he said again, stiffly. 'That's awful.'

'Truth is,' Mansfield confided, 'when they were talking about switching the machine off and organ donation it actually came as a relief, deep down. I thought I'd end up being a full-time carer for a vegetable.'

Talith couldn't think of anything else to say except to repeat for a third time, even more awkwardly, 'I'm sorry.'

Mansfield was expansive. 'Don't be,' he said, waving his hand around. 'Him up there. It's all for a purpose.'

'And Daisy,' Talith queried. 'How do you feel about her? Who would look after her if . . . ?'

Neil looked flummoxed by the question. He gaped at the sergeant and it was obvious he didn't know what to say. Talith made an effort to be helpful. 'Perhaps Tracy's mum or her sister?'

Mansfield blew out his cheeks and shook his head decisively. 'If – when – she turns up then Tracy's mum . . . no chance,' he said. 'No good with kids. And if Sofia, Tracy's sister, stepped forward to look after Daisy, which I doubt, the poor kid's life would be hell. Sofia, two years younger and built like a dumpling, would make the child's life a misery too. No,' he said cheerfully. 'Daisy's well out of it.'

Talith felt very uncomfortable. It seemed to him that Neil Mansfield simply didn't get it, or was in some kind of denial over Daisy. Hadn't he realized the poor little thing was probably dead?

Mansfield's cheerful manner had robbed him of any ideas how to respond. He opened his mouth to speak. Normally he trusted that if he opened his mouth something sensible would come out. He didn't expect anything hugely sensible this time, just something appropriate that didn't do any harm. But this time he was out of luck – nothing. His brain and his mouth had disconnected. He simply gaped like a fish.

'Anyway,' Mansfield said brightly.

Was he on antidepressants?

'What was it you came about?'

'Just a couple of simple questions,' Talith managed. 'We've found traces of black paint on Tracy's car. To your knowledge, had she had a prang in it recently?'

Mansfield frowned. 'She wasn't a great driver,' he said, 'and she wasn't above hiding from me if she'd had a bump in the car but I don't think she'd had a collision in it – not recently anyway,' he said. 'Not that I know of, at least.' He scraped his throat noisily. 'Of course, I might not have noticed.'

Talith wondered.

But Neil's next words began to convince him otherwise.

'I have to say,' he said, 'when I went I went to the pound and saw the state it was in I grieved for it. Tracy loved that Polo. She treated her cars well, for a woman.'

Don't bother with PC talk, will you, Mansfield, Talith thought.

Neil continued. 'She'd have been really upset if she'd had a bump. Probably would have booked it in asap to get it *tidied up*.'

Talith had noticed before how these random little quotes gave him a picture of the victims. He could imagine Tracy as he had seen on her photographs – not the thing in the hospital – being fussy not only about her appearance but that of her car too.

Neil's face clouded as though he had also had a glimpse of Tracy before everything went so wrong. His last view of the beloved VW had been at the scrapyard – after it had been released by the police. He'd had to go, accompanied, to collect Tracy's things. There hadn't been much there: a windscreen ice-scraper, some CDs, a toy of Daisy's, sugar-free chewing gum. He gulped. He'd seen the damage and he'd seen the blood. He didn't want to remember the car but he had a feeling it might invade his nightmares.

'Sorry,' he said. 'I can't be absolutely sure but I don't think she'd had a bump in it – not before the accident.'

Talith had a warm feeling inside his stomach. He was sure this information was important.

THIRTEEN

Friday, 19 April, 4 p.m.

The story was obsessing the nation. Who was the mystery caller? Why had she rung and then vanished? The TV channels, local and national, had played the emergency tape over and over again, hoping someone would recognize the caller's voice. No one had. Yet.

They had appealed for anyone who could give them information to come forward. Again, no one had. Yet.

A local businessman had offered a reward for any information which led to the whereabouts of Daisy Walsh, but even this had not borne fruit.

It was most frustrating but the papers didn't give up. They still ran the headline:

WHERE IS THE CHILD?

And waited.

I have her.
Why do you have her?
You will find out. I have a purpose.
Will we have her back?
Wait and see.
Is she dead?
Again, wait and see.

Randall had returned to Carding Mill Valley, which was now open to the general public – the usual assortment of voyeurs and amateur detectives as well as the more normal dog-walkers and hikers. The police tape still cordoned off the area where the car had rested. There were oil and scorch marks and a deep furrow in the soft soil. The bunches of flowers around the area had grown. Messages, good wishes, blessings, pleas for the return of Daisy and the customary:

why? He looked away from the flowers and glanced up at the Burway, following the trajectory of the car, and climbed back up the steep bank, puffing a little when he reached the top. There were more flowers here. Roses, lilies, carnations and . . .

Something caught his eye.

A photographer he recognized as being from the *Shropshire Star* was recording everything, including the flowers, with an impressive-looking digital camera. Randall called him over. 'Tony,' he said, 'take a picture of this, will you?'

It was an odd concoction of plants. Not a pretty floral tribute. More like a bouquet garni – something you'd stick in a stew pot. It was a bunch of herbs. Surely? Randall stared at it. It looked so incongruous. Was someone playing a joke? He bent down and read the card with it, then almost recoiled. There was no *why?* or *rest in peace* or *to a lovely girl*. It was a message clearly aimed at him.

Read the meaning of the plants, it said. *Follow the message and find the child.*

Someone was playing games with them.

Randall's face became grim. He slipped a pair of latex gloves on and drew out a forensic bag.

Two can play cryptic games, he thought, and slipped the floral tribute inside.

Friday, 19 April, 4.30 p.m.

Now Tracy Walsh was dead her case and therefore her family had moved into Martha's jurisdiction. Her mother, Pat, had long, dark hair and, according to their records, was in her early fifties. Her face, however, was that of a sixty-something-year-old who had led a very unhealthy life, smoking and drinking and generally *doing her own thing*. She walked into Martha's office, hostility bouncing her step, adding a certain arrogance to her air. She was skinny with stained teeth and nasty little eyes that peered at Martha with suspicious hostility and a certain amount of defence, as though the coroner blamed *her* for her daughter's unhappy circumstances and eventual death.

The very cheek of it, her manner said, her sharp shoulders almost pugnacious.

Sofia Waterman, Tracy's sister was, in contrast, a soft and podgy little dumpling of a woman, but with the lovely skin that frequently blesses the overweight. She had a strange, affected way of speaking, adding 'Yah?' to the end of every sentence. It sounded like something she had learned. She was copying someone, probably an A-list celebrity.

Both expressed anger and righteous indignation at the 'pathetic' police investigation and affected a maudlin sympathy for their daughter and sister. But when Martha mentioned Daisy their emotions were hardly different. 'We hardly knew her,' Pat said, her daughter nodding in loyal agreement. 'Tracy and Neil – they kept themselves to themselves, see. So we never built up a relationship with little Daisy.' Pat seemed to realize that, as the child's grandmother, something more was expected of her. 'I did try,' she said, 'but our Trace, she shut me out.'

'Yah,' said Sofia and couldn't resist having an extra dig. 'We would love to have got to know the little kid,' she said, her face as impassive as dough, 'but Trace and Neil . . . They was having difficult times. It was best we left them alone. That's what we told the papers. When Daisy's found they're willin' to pay for the full story. Yah?' she finished brightly.

Martha resisted the temptation to echo, 'Yah.'

Pat and Sofia couldn't resist pronouncing judgement on the dead Tracy, saying that she had a lot of 'problems' which they enlarged on as being 'drink' and 'relationship difficulties' before expressing relief that she was being 'put to good use'. Martha assumed they were referring to the organ donation. She was relieved when they finally rose, muttering something about funeral arrangements and making a note of the date of the inquest.

They still need more help; I must visit the cottage again and leave something more obvious. I spend as little time as I can in this place. For all its contemporary air I can sense, underneath, the black oil of evil, the dirty stink of wickedness. It is here – it is all around . . .

Sunday, 21 April.

Tracy's thirty-fourth birthday was marked by no one. Not even Neil. He was aware of the date and wished he wasn't.

FOURTEEN

It is a truism that where there is mystery, instead of diminishing as the days go by without a solution, it compounds. Look at Jack the Ripper. Look at the *Marie Celeste*. Look at the Bermuda Triangle. The folklore surrounding the unsolved mysteries compounds, grows, adds fantastic detail and finally finds a life all of its own, independent of the truth.

The longer Daisy Walsh was missing the deeper the mystery, and the more her whereabouts were swamped in mist and folklore. The explanation for her continued disappearance resulted in stories ever more mysterious and bizarre. The local press stopped just short of printing the fable that she'd been spirited away by fairies, taken by demons or spirited into the bog by will-o'-the-wisps and their mischievous lanterns, but they'd explored almost every other possibility, including the patently silly one that she'd been swept down the stream at the bottom of Carding Mill Valley. In fact, the stream was little more than a trickle and wouldn't have swept anything down it. Even the sodden pink slipper had been found no more than six feet from the heavy impact of the car. It was not possible that it could have borne the missing child right down the valley and out of sight, thought Martha as she read the story. She was familiar with the stream. Sam had fallen in it when he had been a three-year-old. He had been soaked – rainfall had been heavy for that entire month and the stream had been in full flow. But there had been no danger of him drowning, much less of him being swept downstream. He had simply been very wet, a little frightened and extremely cold. So this was not what had happened to the missing child. The stream could not have swept anything down it except a leaf or a twig. Certainly not a child.

She looked closely at the little girl's face peeping around the edge of the door, laughing, curls bouncing like Shirley Temple's. Her dark eyes were sparkling and her small milk teeth were exposed.

She was wearing a sprigged cotton dress and her hand, holding the door, was chubby and child-like. She was a pretty, endearing child; no sign here of the screaming little girl who wet the bed and was dragged into a car by a drunken mother at two in the morning. How could it have happened to this child, a little girl anyone would surely love to claim as a daughter?

Martha put the paper down with a *tut* of irritation. This was a difficult enough case without facts being so clouded by fable and fantasy.

Her morning was interrupted by a tetchy Jericho putting his head round the door and asking if she had time to speak to Detective Inspector Alex Randall on the other line. Tempted to say *of course* far too enthusiastically, she modified her response to a simple, 'Yes.' Her curiosity was pricked. Could they have found the missing child at last?

But when Alex was put through to her office phone his question, put abruptly, threw her in quite another direction. 'Do you know much about flowers, Martha?'

She didn't know whether to laugh or challenge his sanity and in the end decided to play it perfectly straight. 'In what context?'

'The *language* of flowers.' He spoke earnestly.

'Probably about as much as most people,' she said cautiously, 'roses for love and all that. Although Shropshire does have a bit of a reputation for horticulture thanks to good old Percy Thrower.' She couldn't resist smiling as she wondered where all this was leading.

'Yeah,' he said, his tone lightening so she knew he was smiling too, 'though, as I said, this is more about the *language* of flowers than how much manure to put on the roses.'

'I'm intrigued.'

'Look,' he said awkwardly. 'I'm just heading back up the A49 from Church Stretton now. I'll be passing through Bayston Hill in about half an hour. Is there any chance I could pop in and we could discuss this? I want to show you something.'

'I'll ask Jericho to put the kettle on,' she said lightly. She hadn't seen Alex Randall for a couple of weeks and, quite apart from looking forward to seeing him, she was dying to know how the investigation was progressing. Was there any news of Daisy?

She also felt some sympathy for Alex Randall. As senior investigating officer he had come under intense scrutiny and criticism at his handling of the initial investigation. The newspapers had been increasingly critical of the police: how thorough had the initial search of the Long Mynd been?

Was it absolutely certain, beyond all doubt, that Daisy Walsh had been in the doomed car? What explanation did they have for Tracy screeching to a halt on a remote road at two a.m. when no one had come forward to say they had seen her or collided with her?

Had there been a collision between two cars on the the Burway that night or had the dent been made on another occasion?

How thorough had the initial search been of Charity Ignatio's house?

And again and again they came back to the same question: why had they failed to find the child?

The questions had gone on and on. With no response from the police, the word *failure* was increasingly prominent in the editorials. It was at times like these that Martha felt most sympathy for the police. They were doing their best, for pity's sake. But how on earth did DI Randall think *she* could help?

And the *language* of flowers? What was that all about? Intrigued hardly described her manic curiosity. The thirty minutes between the phone call and Alex Randall's revelations dragged. To try and stop herself from nibbling her nails in impatience she focused on upcoming events.

She had set a date for the inquest to be opened. She already anticipated that the case would be opened and adjourned pending police enquiries. In her heart she could already hear her pronouncement, *open verdict* or *death by misadventure*. No one had *murdered* Tracy. No one had pushed the car off the Burway. She had died by her own drunken hand. Had Daisy's body been found alongside her mother's Martha would have had a joint inquest, mother and daughter together – if Daisy was dead it was fitting that they should be buried together. She had not needed to attend Tracy's post-mortem but Mark Sullivan had rung her with the results. Tracy had died of major organ failure following multiple injuries sustained during a road traffic accident. Already half of her bits and pieces had been sewn into other bodies, hopefully to relieve them of a lifetime's ill health.

Martha had read through the reports with an odd sense of the futility of life but not necessarily of death. Tracy Walsh had achieved something in her death that perhaps she had not managed in life: she had helped and benefited someone.

Alex Randall was actually with her twenty-five minutes later.

She heard him climb the stairs, his long legs taking them two at a time, greet Jericho and a moment later his brisk knock rapped on her door. She pulled it open herself and couldn't smother the broad smile that displayed her pleasure at seeing him again. 'Good to see you, Alex,' she said warmly.

He entered the room and stood still, his face close to hers, smiling into her eyes, breathing in her air. Had this been a cocktail party they would have been close enough to kiss. At least a *mwah mwah* social kiss. It would only have taken one of them to move forward less than one inch. They were that near. She was very aware of him as a man: the scent of him, the sound of his breathing, the rise and fall of his chest, the angles of face and body, the energetic vibes he emitted. They both froze, neither moving a muscle.

Then the spell was broken. He took a step back, still facing her, still smiling but unmistakably backing off. He looked glad to see her but there was a tangible cooling in the atmosphere. The happy light in his eyes dimmed. Perhaps her welcome had been a little too warm. Too intimate. Too open. She was a woman who found it hard to conceal her emotions. She had been overly glad to see him and now she had embarrassed him with her warmth.

He broke the silence with a dry laugh. 'I do bother you with some things, don't I, Martha.'

'I love the intrigue,' she confessed. 'It makes life interesting. Besides, as coroner, I'm involved in the case now. With Tracy's death it comes under my jurisdiction. Tell me first, Alex, have you found Daisy?'

He shook his head. 'Regretfully, no.'

'Not a sign of her? No clue as to her whereabouts?'

Again he shook his head and gave her a rueful smile. 'No. But let's look on the bright side: at least we haven't found her body. Whatever's happened to her she isn't lying somewhere on the Long Mynd, injured or dead, missed by a careless police search. We've combed the entire area thoroughly.' A shadow fleeted across his face. 'And while she's still missing there is, at least, a chance that she will be found safe and well.' His hazel eyes looked hopefully at her.

Not much of a chance as time goes by, Martha wanted to say but desisted, substituting it for, 'So where do you think she is?'

'I'll be honest, Martha, I don't have a clue.' His eyes looked frankly into hers. 'I have no idea,' he said simply. 'Absolutely no idea whatsoever. I'm stumped.'

'What about your mystery caller? Have you tracked *her* down?'

He gave a deep sigh. 'She's vanished. We've had officers calling on practically every isolated cottage, farm and homestead within a ten-mile radius. We've nearly finished. We haven't come across anyone who fits the bill. We've broadcast the nine-nine-nine call over and over again on TV. No one's come forward to say they recognize the voice. If our mystery caller is a real person and not a fantasy, she must lead a life practically without human contact.'

'Hmm. And what about the possible collision?'

'Again, no one's come forward,' Alex said wearily.

'Surely you have identification on the paint?'

Alex blew out a frustrated breath. 'We think it's a Honda or a Chevrolet,' he said. 'But we're not absolutely certain that the collision happened on the Saturday night of Tracy's accident.'

'What about your forensic linguist,' Martha asked. 'The *Shropshire Star* said you'd involved someone from Birmingham. Did she help?'

'Yes and no. Some of what she said was plain odd. Mumbo jumbo, I suspect, but as I've said I'm clutching at straws here. She mentioned some stuff about the mystery caller being a country woman who was socially isolated; someone whose speech wasn't polluted by contemporary phrases. She said she sounded as though she came from another era. She suggested a farmer's wife, a country dweller.' He frowned and said in a spooky voice and a wriggle of his bony fingers: 'From the past.'

In spite of the gravity of the situation, Martha couldn't prevent a smile.

He looked embarrassed. 'She said something about superstition, folklore, pagan beliefs. Black magic, white magic. All that stuff.'

Had the situation not been so serious, Martha would have laughed out loud. 'I thought forensic linguistics was meant to be a scientific study, Alex.'

'I know,' he said, suddenly looking weary. 'We know we're clutching at straws. But what else can I do with so little to go on and the possibility that the life of a four-year-old is at stake?' He leaned in so close she could read his troubled eyes. 'At night I dream I've found her body and she's freshly dead, so if we'd found her sooner she would still be alive.'

She reached for his hand in sympathy and for once he didn't draw back, seeming happy at her touch.

He continued, 'No one has come forward who knows of someone

who might have had a prang at two a.m. in the early hours of Sunday the seventh of April on the Burway, and no one appears to recognize the voice of our mystery caller. And that is the sum total of everything we know about the whereabouts of Daisy Walsh. Nothing. Quite honestly,' he said despairingly, 'we may as well say she's been spirited away by fairies or taken by the Devil. We haven't got any better ideas.'

'Are all cases like this, Alex? So confusing?'

'Mostly.'

'But she exists,' Martha pointed out. 'She's not some wood nymph to disappear into nothing. She's a real child.' Even as she spoke the words something pricked at her consciousness, causing her to frown.

'Yes. She exists,' Randall responded a little testily, not noticing. 'And I believe our caller is a local woman but we can't seem to find her. The team have been all over the place, knocking on doors, asking questions. We've covered everywhere.'

Martha searched his face for the slightest beam of hope. It wasn't there. Only grey depression as heavy as lead. She tried to encourage him. 'She's out there somewhere, Alex,' but the words had the opposite effect. He tightened his lips.

'Usually I find it helpful talking to you about a case,' he said frankly. 'It gives me a different perspective.' Then he grinned even wider, almost apologetically, and met her eyes. The gleam was back. 'Don't take offence, Martha, but this is really *not* one of those instances.'

'No offence taken, Alex,' she said briskly, responding to the warmth in his eyes. 'I'm just sorry I can't inspire you.' She couldn't resist glancing down at the newspaper on her desk and tacking on, 'It must be very frustrating having your shortcomings pointed out so graphically.'

'Yeah, but you've got enough to do. I really shouldn't keep bothering you.'

She cut him short and sat down at her desk, her mind a swirl of emotion. 'My life would be an awful lot duller if you didn't, Alex. You know you're welcome at any time.' She met his eyes. 'You must know that.'

He simply nodded. 'But it would be only too easy to take advantage of that, Martha.'

And like a pubescent girl she felt her face flush. It was all she could do not to cover what she knew would be flaming red cheeks with her hands. Alex Randall sat and watched her, the glint of humour dancing in his eyes. She waited until they were drinking the coffee that Jericho had brought before prompting him. 'So what is all this about? Flowers? Gardening?'

'We-ell,' he began, 'you know how people leave flowers when there's been a tragedy?'

'Yes.' She couldn't work out where this was leading.

'Some were left on the Burway, just at the point where the car left the road.'

'But Tracy died in hospital. Not there. And Daisy – well, we just don't know.'

'Perhaps someone does.'

They had returned to the circle.

'Then why conceal her body?'

He shrugged. 'I wish I knew.'

'Don't we all? It would bring some relief.'

'Well,' he said gloomily, 'we're never going to get Tracy's side of the story now, are we?'

'No.'

'There were quite a lot of flowers.'

Martha couldn't work out where all this was heading. 'So? I expect a few people felt sympathy. It's generally done.'

'Not like this.' He produced a bedraggled bouquet tied up with blue ribbon. She stared at it. It was hardly decorative; not the usual wrapped bouquet. In fact, they weren't really flowers at all. They looked more like a bunch of herbs. She looked across at Alex, a question in her eyes. He shrugged and she picked the bunch up, frowning and sniffing them.

'Well, as to flowers being left at the site,' she ruminated, 'as Tracy didn't die *there*, and Daisy's fate is a mystery, it may just be a token. Or . . .' Her voice tailed away.

'That's not all,' Alex said and produced the forensic bag. Like him she read the message. *Read the meaning of the plants. Follow the message and find the child.*

'So there's some significance in the plants,' she said and began to identify them, then looked up. 'You said the meaning of plants. A hidden message.'

He leaned forward, hands on his knees. Curious. 'Go on,' he urged.

Her fingers lingered over the sprig of lavender. 'So these flowers are not the usual message of love, sympathy or hope but something a little more subtle. Something we need to interpret.'

'That's exactly what I meant,' he said eagerly, 'when I used the phrase *language* of flowers. Can you imagine what the papers would make of these?'

'Yes,' she responded, lifting her eyes from the plants to his face.

'Nothing good.'

His eyes were bright and hopeful. 'I don't suppose you could have a go at interpreting the message for me?' He leaned far back in his chair, relaxing now, half closing his eyes but watching her from lowered lids, hawk-like.

'I'll have a go,' she said, 'though I worry I might *mis*interpret the message.'

'It's a possibility,' he agreed, 'but . . .' After a brief pause, he continued, 'I wasn't sure what your horticultural identification skills were so,' he took a list out from his pocket, 'I got one of the people at the Percy Thrower Garden Centre to identify them all.' He read from the list. 'Lobelia, azalea, lavender, mint, rosemary, myrtle.'

Had it not been for Alex's face earnestly searching for help and the gravity of the situation, Martha would have giggled. 'Sounds more like a recipe for a casserole to me.'

'We-ell, it certainly looked different from the other floral tributes, which is why I picked it up and brought it here. It was left a little apart,' he added. 'And then I read the message.'

She studied the list then fingered the sprigs. It did look more like a bouquet garni than a decorative flower arrangement, and there was no mistaking the direction: *Read the meaning of the plants. Follow the message and find the child.*

It didn't say whether the child was alive or dead, but it was a clear challenge.

Martha looked at Alex's list, then at the plants again. Without another word, she stood up and crossed the room.

She took a book down from the shelf and turned to face Alex Randall. 'Luckily for you, one year, when my mother didn't know what to buy me for Christmas, she bought me this.' It was a heavy tome with plenty of pictures of plants. She laid it on her desk, leafed through the pages, found the plants and made a few notes.

Ten minutes later, she met Alex's eyes. 'The message,' she said, 'is a very negative one. Lobelia stands for malevolence. Azalea's a warning to take care; it also stands for temperance and fragility.'

She looked up. 'That could possibly refer to Daisy. Tracy certainly wasn't temperate though she was ultimately fragile.'

Randall nodded, listening hard as she continued.

'Lavender stands for devotion but also for distrust. Mint for suspicion. And rosemary for remembrance or to look at it another way to make sure you never forget.' She leaned back in her chair, thoughtful. 'Myrtle doesn't quite fit in – not according to this, anyway. Myrtle stands for love, Alex. Apparently it's the Hebrew emblem of marriage, used under the canopy or *chuppah*. Perhaps it stands for the love Tracy surely must have felt for her daughter?' She wished she could have taken the questioning upward inflection from the end of the sentence but she was not sure what Tracy Walsh's feelings had really been towards her little girl; certainly not at the point when she had snatched her from her bed and driven her, drunk as a skunk, up such a dangerous road.

'If I'm reading the message correctly,' she said, 'there is love, a warning never to forget, distrust, suspicion and malevolence. At a guess the person who is sending us this message knows a little more about Tracy Walsh and her daughter than we do.'

'And the message is meant for?'

She met his eyes. 'I think it's meant for you, Alex, as senior investigating officer.'

Randall looked troubled. Then he spoke quietly. 'Hidden messages? So we probably have the same person who made the phone call, the very same person that we're assuming removed Daisy alive, dead or injured from the scene of the accident, and this person is sending me an indirect and deliberately obscure message of malevolence, distrust, a warning we must never forget and suspicion, together with an ancient Jewish message of love and commitment, and in the centre is a four-year-old girl who should take care and who is fragile, temperate and currently missing. It's as bad as those awful people who are addicted to crossword puzzles and talk in riddles. That's what this is, Martha. Talking in riddles.' His expression was strained. 'And I suppose the negative messages all relate to Tracy?'

'Or Neil,' she added softly. 'I take it the grandmother and aunt are not in the picture?'

'I hadn't even considered that possibility,' he said, heaving a great sigh. 'Why on earth would they abduct a child whose future would almost certainly lie with them?'

'I can only think of one reason,' she said, 'and it's not a very good one. Chequebook journalism?'

'A very risky strategy,' he said.

'I met them today,' she said, 'and was fairly unimpressed. They appeared to be fake. I don't think they really cared at all about Tracy's death – or Daisy's disappearance, for that matter. I just got the impression they . . .' She stopped. 'They were talking about speaking to the press. They seemed a pair who only thought of themselves. There wasn't any real grief or concern over the plight of Daisy but, you know, I can't see them abducting the child and hanging on to her, hoping to make a bit of money out of it. They didn't seem that conniving.'

Then another thought struck her and she touched the sprig of myrtle. 'Does anyone actually *love* this little girl or has she been a pawn in a relationship, a way for Tracy to get back at Neil for his perceived infidelities? Is that why she grabbed her that night instead of leaving her safely in her bed?'

Alex didn't comment but something in his face looked haunted and sad. Regretful. It was as though he was reliving some personal painful memory. Martha wondered, was it the phrase *love this child*, or the word *pawn*? The next minute he had recovered and was his old self, balanced but secretive, hiding behind a screen of politeness. 'When we find Daisy's abductor,' he said, his face grim, 'we will charge her at the very least with wasting police time and abduction, and possibly concealment of a body, if not with something far, far worse.' He was staring into the distance, his face haunted but determined. 'I still have so many more questions,' he confessed.

'Like?'

'Why *was* this person on the scene in the first place? Was it accident or design?' He indicated the sprig of plants. 'Why leave such an obscure message when we might easily have failed to pick up on it?'

'The message,' Martha said slowly, 'was left deliberately obscure. Only the right person would read it.' She looked up. 'They knew it would end up with you, Alex.'

He took a moment to absorb that one. 'What it doesn't tell us,' he said, 'is whether she's alive or dead. Presumably if she's injured it would be as a result of the car accident? If so why not simply bring Daisy to us? We'd take care of her. We'd make sure she was safe and had any medical treatment she needed.'

The sentiment sparked Martha off thinking. 'Wait a minute, Alex.

Realistically, what will happen to Daisy if you find her safe and well?'

He shrugged. 'Relatives, usually. They generally step in – with the encouragement of social services.'

'Exactly. And Tracy's relatives are?'

'Well, there's her father,' he said dubiously.

Martha dismissed him with a purse of her lips and a shake of her head.

'Daisy's father? I don't think so.'

'So it will be Daisy's grandmother and aunt.'

'Exactly. Like I said, I've met them, Alex.' She paused, picking her words out carefully, like chicken bones. 'They don't want her. The general impression is that there was bound to be a tragedy someday with Tracy's drinking, yet they've shown little interest in Daisy. But they are her next of kin. Realistically, who else is in line to take care of Daisy if she's still alive? Neil?'

'What do you think they think of Neil?'

'To be honest they didn't seem that interested in him either but at least they didn't say anything bad about him.'

'Do you think it's possible that if Daisy's still alive grandmother and granddaughter might be reunited?'

Alex snorted. 'Reunited? They hardly saw her. I don't think *if* has ever seemed a bigger word, Martha. She's just not the maternal type, is she? And I think it very likely that if Daisy really is still alive social services will be keeping a very beady eye on her future.'

Martha was silent. Randall watched her, seeing her face thoughtful, pensive, anxious. Finally she looked up. 'I'd be very tempted,' she advised slowly, 'to look very deeply into Tracy and Neil's lives,' she said. 'Not just their life together but their lives as individuals. I suspect something very murky is behind this. And I simply can't believe that the little girl was discovered by chance at six a.m. in a remote country place by a wandering country person who abducted her, when she was probably injured and shocked, and who is now teasing you with obscure bunches of plants meant to send warnings which you might or might not have read correctly, and which with-hold the vital fact, whether Daisy is still alive. OK,' she said, holding up her index finger. 'So you've got the message now, that there is more to this than meets the eye. But malevolence? Who does that refer to? Our abductor? Tracy? Her family? Neil? Something happened that night up there on the Burway, at two in the morning a few weeks ago, and I don't think it happened by chance.'

The phrase resonated in her head like an echo. *Happened by chance.* What was she saying? That all this had been *planned*? It was an impossible idea.

She focused on him. 'Wherever the little girl is,' she said, 'dead or alive, injured or healthy, happy or not, she shouldn't be there.'

Randall's grey eyes were very troubled. 'Where *should* she be, Martha?'

'Possibly with Neil, but that won't happen.' She was temporarily distracted. 'Tell me. Did Tracy's sister and mother visit her in hospital?'

'I think they had to go there to sign the organ donation forms.'

'Mmm.' She screwed her face up. 'A four-year-old child is naturally suspicious of strangers. I wonder if Daisy had met her abductor before.'

Randall shrugged. 'Who knows?'

She could follow his train of thought – how very little they knew – for the time being.

'Well, I have plenty to chew over.'

'Good,' she responded lightly.

He still didn't move. She put a hand on his arm, less as a physical contact than a way of emphasising her words. 'The sort of person who would send this message, Alex, is exactly as your forensic linguist thought – a country person with an eccentric character. Someone who lives in the past, in the realm of witchcraft and folklore, of legend and fantasy, someone whose values are not like ours. Someone who believes they are above the law. Someone without conscience or pity. Someone who does not care about a four-year-old child who, if she's even alive, must be confused and frightened if not in actual pain or danger. Find her, Alex, for goodness' sake. This person is pure evil. She is playing with you and deliberately using an obscure way of communicating to taunt you. She'll let you have the truth when it suits her.'

Even as she spoke the words something pricked her mind. It was the phrase she had just used, *obscure way of communicating*. Somehow it connected with another phrase she had used in the past, together with *without conscience or pity*. She had been here before, to this dark and troubled place. It was connected with a girl. Not a child. A girl. There was, in her mind's eye, another image, faded, indistinct and blurred at the moment, but the image would come into focus at some point. Just not yet. She was not ready for the revelation. *All in good time* (one of her mother's favourite phrases). She looked down at the plants and knew she must do something here apart from simply translating. She must interpret too. Interpret and anticipate.

Alex was watching her. 'What is it, Martha?' he asked gently.

'I can't say,' she said. 'Not now. Not yet, but I fear for the child.'

It was the name. Why had it seemed familiar?

He said nothing but still watched and waited.

Finally she spoke. 'Something in this case is reminding me of a previous case long ago. I'll have to ask Jericho if he can help me out here.' She laughed. 'He has the memory of an elephant. Leave it with me, Alex. I really can't say because it might be nothing. I might be barking up the wrong tree.' She stopped then added, 'I hope so.'

He simply nodded. Then, quite out of the blue, he spoke. 'Martha,' he said tentatively.

Sensing something she turned, her eyes on him.

But she knew from the quick drop of his gaze that he had lost his bottle.

'It doesn't matter,' he said and she knew if she had pursued the subject he would have sidestepped whatever it was he had been about to say.

He left and she watched the still-swinging door. How bloody typical, she thought. The only man I have the slightest feelings for and he's married, plus he doesn't appear to have any affection for me whatsoever. A moment later she stood up decisively and opened the door.

'Jericho,' she called. 'Can you help me out?'

FIFTEEN

Wednesday, 24 April, 10 a.m.

Charity Ignatio's homecoming was different from other occasions. Not quiet and private but very, very public. The police had been in constant contact with her while she had been in the Middle East and they knew she would be back today. Apart from a few days off early in April her schedule had been far too tight to return any sooner and they had had to be patient. It was hardly likely that Charity would hold any key to the child's whereabouts. She was out of the picture, having been in the Middle East at the time of the crash and Daisy's disappearance.

But, as Daisy remained missing, media interest had swelled so not only the police but the press, noisy and jostling, long lenses poised, were waiting for her outside her front door on that chilly April morning. She arrived back in the UK tired and jet-lagged after an overnight flight and voicing her outrage. How dare someone break into her cottage, make a telephone call and then vanish into thin bloody air. By the time she'd picked up her car from Heathrow airport, paid the exorbitant fee for being away for almost a month, battled her way up the M40 and across to Shropshire on the M54, finally arriving at Hope Cottage at 10 a.m., her mood had not improved. And when she saw the police car, standing patiently, waiting for her return, and behind that the feeding frenzy of the world's papers, she finally snapped.

But what the world loves more than anything else – more than romance or scandal, more than a grisly murder, more than embarrassing failure or even runaway success, is a mystery. And this mystery was sticking to the front pages of papers and media sites like a fly to flypaper.

WPC Delia Shaw stepped forwards to introduce herself but she had her work cut out soothing the irate and exhausted woman. She looked behind her apologetically at the long lenses and furry sound equipment that was being thrust forward. 'I'm so sorry,' she said. 'If we could have stopped them we would have but . . .'

Charity Ignatio simply scowled. She was somewhere in her mid-twenties with swarthy, Hispanic, thick-set features. She had beautiful dark eyes and fabulously long, curling eyelashes that couldn't possibly be a gift of nature, could they? She also had a wonderful complexion and a strong, square, almost masculine chin. The thought flashed through Delia Shaw's mind that she would have made a great Carmen.

Charity's scowl deepened as she met the officer's eyes. 'Look,' she said in a very patrician voice. 'I'm bloody knackered. I haven't had any sleep for two nights and I need to rest. It isn't my fault that someone's used my cottage.' Her eyes scanned the press and their intrusive lenses with frank hostility. 'And if that lot think I'm giving them an interview . . .' Her eyes narrowed, '. . . about bloody nothing . . .' She didn't need to complete the sentence.

'I know that,' WPC Shaw said sympathetically. 'We just want you to take a quick look around and see if anything's been moved or is missing. Or . . .' she began, with a flash of inspiration, 'if anything's there that shouldn't be. We can take a statement and your fingerprints sometime later.' She flashed a winning smile. 'When you've had some sleep.'

'Right,' Ms Ignatio said, stomping round to her boot and dragging out an enormous suitcase.

PC Gary Coleman hastened to help. 'Here,' he said. 'Let me.'

And she did.

The cottage felt cold and unwelcoming. Charity looked around her, still grumpy. 'I take it you've already had a look around.'

Delia Shaw didn't think it was quite the right moment to point out that a front door key hidden under a flower pot was not a good idea. Ms Ignatio was in a bad enough mood as it was without police criticism of her security arrangements.

She continued with her grumbling. 'You'd have thought Shirley would have made a bit of an effort,' she grumbled. 'Put the heating on or something.'

'We asked her not to come,' Delia Shaw responded smoothly. 'We know that our mystery call was made from here.' She ignored the outraged, '*Bloody cheek*,' and continued. 'We don't know who she is and we didn't want your cleaning woman to destroy any potential evidence. We think our caller is the key to finding the little girl.' She dropped her eyes. She didn't want Charity to read her private fear that either they never would find Daisy alive, or that they would find her decomposed body.

Somewhere.

But if she'd thought that mentioning Daisy Walsh would soften Charity's anger she might have considered again. It did nothing. She marched around the rooms, her aggression as obvious as steam coming out of a dragon's furious nose.

Belying its Victorian exterior, the cottage was very modern inside and it was obvious that Charity's tastes were for the ultra-contemporary. Everything was Spartan white. Even the sofa was spaceship-white leather and looked very uncomfortable, the sort where the cushions slide off and is always cold to the touch. Delia Shaw took a surreptitious glance at Ms Ignatio and added, *like its owner*, to her observation.

Charity might have a warm, traditional name but there was nothing either warm or traditional about her or her abode. In fact, the puzzle was why on earth did she choose to live *here*? Of all places? She would surely have been much more at home in a Mayfair flat. It would have been more convenient too for someone who spent their life travelling between international airports. So she watched her closely and with scarcely concealed curiosity.

The two officers followed Charity around in their stockinged feet, Ms Ignatio having insisted they remove their shoes first. They didn't mention the fact that forensics had done a thorough hovering job and was currently analysing every speck of debris that had been lifted from the carpet. If Ms Ignatio thought the carpet looked extra clean she didn't say so.

The kitchen was Tardis spacious with white wood units and pale granite tops, and it had a wonderful view out towards the sheep scattered along Carding Mill Valley and the Burway which looked a thin, precipitous ribbon of tarmac heading upwards and out of sight. Charity stood in front of the window and stared out, apparently lost in thought.

Delia Shaw cleared her throat. '*Is* anything out of place?'

'No. But . . .' Charity turned around. 'You'll think I'm being fanciful,' she said, embarrassed, 'but I can feel a presence.'

'It's possibly because you *know* someone's been here,' Coleman said, ever the pedant. 'It's quite common when there's been an intruder to feel that they've left their mark somewhere.'

'Is anything out of place?' Delia Shaw persisted.

Charity looked around her, frowning. 'I can't work out what it is,' she said, 'but something is different.' Her eyes scanned the room as she scowled.

Both Shaw and Coleman would dearly have loved to press her or even mention the intensive forensic 'scrub' but Charity's shoulders dropped and she continued with her tour without saying anything more.

They trailed after her around the small, two-bedroomed cottage, her misgivings translating to them and altering the innocent character of Hope Cottage. Instead of appearing a tidy, hardly lived-in home it seemed to be holding its breath, waiting for them to discover something. Delia Shaw glanced at her colleague. Was it possible the child *was* here after all?

It appeared that Charity felt the same. She was opening cupboards and searching under beds, her fingers spread out, her features puzzled.

As the cottage had a sloping roof upstairs the loft was very small, with only room for the water tanks and a small, wooden boarded area, no more than three foot square. The police had already searched up there and found nothing but Charity had the eyes of a hawk. She dropped the ladder down and climbed right into the loft, switching an electric light on as she went while the two police waited at the bottom of the ladder, looking at each other, their shoulders up, querying.

'Aha,' Charity said, scrabbling around up there. 'Not mine, I think.' And she dropped a small fluffy pink slipper right into Delia Shaw's hand. It had a scuffed plastic Barbie doll on the front and was a twin for the other.

Delia Shaw felt her face flame, while Coleman gave an embarrassed scrape of his throat.

Martha, meanwhile, was speaking to her officer. Jericho was listening intently, his head titled to one side, his eyes gleaming. He loved playing detective and his memory for old cases was prodigious, much better than Martha's. His mind was like a filing cabinet, everything neatly placed in chronological and alphabetical order.

'Did I dream it, Jericho,' she was saying, 'or did it really happen?' And then she told him about the bunch of herbs and the message it had conveyed, which had led to her question about a past case.

Jericho was silent for a moment, his mind flicking through cases as though they were cards in a pack. King, queen, ace, jack. He looked at her. It was the jack. The jack of clubs. A naughty card not, in this case, a male, but a female of the species. Jericho Palfreyman felt happy. He so loved a cliché.

'Deadlier than the male,' he murmured appropriately.

And Martha had got her clue.

'In 2002,' he said decisively. 'It were a wench what cooked tea for her family. You remember,' he prompted. 'They lived in Hope Bowdler. Father, stepmother and half-brother.' He screwed his face up in concentration. 'The girl made some sort of a soup and they all fell ill.'

Martha looked dubious. 'I'm not sure whether . . .'

'Aye, but she must have had a witch's knowledge of plants,' he said. 'There was no proof what she'd bin up to but someone left some Death Cap on 'er doorstep.' He looked at her in some surprise. 'Don't you remember, Mrs Gunn?'

'Not as well as I should,' she said. 'Who did you say died?'

'The whole family,' he said, 'except 'er.'

Martha screwed up her face. She still didn't remember the whole story – only fragments. It had always been a jigsaw with too many pieces missing. 'I remember the verdict,' she said. 'Misadventure. I had no option. I just remembered the case. I wonder what happened to her.'

Jericho looked very slightly irritated because now he didn't quite have all the answers. 'Give me a few days,' he said.

Randall was still pedantically pursuing leads, his officers increasingly frustrated.

WPC Lara Tinsley had the pleasure of PC Sean Dart's company when they went back to interview Lucy Stanstead at DI Randall's insistence. He didn't feel comfortable with the role of the naval captain's wife in all this. Tinsley watched the PC concentrate on driving the squad car and wondered. She hadn't quite made up her mind about Sean, whom she'd privately christened Sean Dark Horse. He'd recently transferred to Shrewsbury from Halifax but no one really knew why. She suspected it was to do with a marital breakup – he had a bitter twist to his mouth and never mentioned his family. Not his partner (male or female) or children, not even his mother or father, or anyone, in fact. He really was the proverbial dark horse and Lara Tinsley, who had a slightly nosey streak to her, had made it her mission to winkle out his backstory.

She thought this was possibly a waste of time and didn't quite see how Lucy Stanstead could possibly further their enquiries into Daisy's disappearance but hey, this was a major investigation. Sometimes you prodded around in a dark hole and found something surprising.

She just hoped that Lucy would provide something.

But it was their bad luck that the woman Neil Mansfield was suspected of having an affair with was not alone. However much he was away her burly Royal Navy captain husband was very much at home now. All six foot four of him. And he was not in a good mood.

He snatched the door open with a bad tempered scowl which only slightly meliorated when he registered the fact that they were in uniform.

'What?' he snapped.

Lara Tinsley gave him her nicest smile. 'I'm *so* sorry to bother you,' she said, oozing out all the charm she possessed, 'but we're investigating the accident that happened on the Burway and the disappearance of a little girl, Daisy Walsh.'

His fury was as intense as an Australian bush fire. 'What the hell do you think it's got to do with us?'

This was a tricky one. At her side Lara saw Sean Dart's mouth drop open as he waited for her to squirm out of this.

'The child's stepfather is currently doing some decorating here,' she tried, knowing it was as an excuse as weak as water.

Captain Stanstead scowled. 'That's a *nice* way of putting it,' he sneered.

Lara's shoulders dropped and she sneaked a glance at her colleague, with a mute appeal. *Help me out here, Sean?*

He did not respond but stared woodenly ahead.

Thanks. Thanks a lot.

Behind the captain they caught a movement. A petite woman in her thirties, eyes wide with fright, met their eyes, gave a very slight shake of her head and then there was another mute appeal. *Please.*

'Look,' the captain said, directing a very threatening-looking index finger at them. 'You get that bastard to finish his bit of *decorating* and then he can get out of our lives for ever.'

'We-ell, he's having a difficult time at the moment,' Tinsley tried. 'He's been spending a lot of time at the hospital with his partner and now, of course . . .' She dropped her eyes then sneaked an upwards glance. Lucy Stanstead was holding her breath while her husband had not lost any of his anger. 'She died, then,' he snapped.

'Unfortunately, yes.'

Stanstead gave a cynical snort. 'She's better out of it,' he said.

'Can we talk to your wife?'

Stanstead's eyes narrowed in suspicion. 'How do you think she can help you?'

Tinsley bounced his suspicion back with a bland smile. 'We don't know,' she said, 'but we do need some help.'

Ideally they would like to have spoken to Mrs Stanstead on her own, but the captain was patently not going to allow them this.

Lara Tinsley and PC Dart followed the couple into a large sitting room at the back of the house. There was still a strong smell of paint, even though Neil couldn't have been here for more than two weeks now. He'd been largely staying at home in case Daisy 'turned up'. It was a very optimistic point of view but no one had had the heart to disillusion him.

The room was light and bright, a conservatory leading off into a garden which was spring bright and full of flowering bulbs. Someone was a good gardener. Tinsley had never got her garden to look anything near as lovely as this. She glanced out of the French windows in admiration then turned back into the room.

'So?' the captain demanded.

Tinsley directed her questions at Lucy. 'Tell me about Neil Mansfield.'

Lucy licked her lips. 'What do you want to know?' Her voice was faint with a slight tremor. Lucy Stanstead was very nervous.

'How did you find him?' Lara Tinsley asked conversationally.

'He . . . he'd . . . he'd done some work for Mrs Price – the lady who lives opposite.'

Tinsley wondered exactly what nature of work Mansfield had done for Mrs Price. More of the same?

Lucy was gaining confidence. 'She said he was neat and clean, did a good job and didn't charge extortionate prices.' She was patently on safer ground here.

'So I rang him.'

'What was your impression of him?'

'He seemed polite. He listened to what I wanted doing and turned up on time.'

Her eyes were still begging for them to keep her secret.

'Did he ever mention his partner, Tracy?'

Lucy had a swift look at her husband, whose eyes were fixed on her, a tautness to his mouth that Lara didn't like. She'd seen enough cases of domestic violence to recognize the tension that existed between Captain and Mrs Stanstead.

Lucy gave her husband a nervous look that reminded Tinsley of bushbuck or fawns – always wary – then bravely answered the officer's question.

'I got the impression they weren't very happy,' she said.

Her husband gave her a warning sign, clearing of his throat.

But his wife was past caring now. 'I think he planned to leave her.'

'Really?'

Lucy Stanstead tucked her thin, pale hair behind her ears and nodded.

'And Daisy, the little girl?'

'I think that was what had stopped him leaving before. You see, he hadn't legally adopted her and he wasn't her father so he would have no right to see her and he didn't . . .' Another swift glance at her husband. 'He didn't,' she repeated, 'think that Tracy was a very good mother. What he said was that if he left Daisy would have no one who cared about her.'

Something struck Tinsley. She looked at Sean Dart and wondered if the same thought had entered his brain – if he had one. She wasn't convinced. Yet.

'Did you ever meet Daisy?'

Now Lucy Stanstead did look anxious. She gave a tiny nod without vocalizing, as though she thought her husband might miss the affirmative movement. 'He brought her here once or twice when Tracy was working.'

When Tracy was working. The phrase seemed important to Lara Tinsley. She would bring it up at the next briefing. Apart from an initial superficial interview with her employer they had largely ignored Tracy's place of work. What if there was something or someone there that had some bearing on the events of 6 and 7 April?

'Do you have any children of your own?' She'd deliberately addressed the question to them both. Captain Stanstead merely tightened his lips while his wife shook her head – with a tinge of sadness, her mouth drooping in unhappiness. Lara Tinsley decided not to pursue the reason why they had no children, instead turning the focus of her questions back to Neil Stanstead.

'Is the job nearly finished?'

Lucy nodded. 'I think one more day will do it,' she said, her eyes dropping to the floor.

'Have you heard from him since the accident?'

A shake of the head this time.

'And have you rung him?'

Another shake of the head, then, 'I thought I'd wait until after Tracy's funeral.'

Tinsley glanced at her colleague. Have *you* got any questions? she mouthed.

He took the cue. 'Neil Mansfield has the reputation of being a ladies' man.'

Tinsley almost groaned. *Oh, no, I didn't mean that.*

It didn't throw Lucy. 'Not with me,' she said. 'With me he was the perfect gentleman.' The words were accompanied by a defiant look aimed directly at her husband, as powerful and focused as a laser.

'Thank you,' WPC Lara Tinsley said, and they both stood up.

The Stansteads both saw them to the door, the captain patently not wanting his wife to be alone with the police.

They stopped at the car. 'While we're out here we may as well just check on Mrs Price before we head back to the station,' Lara said. She wondered if Mansfield's other customer might give them a little more insight into the man.

Mrs Price proved to be in her middle forties, a slim woman with very sharp, all-seeing eyes. She was plain in a business-like way, no make-up, hair scraped back from her face, wearing a shapeless black dress and cardigan and flat black leather ballet slippers. She blinked as she registered who they were.

'Ye-es?'

Quickly WPC Tinsley flashed her card and explained why they were in the vicinity.

'We understand that Neil Mansfield did some work for you?'

'That's correct.'

'And you recommended him to your neighbour?'

'That also is correct.' She spoke in a clipped, precise voice, reminding WPC Tinsley of her old English schoolmistress.

'His work was good,' she continued. 'He *never* left a mess and he was pleasant. Also, his prices were not out of the way. Lucy wanted to have some of the upstairs decorated while her husband was at sea. I knew Neil was reliable, would turn up on time and the job would be finished before Captain Stanstead was back on leave.' She said disapprovingly, 'He runs a tight ship,' without cracking her face at the appropriateness of the analogy. 'He wouldn't tolerate the house being decorated while he was there. And the work *would* have been finished had events not intervened.'

Then, oddly enough, it was at that point that she smiled. No more than a tight rictus but unmistakable for all that. 'I got the feeling,' she chortled, 'that Lucy was planning to pretend that it was *she* who had done the decorating. The captain can be a little mean with his money and might well have objected to the cost of paying someone to do something he would consider his wife should do.'

Lara Tinsley met Sean's dark eyes. He made a strange, resigned sort of face accompanied by a shrug, still leaving the questioning to her.

'Is there anything else you can add that might throw some light on the fate of little Daisy Walsh?' She'd asked the question more in desperation than believing it would lead to anything concrete.

'I saw them once,' Mrs Price said reflectively, 'the three of them.'

For a moment both the officers thought she was talking about Mansfield, Daisy and Tracy. But when she continued they realized how wrong they had been.

'Neil, Lucy and Daisy,' she said, her head on one side. 'They just looked like a happy family.'

The phrase startled them both. Food for thought.

Lara Tinsley waited until they were outside before turning on her colleague. 'Well, you were a fat lot of good in there!' she exploded.

PC Sean Dart grinned at her. 'Sorry,' he said. 'I just thought you were making such a good job of it there was no point my distracting you.' His accent was stolid, Yorkshire, slow, but friendly and for the first time she caught a hint of a sense of humour.

'So,' she ventured, 'what did you make of that?'

'Puts a different light on it, doesn't it?'

'You bet it does. Happy family? Neil, Daisy and *Lucy*? Interesting, don't you think?'

'Aye.'

'I wonder what the captain would have made of that.'

Sean simply grinned at her.

And WPC Tinsley caught the first hint that she and PC 'Dark Horse' might become buddies. One day.

SIXTEEN

Randall hadn't held out much hope for the letter that had accompanied the bouquet of herbs. He had submitted it to forensics for DNA and fingerprints but he knew their perpetrator was too smart to have left such obvious clues. He'd even taken a photocopy and submitted it to a handwriting expert who came back with the observation that children who had been to school in the sixties had been taught lovely handwriting – just like this.

'Village schools,' he'd said, with the pride of a magician pulling off a difficult and seemingly inexplicable trick, 'were taught copper plate writing. It was considered important,' he finished loftily.

Randall felt frustrated. Oh, yes, it all fitted all right but it still hadn't found them their mystery woman. Or the child.

The slipper had proved to be the partner of the one found in Carding

Mills stream and it hadn't been there during their initial search of the cottage. Gethin Roberts had searched the tiny attic. 'Not a chance, sir,' he'd said when questioned. 'It was put there some time later.' And Randall believed him.

Wednesday, 24 April, midday.

Martha scanned her court. She had anticipated, if Daisy's body had been found, to have had a joint inquest for mother and daughter. But she couldn't put off at least opening the inquest on Tracy Walsh any longer, while she waited to find out the fate of her daughter. She gave a slight smile and a nod in DI Alex Randall's direction and another one towards Mark Sullivan, the pathologist who had performed the post-mortem on Tracy Walsh. He returned the gesture with a reflected friendly nod.

She sat back in her chair, thinking. Dr Mark Sullivan was a brilliant pathologist. Of all the doctors she had worked with in her time as coroner, Sullivan was the one she trusted most. He was not one to fudge the evidence, to skimp on the initial post-mortem, and above all he never ever tried to extrapolate too much from the evidence. So many pathologists thought they were police, judge, jury and executioner as well as coroner, trying to push the verdict into her mouth and sensational headlines into the papers.

But Sullivan? She met his clear blue eyes and smiled again. At one time, she had worried about him. He had had a drink problem which had been solved by divorcing his wife. These days he looked a happy and confident man, particularly in the rather snazzy navy suit he was wearing with a varsity tie of maroon and pale blue. At least she hoped it was a varsity tie and not the colours of Aston Villa. She smothered a smile. She wouldn't put it past Sullivan to turn up to an inquest in a tie bearing the colours of his favourite football team.

She continued looking around the room, happy to observe everyone before she opened the inquest. Alex Randall was also smart in a grey 'court' suit. Policemen always dressed up for an inquest, unless they wore uniform. She felt DI Randall's gaze on her and gave him a shallow smile.

A grin would be out of place.

Her glance drifted across to Pat Walsh in tight jeans and her customary sour expression and Sofia at her side, unable to supress the excitement she was obviously experiencing at being the focus of attention. Martha had seen her being interviewed by a reporter before she'd entered the court, and it had looked business-like: Sofia, hand on plump hips, had been frowning and shaking her head, while the reporter had appeared persistent. In anticipation of the inquest and her role as victim's sister Sofia had had her hair professionally streaked and her long, red fingernails sparkled with crystals, indicating the attentions of a professional manicurist. Martha stifled a cynical smile. To Tracy's mother and sister this was simply a day out with maybe a cash bonus at the end. There was no hint of either grief for Tracy's untimely death or concern for the fate of the little girl, their niece and granddaughter. As she met the younger woman's eyes Sofia gave a cud-like chew of her gum and a bovine smile.

Observing Tracy's relatives, Martha wondered what the dead girl had really been like. This was the trouble with her job: she never met the people whose fates she became bound up with. She heard about them, sometimes from people choked with love, at other times their opinions skewed by jealousy, simple dislike or even guilt, but to her the subjects of her inquests always remained shadowy strangers; people never met, only peeped at through a gauze curtain which shifted in the wind, depending on who was speaking. So she could only ever speculate as to their true character. She never, ever caught the flavour of the real person however many eloquent eulogies were made. Before opening the inquest she trawled through what she knew about the dead woman. From the descriptions and photographs Tracy had been slimmer and prettier than her sister. But had she been cast out of the same miserable mould as her mother and sister? She would never know, and so she turned her gaze back on Sofia, who gave her another long, slow, insolent chew before turning to speak to her mother. Pat scrutinized Martha from across the room, displaying stained teeth and the fidgety fingers of a smoker who is planning her next cigarette.

In the front row a portly young man in an ill-fitting suit was frowning and nibbling his nails. He was hyperventilating with great scoops of breaths and he looked pale and uneasy. Uneasy, Martha wondered, or was there an element of guilt? She recognized Neil Mansfield, whom she had only spoken to on the telephone, from his picture in the newspaper. He was clearly avoiding meeting the glances of Tracy's relatives.

Martha cleared her throat.

Time to open the inquest.

She gave her customary speech about the formalities to be observed, made a passing reference to the child who was still missing, using the platform to appeal for anyone who thought they might be able to help to speak to the police. Then she outlined the procedure and function of the inquest – to ascertain who had died, when they had died, where they had died and how they had met their death. She described the circumstances of the crash without dwelling on the alcohol-fuelled row which had provoked the evening's events and began with Neil Mansfield, who took the witness stand nervously, by asking him to describe the events of the night of Saturday, 6 and early morning Sunday, 7 April. After a lot of clearing his throat Mansfield made a good witness, surprisingly unemotional now, having conquered his nervousness, but Martha noticed he continued to avoid meeting Tracy's mother or sister's glances. It was obvious there was no love lost between them. His face was very pale but he appeared resolute. Now he was factual, growing in confidence, giving his evidence in a firm, clear voice and responding to her request that he run through the events of that night in chronological order, answering the questions she put to him with impressive clarity considering what must at best have been a rather fuzzy memory.

'We'd been drinking in the early evening.' He scanned the room, challenging any negative response. There was none, only sympathy, even from Tracy's mother and gum-chewing sister. Mansfield cleared his throat and continued in a low voice, not fixing his gaze on anyone in particular. 'We'd wanted to go out but we didn't have a babysitter for Daisy.' Mentioning Daisy made Mansfield suddenly lose his control. He gripped the front of the witness box and screwed up his face as though tightening and contorting his features would prevent him from crying. But he recovered in the briefest of moments. He went even paler, almost a greenish white and gasped, cleared his throat and continued. 'We, erm . . . we couldn't decide what to watch on the television.'

There was not a person in the court who did not realize that this phrase was a euphemism for *we argued over the channels*. Mansfield's eyes flickered around the room, his face set. He was going to tell this tale. 'We had a bit of a row. Daisy started crying. Tracy ran upstairs and fetched her out of her bed then she came running back down with her.' His voice was gruff. Martha recognized the symptoms. Neil Mansfield was still finding it hard to keep control and stop himself from crying.

She gave him a sympathetic look. 'Take your time, Mr Mansfield,' she said gently. 'Would you like some water?'

Jericho's head shot up. This was one of his duties.

'No, thanks.'

'She went off.' Mansfield swallowed. 'That's all I know. Sorry.' He seemed to be apologizing to the entire room. 'I fell asleep. Next morning . . .' He looked around him desperately. 'Next morning I realized she wasn't back. Then . . .'

'All right,' Martha said kindly. 'That's enough. Is there anything else that you can add that might shed a light either on the events of that night or help the police to find Daisy?'

Mansfield shook his head and now she could see that tears were not far away. His face was twisted like an anguished child.

Detective Inspector Alex Randall was next to take the stand, explaining the circumstances of the accident, using maps and photographs to clarify the geography of the area. Martha sat back in her seat and watched him. It was always good to observe a professional, particularly when he was tall and attractive with a clear, pleasant voice. Randall's voice was curt, clipped, accentless. She could not have guessed where in the country he came from or what his background was. He was classless, polite. Not bland exactly but difficult to pin a label on. Even his vocabulary gave no clue to his geographical origins. She wondered when he had developed this closed aspect of his character. And why. Why did he need to be such a closed book? Had he always been like this or was it something he had developed? His face was animated as he spoke. He enjoyed giving evidence, putting across his side of the story. Luckily Randall was so engrossed in his story that he was unaware of Martha's scrutiny. Or so she thought. Quite suddenly he stopped looking at his notes, turned away from the people watching and moved his head to the right to look directly at her, his eyes seeming to look beneath the surface as though he could guess what she was thinking. She flushed as only redheads can.

Randall left all guesswork and supposition out. His statement was completely factual as he related the findings of the crash investigation team. 'Tracy Walsh drove up the Burway, a narrow and precipitous road which climbs up to the Lond Mynd.' He displayed maps and photographs to illustrate his point. 'Forensic examination of the area suggests that near the top, for some reason, she braked sharply and then tried to reverse back down the Burway.' He leaned forward slightly. 'There is no evidence to illustrate why she did this. Whether it was something real such as a collision with another car as suggested by a graze of black paint found on her offside wing or perhaps an animal or even something imaginary, possibly due to a combination of her disturbed state and the high alcohol content in her blood, is a matter for conjecture. We have no evidence to point us one way or the other. We have found no hard evidence that another vehicle was involved, although . . .' His natural honesty drove him to confess, '. . . it is possible that the collision with another car did not take place on that particular night. It could have happened at another time. Also, no one has come forward to say that they were on the Burway on that night at that time and there is no evidence of tyre tracks on the road apart from Tracy's. The only evidence is the scrape of paint found on Tracy's VW Polo and her tyre marks. There is no report of a collision on the Burway that night, so if there was an encounter the police are unaware of it. Tracy then reversed and slipped over the edge, the vehicle rolling down the side into Carding Mill Valley, a drop of over three hundred feet. The emergency services were alerted at six a.m. by a caller who has, so far, failed to come forward.' Randall paused and scanned the room. 'If the caller is here today or anyone has any idea who our mystery woman is I would appeal to them to speak to us. It may well be the key to finding Daisy.' He continued with his evidence. 'Tracy was taken to the Royal Shrewsbury Hospital on Sunday morning, the seventh of April at seven thirty a.m. but regrettably died eight days later from her injuries.' Randall paused. 'While we believe that Tracy's daughter, Daisy, was also in the car we have not yet found her in spite of an extensive search of the area and a high-profile press focus. No one has come forward to help us find her.' Randall blinked and fell silent. His words had held real pathos, particularly when he held up Daisy Walsh's photograph, the pretty, smiling four-year-old peeping around the door, her eyes, like the Mona Lisa's, seeming to meet everyone's in the room. They all looked at the picture and read the innocence in her eyes. A few muttered. All were mesmerized, Randall himself staying silent as the people studied the image. No one in the courtroom could have been thinking anything but *where was she?* What had happened to her after the car crash? Would they ever find her? Martha took a swift peek at Pat and Sofia and would have sworn that even they were moved by the picture, which needed no embellishment. The child spoke for herself by her sweet expression. Only one person in the courtroom couldn't bear to look at it: Neil Mansfield. After one millisecond of a glance he had put his hands over his eyes and blocked out the image. An almost audible sigh was breathed around the courtroom before Randall's clear voice broke through the whisper, as soft as a summer breeze through pale green leaves. 'The caller was a woman who made no mention of the child, only saying that some*one* was hurt,' he added.

'Thank you, Detective Inspector Randall,' Martha said. 'Do you have anything else to add?'

'Only this.' Alex faced the courtroom, his face taut and serious. He had to keep trying. 'If there is anyone – anyone out there – who can shed light on the whereabouts of little Daisy Walsh, who, I might remind you, is only four years old, I would be very grateful for the information.' The room was silent now, all eyes fixed on the tall detective, but no one spoke. They were all holding their breath. Martha scanned people's faces and read no cognition. Daisy's whereabouts, it seemed, were to remain a mystery for now.

For now, she wondered, or *for ever*? It was a terrible thought. Agonizing, it would appear, for Neil, who had dropped his face into his hands.

After a brief pause and a nod from Martha, Alex left the stand and his place was taken by the pathologist.

Dr Mark Sullivan looked very dapper in his dark suit and elegant tie. He took the stand with a confident, clear gaze and none of the hesitation and tremor of his earlier days. His manner was grave yet light. He deliberately spoke in words that everyone sitting in the courtroom could understand, never hiding behind jargon. When he needed to use medical expressions for precision's sake he explained the meaning in layman's terms. An aneurism became a 'bulge in an artery', contusions were 'bruises', a compound fracture explained as 'a broken bone projecting through the skin'. And everyone could understand the word 'coma'.

Sullivan carefully explained Tracy Walsh's injuries. 'Three skull fractures, multiple chest injuries including rib and sternal – breastbone – fractures. She had a haemathorax plus a large pleural effusion, which translates as blood and fluid in her lungs. Also a fractured pelvis and compound fractures of both tibia and fibulae, the bones of the lower leg.' He paused. 'These injuries were so severe that in spite of the best medical attention Tracy developed major organ failure and died on the fifteenth of April, eight days after the accident.'

Again, he paused before continuing, factually giving the milligrams of alcohol in her blood without sounding judgmental, then he stopped speaking and waited for any comments. Martha gave him an approving nod and he sat down.

The words *accidental death due to road traffic incident* hovered on her lips but she did not pronounce them. There were still anomalies and inconsistencies that needed explaining before she could be absolutely certain that there had been no design, nothing planned, in the death of Tracy Walsh and the disappearance of her daughter. Also, she still hoped to know Daisy's fate before closing the inquest. And so she waited. It was still possible that this would turn out to be a double inquest, both deaths due to the terrible careering of the VW over the side, dropping the three hundred feet into Carding Mill Valley. It was also possible that the entire backstory would still prove much more complicated than anyone here had so far suspected. Like Randall, she could not work out exactly where the clues that had been left fitted in, so they had decided to suppress the taunt which had accompanied the strange bunch of herbs and the appearance of the second slipper. It would, they hoped, in the end, fit together, but for now there were too many pieces of the jigsaw still missing.

Finally Martha adjourned the inquest and set a date well into the future. She also released Tracy's body for burial. They all knew how she'd died. They knew when and where and who she was. What they didn't really know was why.

Alex was waiting for her in the hallway. He gave her a tentative grin. 'How did I do?'

She couldn't help but warm to his self-effacing humour. 'You did all right,' she said, knowing the light in her eyes would voice her approval more eloquently than words alone. Then she added impulsively, 'Have you got a minute, Alex?'

'Yes. Of course.' He looked and sounded surprised.

She led him into one of the private interview rooms. 'It was that business of the flowers,' she said. Randall's eyebrows lifted but he made no comment.

And suddenly she lost confidence in what had seemed such an inspirational idea. A real help to direct his investigation. Was she simply sidetracking him from his case? Wasting time? Was this nothing more than a red herring, a strange coincidence? *She* was out of the picture – surely? The trouble was that for all Jericho's digging into the past and unearthing something she couldn't see where it fitted in. She ploughed on but dejectedly. 'You're going to think I'm nuts,' she said. 'And I don't know how it fits in, except it does.'

'Let me be the judge of that.' He was smiling with more than a hint of indulgence.

'It was the bunch of herbs. It was the—' She was finding this much more difficult than she'd thought, doubting now the logic of her ideas. 'It was the . . . Oh, I don't know.' She wished Alex would say something. Anything instead of watching her with that faintly puzzled look. 'You *are* going to think I've lost the plot. I just wanted to go over it with you.'

'Are you going to give me a clue so I can make a judgement?' And his face was still warm and kind – almost tender – which gave her the confidence to continue.

'All right,' she said, the words now coming out in a tumbling rush. 'It was the name.'

'Yes?'

'Combined with the planting of the bunch of herbs. The message, the way of speaking and the idea that it was someone with a rural bent. The geographical location of the Long Mynd together with a crime committed.'

He bent his head even nearer to hers, as though to listen more intently but now he was frowning.

'I don't *know*,' she said, 'but I felt that there was a connection with a case I was involved with a little more than ten years ago. It was an odd one and ultimately came to a very unsatisfactory conclusion. I had to give a verdict of accidental death then but, Alex . . .' She locked eyes with him, wanting to emphasize her words. 'In spite of a dearth of evidence and nothing turning up in the police investigation I could never shake off the idea that it was a deliberate felon. *All* my instincts screamed to me that it was murder.'

'Just go through the circumstances again. I haven't got a handle on it.'

'It was a teenage girl, fourteen years old. She made home-made mushroom soup for her father, her stepmother and her half-brother. They all died. *She* was very slightly ill but survived.'

'Tell me more.'

'The girl had gathered what she claimed to believe were chanterelles. She was no expert on fungi. They turned out to be the Death Cap.'

Randall waited.

'Before the inquest the girl's aunt came forward and spoke very frankly to me, thinking I would not be connected with the police. She didn't want to get her niece into trouble but she did want to voice her misgivings and point out how strange the entire thing was. The girl was a rebel, she told me. Disruptive and vicious. It was uncharacteristic for her to gather mushrooms in the first place. She was the sort who, if she did any food shopping, would have bought it at the local supermarket, neatly labelled and on a polystyrene tray ready to microwave. The girl was no cook. According to the aunt this girl *never* cooked for the family. *Never*, Alex,' she emphasized. 'Added to that she *hated* her stepmother and bitterly resented her parent's divorce and the fact that her father had remarried. Her own mother was extremely bitter too and had attempted suicide on a number of occasions, which was why the girl lived with her father and his paramour. Her mother was deemed to be unstable so her father had custody. When her half-brother was born she became very, very difficult. The hostility was judged to be so great that the aunt told me that she was never allowed to be alone with her half-brother. That was how bad the situation was.' Martha waited for a moment to allow the facts to sink in before continuing. 'Even with all this evidence I might still have bought the "terrible accident" verdict apart from one thing: the police found a book at the property which had been borrowed from the library. The subject was on recognizing various fungi. The trouble was that it had been taken out in the stepmother's name and the library couldn't remember who had actually picked the book up.'

'Hmm. Intriguing and very hard to prove intent.'

'Very hard,' she repeated, more slowly.

Randall was thoughtful for a moment, then looked up. 'There's something else, isn't there?'

She nodded. 'The family lived in Hope Bowdler, in an ancient thatched cottage there. The day of the funerals a small basket of Death Cap fungi was placed on the front door step.'

'By the girl?'

Martha shook her head. 'She was still in hospital at the time. They'd kept her in for observation in case she developed symptoms later. We never knew who'd left the basket of Death Caps on the step but I'm pretty sure it was someone who shared my suspicions.'

'So . . .' He looked up. 'Martha?'

'It wasn't just the unusual nature of the case,' Martha said. 'It was also the name of our lethal chef which was unusual enough for me to remember it. Or at least,' she added with blunt honesty, 'for it to ring a bell in my mind and ask Jericho to fish out the file and refresh me of the details.'

Randall waited.

'The name was Ignatio,' Martha said. 'Charity Ignatio.'

Randall gaped. It was not what he had expected.

'But the herb message couldn't possibly have been put there by her,' he said. 'She was out of the country.'

'I still think there's a connection,' Martha insisted. 'I believe the person who placed the Death Caps on the step of the cottage in Hope Bowdler was the same person who placed your bunch of herbs at the point where Tracy's car began its roll down into the valley. Note, Alex: the point where Tracy's car *left* the road.'

His hazel eyes looked deep into hers, displaying – or was she imagining it – warmth, affection? It gave her further confidence to continue with her strange idea. 'Under the circumstances, don't you think it's odd that Ms Ignatio should choose to live out there, in a backwater, when she has a job that requires her to travel the world? Why not live near an airport or at least a station that has a mainline to London rather on a rural line that means she has to change at Birmingham? And why cling to an area where it is perfectly possible that people will always connect you with a crime and a question: what did you do to your family?'

Randall frowned. 'So what happened to her subsequently? Was she found guilty of attempted murder?'

'No,' Martha said. 'Nothing happened to her. Whatever my private instincts I had no hard evidence and neither did the police. I passed an open verdict.' She felt she had to justify her decision. 'I had no choice, Alex. It was all put down to a tragic mistake. Like the case, the book on fungi was returned to the library and put back on the shelf, as it were. In fact, young Charity came out of it rather well. The light that was put on it was a rebellious teenage girl who was trying to make amends for her previously unruly behaviour by organizing a banquet.' She couldn't prevent a look of disgusted cynicism passing across her face. 'I couldn't have handled the PR better myself. Instead of being labelled a Borgia she was pitied and indulged and always insisted it had been a terrible mistake. She was put into care, for a while, and then fostered, probably inheriting all her family's money, including her stepmother's whom, I believe, was quite wealthy, coming from a farming, land-owning background. And from there to the present day, who knows? Dubai's a glamorous city – it sounds like she's done well for herself.'

Randall's face was grim. He was thoughtful for a moment before saying, 'But the crimes are, surely, different? Besides, Charity was quite definitely out of the country when Tracy had her accident. We've checked.'

'Accident?' Martha queried.

Randall regarded her, his face still frowning. 'She can't have orchestrated . . .' He paused. 'I don't understand,' he said. 'What are you asking me to do about this?'

'Nothing. I just wanted you to be aware, Alex.'

WPC Lara Tinsley had waited for DI Randall to return from the coroner's court before she discussed with him the results of her and PC Dart's morning's work and soon realized her inspector's mind was distracted. It was even worse than that. His mind had been buzzing with the possibilities Martha's revelation had provoked. But none seemed to fit the case. He had watched too many officers struggle to make facts fit an odd-shaped theory. Until the fit was perfect and watertight he knew whatever he came up with it would be the wrong one. And though he hadn't wanted to tell Martha this, this was what it felt like. The wrong connection.

He listened to his officer's story without comment, then asked, 'And how are you getting on with PC Dart?'

It was not quite what she had expected. 'We-ell,' she began before saying, 'he keeps himself to himself, sir, doesn't he?'

Randall nodded. 'And how is he to work with?'

'I've no complaints, sir, though he doesn't volunteer much in the way of ideas.'

'Give him time,' Randall said. 'I think he'll be all right once he's got over . . .'

Tinsley looked at him enquiringly.

'Once he's settled down,' Randall substituted. 'So have you any suggestions that might throw a light on this case, Tinsley?'

'No, sir,' she eyed him speculatively, 'but I had a few thoughts.'
'Go on.'

'Well, firstly, I felt I could have got a lot more information out of Mrs Stanstead if her husband hadn't been there.' She hesitated. 'He's quite intimidating.'

'Really? What sort of information?'

'I don't know, but she's obviously terrified of him and there was something else. Something she was keeping back. A neighbour saw the three of them together, Lucy, Neil and Daisy.' She leafed through her notebook then looked up. 'She said, and I quote, that they "looked like a happy family".'

Randall recalled the conversation he had just had with Martha. Charity Ignatio had kept something back too. She had hidden her past. 'She's not the only one keeping things to herself,' he muttered.

'And then I wondered a bit more about Tracy,' Tinsley continued. Randall looked interested. 'Go on.'

'I wondered more about her life.'

'Specifically?'

'I wondered about her work, sir.'

Randall grinned at her and clapped her on the shoulder. 'Too right,' he said. 'And I'll add to that we need to know a bit more about Neil Mansfield.'

Perhaps it was Lara Tinsley's hopeful, eager face, but at the briefing Alex Randall began to feel a little more optimistic, as though the smallest glimmer of light was there, just over the horizon, a glowing ball of hazy pink. He didn't know yet what to do about Martha's revelation. He couldn't quite fit it in to the scenario. Yes, they needed to recheck passport control and make absolutely sure that Ms Ignatio hadn't sneaked back to the UK on 6 and 7 April. What irony if she had made the call herself after all their searching for the 'mystery woman'. But even if Ms Ignatio had somehow spirited herself back to Shropshire it still didn't explain the whereabouts of the missing child. She wasn't at Hope Cottage. That was for sure.

But the slipper had been planted there between their initial search and Charity's homecoming.

Lots of ideas were buzzing round Randall's head as he faced his team of officers. Charity Ignatio and her disturbing past; Neil Mansfield with his Lothario ways; Allistair Donaldson, Daisy's apparently uninterested father, and Tracy herself, the cause of all this. Cause or catalyst?

So many unanswered questions.

Perhaps he should take a trip up to Scotland and see if he could get some answers from Allistair. Maybe he should not have relied on the local police to speak to someone who could prove so significant. After all, he was the missing child's next of kin. He was the person who had a right to her. Even if *he* wasn't interested in his daughter, perhaps he had family who were. There was a mystery caller to be found though he couldn't work out why, if she existed, she had not come forward. After all – *she* had done nothing criminal except abduct the child, if indeed she had. It was Daisy's disappearance which had escalated the police interest from a simple RTI and initiated the major police investigation. Had the little girl not been missing this case would have been done and dusted by now – a simple car accident with a drunk driver. In the light of no corroborative evidence they would not have looked terribly hard into the scrape of paint on Tracy's offside wing. After all, drink drivers, while they may be in a regrettable state, are not exactly a rare occurrence; neither are they known for their skill as drivers. But without the one ingredient of the vanished child there would not have been the attention this had provoked. And this caught Randall up short. Was that *why* the child had been abducted? To focus attention on a road accident? He pondered this point for some moments but found no answer. In fact, he was no closer to any answers at all – still only questions. Questions. Still questions and more questions.

However, he added it to the board: *Why take the child?*

Underneath he wrote a point they had glossed over: *Something or someone real or imagined stopped Tracy Walsh in her tracks. Who or what was it?*

Randall frowned. There was another point they had not explored well enough. It was the direction Lara Tinsley had suggested, Tracy's place of work: the Long Mynd Hotel.

And central to the entire case was an area with an evil reputation, borne out by places for names and events: Dead Man's Beach, Dead Man's Hollow, Dead Man's Fair, the Devil's Chair. Church Stretton and its surrounds were full of tales of death and disappearances, riddled with folklore and inexplicable disappearances; miraculous appearances such as that of the Reverend E. Donald Carr after his night struggling with the blizzard in Carding Mill Valley. Carding Mill Valley was the very same place Tracy Walsh's car had made its final resting place. Randall's hand hovered over the board, reluctant to wander into a place of fantasy, then he set his mouth. One might believe anything in these strange hills.

SEVENTEEN

N ow he had the list in front of him it was beginning to feel complete: he stood back and studied the board. This looked well rounded.

He could allocate tasks and focus their attention. Randall felt his mood improve even further. It really did feel like dawn, the beginning of a new day. The room warmed as the officers sensed the lightening of their DI's mood.

Randall stood back to study the first name on the whiteboard, reflecting on his new knowledge concerning Charity Ignatio. Then he turned back to face the officers and filled them in on the old story, the family tragedy, wondering still if the poisoning of the soup had been accident or design. The trouble with events like that was that even years later one could never be absolutely sure, and as time rolled on the deaths became even more fuzzy and blurred, ever more out of focus. Unless there was a witness or a confession, poisoning cases were notoriously hard to prove, hard to bring to court and slippery as eels. And then there was the sequitur. Why on earth would someone place the Death Caps on the doorstep except to point the finger of suspicion? But if they knew something why not tell the police and see justice for the dead family? Randall narrowed his eyes. Unless that person had their suspicions but was unable to prove anything beyond reasonable doubt, and that was what the law demanded. *Beyond reasonable doubt.*

He thought for a minute. Perhaps the Death Caps were placed on the doorstep to send a message to Charity. *I know what you've done. I have my eye on you. Don't even think you'll get away with it ever again.*

Maybe that was it.

A couple of the officers were resurrecting the background on their iPads. All agreed it made Ms Ignatio a lot more interesting. But the fact remained, incontrovertible: she'd been out of the country.

Randall scanned the room and picked out WPC Lara Tinsley, whose cow-brown eyes were fixed on him with particular alertness.

'Lara,' he said, 'I want you to go and talk to Ms Ignatio about the event. Let her know that we're aware of her past. See what you make of her.' He found it difficult to explain about the connection between the fungi that had been left at Charity's door and the plants that had been left at the scene of the crash. He wasn't sure himself. He could see a few of the officers frowning, as though they were sceptical. But when he related the fact that Death Caps had been left outside the house where the four family members had been poisoned, three of whom had subsequently died, he saw their expressions change to become thoughtful and he knew they were as puzzled about their significance as he was. If the person who had left the bouquet had had suspicions, why leave a message that at best could only provoke curiosity and point to an old and forgotten case? Why not simply come forward and tell the police what those suspicions were? It didn't make sense any more than this case and the disappearance of the little girl – yet. He trusted it would soon.

'It puts rather a different light on our little globetrotter, doesn't it?' WPC Lara Tinsley kept her eyes on him, tucked a strand of silky hair behind her ears and nodded.

Randall continued, emphasizing the point: 'Suddenly she isn't quite the innocent bystander we initially thought, is she? Hardly someone whose cottage was used *by chance* to make a phone call. It could have been used deliberately to focus our interest in her and evoke the old case, to make us realize she is someone with a devious and at best murky past. Why involve Hope Cottage at all?' Randall continued to encourage, wanting WPC Tinsley to understand how important this task was. 'Maybe that was why. Get a take on her, Tinsley. Speak to her cleaning woman again if you need to. Also check on passport control. Is there any conceivable way she could possibly have slipped back to UK on the sixth and seventh of April?'

'Yes, sir.'

'She's a bit too much of a closed book, that one,' he muttered more to himself than to the gathered team. 'I don't feel I have a handle on her at all.'

Inwardly he was still asking the question *why make the phone call from her cottage?* Was it purely to focus their attention on her and resurrect the old case? And was their mystery caller still frustrated they were not spending more time and consideration on Ms Ignatio? Was that why they had planted the slipper?

He hesitated. He didn't want to influence his officers by voicing his concerns here and now and he didn't want to confuse this case by involving another old, puzzling incident, possibly a murder, which had never been solved at the time so what hope for them now? They should focus on the missing child. But his mind wouldn't stop asking questions. Why? If Charity *had* deliberately poisoned her family what would have been her motive? It could be put down to jealousy of her stepmother and half-brother. Hatred of her father for replacing her; a sort of teenage angst. But there was, as far as he knew, absolutely no connection between Charity Ignatio and Tracy Walsh, and that was a stumbling block. They came from different sides of life. And, if Charity had been innocent, since then she must have led a blameless life. She had no police record. He met Lara Tinsley's eyes, feeling the balloon of hope starting to deflate. He was beginning to realize how very little they had ascertained about this troubling case and he worried how far they would have to go to find one little girl, dead or alive. 'Find out if there is any connection between Tracy and Charity,' he said, 'however tenuous.'

She nodded.

Under his breath he muttered, 'Thank you, Martha Gunn.' He had a swift vision of the unruly, flaming red hair that seemed so incongruous in a coroner. He recalled a pair of mischievous green eyes and her light manner but undoubted dignity when conducting an inquest, those same green eyes displaying such humanity for the families of the dead. That soft, sympathetic look that she had, just a few times, directed at him. How could she possibly know about his own troubled home life? He had never confided in her. There was no way. None of his colleagues was aware of his home circumstances. Yet he felt that Martha Gunn had somehow divined it and if he was honest with himself he knew he might not have spelt his story out but he had certainly hinted at it. She knew something was very wrong in his life and there was something in her gentle concern that helped him. For a moment Randall was struck. He was beginning to realize how much he was depending on her on this case, trusting her judgement and waiting around for her opinions.

But it wouldn't do.

He cleared his throat and focused on the assembled officers and the briefing, aware that, to him, Martha Gunn was a treasured object that he took out of his pocket, admired and polished before returning it to its secret place. His left breast pocket. The one right over his heart. She was his talisman.

Bad thought, Alex.

Lara Tinsley was eyeing him curiously.

'Yes?' he asked.

'Sir,' she began tentatively, 'the person who left the Death Caps outside the door? I mean . . .' she flushed, 'it only focused suspicion on Charity, didn't it?'

He nodded, realizing her mind was tracking in the same direction as his.

'And we understand the message, or so we think.'

'Yes.'

'But the bunch of herbs left at the site of Tracy's crash. Is the message against Charity?'

He waited.

'What's the warning?'

He threw the question around the room. 'Any ideas?'

The faces that met his were blank.

'And why take us back to the old case more than ten years later? I mean, why now?'

No one could think of a reason. Unless . . .

Again his thoughts turned to Martha. He could ask her that same question.

For now he wanted to focus on the present and find the child who had, it was alleged, last been spotted being dragged out of bed in the middle of the night.

He set PCs Gary Coleman and Delia Shaw to interview Neil Mansfield and Lucy Stanstead again. 'Observe the relationship between them,' he urged, adding, 'but interview them separately. WPC Tinsley feels that this is an interview best conducted away from the good woman's husband, if you can manage that. It might be a bit difficult.' Randall frowned. Something was bugging him and after a brief search around his memory he knew what it was. It was the phrase that Neil Mansfield, Lucy Stanstead and Daisy looked like a happy family. It was brazen – and dangerous. Tracy had been a very jealous woman and as for Captain Stanstead – well. But surely he was out of the picture? Surely he had been away at sea at the time of Tracy's accident?

Another point to check.

'Gary,' he added, 'we have a warrant to remove Mansfield's computer. I don't need to tell you what you're looking for. Basically anything that might have a bearing on the case.'

Coleman grinned. 'Good one,' he said. He loved computers and was never happier than when he was in front of a screen, tapping away on a keyboard. Randall, too, swallowed a grin. He knew he'd just handed Police Constable Gary Coleman his dream job. And if there was anything on Mansfield's computer Coleman would unearth it. Inwardly, now, he was beginning to smile. For some reason he was thinking about movies. It was all in the casting, the most important role, matching the right actor to the right part. They had to look right, have the appropriate talents. It could make or break a film. And boy, it was the same in the police force during a major investigation. Match the right person to the job.

And he just had.

Out of the corner of his eye, Randall could see Gethin Roberts twitching with anticipation. Time to put the young PC out of his misery. 'Roberts, I want you to focus on Tracy herself. Villain or victim? Speak to her mother and her sister again. Explore her place of work further. Get up to the Long Mynd Hotel. See if you can get any evidence of further contacts.' Tracy might be dead, he thought, but in the end it was she who had taken the little girl – her daughter – to a dangerous spot in the middle of an ice-cold night, when she had been rip-roaring drunk. Why?

Roberts was watching expectantly. Waiting for a prompt.

'I get the feeling,' Randall said, almost musing to himself, 'that there is something we don't know about Tracy. I wonder why she took the child with her that night. If Daisy had been irritating her by crying, why take her out of her bed and put her in the car? It would be bound to make the child more fractious so why not leave her behind? Was it, I wonder, because she didn't trust Mansfield?'

'But Mansfield looked after Daisy when Tracy was at work,' Roberts pointed out. 'She must have trusted him.'

'True. But I still wonder why she got the little girl up, put on her dressing gown and slippers and bundled her in the car.'

Around the room, DI Randall could sense that most of the assembled team were dubious. To them it didn't appear to be particularly strange behaviour. Not from a drunk, at least.

'As for me,' he announced, 'I'm going to take a trip up to Inverness and speak to Daisy's father and the rest of his family. Check 'em out. See if the connection was as tenuous as has been suggested and if there is one, perhaps a grandmother who takes an interest in Daisy Walsh.'

He turned around to read the next name on the board. 'We've yet to identify our mystery caller who, it is still possible, has Daisy with her. Of course, if it proves to be Ms Ignatio then where is the child? How has she been spirited away when Charity was thousands of miles away when she was abducted? That would involve another person. It is quite impossible that she made the call, so if she is involved in any way she must have an accomplice. Maybe our mystery caller?' His head was spinning with the possibilities but he carried on doggedly. 'Is she with her? Concealed somewhere? If so, where? She's not at the cottage. So is she . . .?' It was quite unnecessary to add, *Dead or alive, injured or not.* They all had imaginations. He didn't need to rub it in. They were all aware of the fragility of a four-year-old. Some of them had children of about that age themselves.

Randall hesitated before reading out the final entry on his list. He wasn't quite sure how to put it. He didn't really want to send his officers hurtling down a route of myth and legend but in his mind there was little doubt that this last thing played a part.

So he plunged in. 'And lastly, there is the area itself. We all know that the Long Mynd and its environs are remote and wild and the place has a bad reputation – partly to do with folklore and partly to do with its geography. I concede that there is something menacing about the hills rising so suddenly out of the Shropshire Plain.' He was choosing his words very carefully. 'So while I wouldn't want you to be influenced by folklore and superstition, bear it in mind, will you?' There were a few dubious nods of acknowledgment but DI Randall couldn't help noticing that there were no smiles, no mockery, no leg-pulling. The faces looking back at him were grim. A few glanced across at the board holding Daisy Walsh's picture as though to remind themselves of the missing child: the sweet little girl with sparkly eyes who peeped around a door and was still missing.

Alex Randall was mischievously aware that he had deliberately left out Sergeant Paul Talith. When the room had emptied Talith still waited, hovering like an expectant father. Randall grinned at him. 'Fancy a trip up to Scotland, Paul?'

Truth was Talith didn't – not really. He'd promised Diana he'd give her a hand tidying the garden up but he could hardly say that to DI Randall, could he? No. So he simply nodded. 'When, sir?'

EIGHTEEN

Wednesday, 24 April, 7.30 p.m.

Martha was at a Stoke City home game in which Sam was playing. She watched the ferocity of his game, the speed of his sprints, his skill with the ball and then, heaven of heavens, he curled one which grazed the top bar and dropped in, rolling innocuously into the back of the net to an accompanying roar from the enthusiastic crowd and a look of dismay from the goalie. She looked around her. Even if she had had the skill she would not have liked to have been in Sam's shoes. All that focus. All that fervour. All that adulation which could so easily and quickly turn sour. But as she watched Sam's glances move left and right she realized something that had never quite hit her before. He did not see it like that. He was not an individual. It was not *his* shoulders that carried the game. It was the team. He was only part of a team. A limb of a whole body. The team members made up the rest. They were his blood brothers. His family. If he let them down *they* would forgive him because they were parts of the whole. It was then that she began to understand why such a fuss was made at affairs between the partners of team members. It was treachery, traitorous. Worse than incest. She looked around her at the others in the members' box. They probably already knew this. One very good-looking man, about her age, with dark hair and wearing a thick jacket, leaned over. 'You must be so proud of Sam.'

She smiled into a pair of warm brown eyes that she didn't recognize. 'I am,' she confessed, 'and fearful too. So much can go wrong.'

'I wouldn't look too far into the future,' he said softly, 'particularly if you're a pessimist.'

She began to protest. 'I'm not,' she said before she met his eyes again and realized he was teasing her.

She sat back and relaxed. The thought that Sam was playing with members of his 'family' was a comforting thought.

She allowed her mind to wander.

Sukey was at home learning lines. She was at a school for the performing arts and loving every minute of it. She still looked young enough to play children's parts and yet woman enough to act the temptress. Seventeen years old with the poise of a woman of thirty. Sukey now had an agent and when the agent was approached with a script for a TV production or, even on one occasion, a movie, she had been auditioned and had been successful for two minor parts to date: a sheriff's daughter in a remake of a classic Western which in Martha's opinion hadn't needed remaking, the critics agreeing with her. But her second part had been in a wonderful adaptation of one of Martha's favourite titles: *A Tale of Two Cities,* where, helped by her wonderful golden hair and innocent eyes, she had played Little Lucie. While not ignoring the fact that she was probably ten years too old to play it, the critics had forgiven the liberty taken with Dickens and had praised her 'wonderful mastery' of the French Revolution story and the child innocent of the horrors wheeling around her. In particular they had praised the scenes played with her grandfather, Doctor Manette, who had been played by one of the leading actors of the time. A friendship had blossomed – the actor had taken her under his wing and there was a suggestion that she would play opposite him again.

Where would it all end? Martha did not have a clue and for tonight she didn't care either. Her children were not such a heavy responsibility any more. She was realizing, like countless parents before her, that they were adults and must make their own choices and career moves. And yes, make their own mistakes too. She was startled out of her reflections by a roar from the crowd. The game was over. Stoke were the victors. She glanced across at the man. He was standing up, his back to her, chatting animatedly to a few members of the crowd. She hesitated then made her way to the exit. She must find out whether Sam was coming home with her or with one of his teammates.

Thursday, 25 April, 8.45 a.m.

Police Constable Gary Coleman was the force's computer expert. A few flicks of the keys and he could discover facts about its owner that even they were unaware of. That was the easy bit. The difficult bit had been removing it from Tracy and Neil's house. Neil had objected – strongly. 'What about my emails? And my business?'

Coleman was soothing. 'You'll have it back in a day or two.'

'But . . .' And Mansfield had fallen quiet, his anger not abated but tempered by something else. What, Coleman wondered, was Mansfield so worried about?

He got to work.

Gethin Roberts, meanwhile, had just reached the spectacular Long Mynd Hotel. Set halfway up the hill overlooking the pretty Victorian town of Church Stretton, it was an upmarket place with some very wonderful views. A year or so ago Roberts and his girlfriend, Flora, had been driving south down the A49. The night had been snowy and the hotel had blazed its light, like a beacon, right across the valley, looking somehow majestic and mysterious at the same time. Flora had touched his arm. 'It looks just like the hotel in *The Shining*,' she'd whispered in awe. And Roberts had been forced to agree.

As he climbed out of the car he reflected that he wouldn't mind a few nights here himself and wondered if it had a swimming pool.

It did. Outdoor *and* heated.

The manager met him in the hall. Roberto Agostino was a small, dapper Italian with oily black eyes and swept back hair. 'Pleased to meet you,' he said with a tight smile. In general, four-star hotels do not like police attention. The visible presence of the long arm of the law is not considered good for business. Knowing this, Roberts gave him a bland smile in return and followed the manager into his small office.

Agostino closed the door behind them. 'Now,' he said, not fooling Roberts for a moment with his friendly manner, 'how can I help you?'

'It's about one of your employees,' Roberts said.

Agostino lifted his eyebrows.

'Tracy Walsh.'

Agostino's face cleared. 'Ah, Tracy. Such a shame. I knew she sometimes had a drink too many but, eh,' he said with a Continental shrug and a pout of his lips, 'this is awful. The poor girl. We have collected for her charity. And the little girl, Daisy. You still have not found her?' There was a note of accusation in his voice.

Roberts coloured. 'No. Unfortunately we haven't.' Something struck him. 'You knew Daisy?' he queried.

Another continental shrug. 'Tracy brought her to work with her once or twice when she didn't have child care. We did not approve,' he added quickly, 'of course. But what can you do?'

'Yes,' Roberts commented vaguely. It was the first time he had ever considered the problem. Child care and work. How did people manage? He had the briefest glimpse into the future. How would Flora manage when they had their own children? Answer – he didn't have a clue. Her mum, he supposed, or child care. And that was expensive. He turned his attention back to Agostino who was speaking, the black eyes narrowed.

'So. How can I help you?'

'Tell me about Tracy. Was she popular?'

Agostino winked. 'With the men,' he said. 'Not always with the women.'

'You mean she was a flirt?'

'She would . . .' Agostino frowned in concentration, trying to locate the right words in his vocabulary. 'Step over the mark,' he said finally. 'But sometimes she would *hit it off* with some female visitor.' He spoke the phrase in a tentative voice, as though testing the water.

'Anyone in particular?'

'Back in November,' he said slowly, 'we had a convention for social workers. One of them seemed to strike up quite a friendship with Tracy,' he said, 'though I wouldn't have thought she was her kind.'

It seemed unimportant but Roberts asked anyway. 'Her name?'

'Sheila Weston. She was from Slough. She kept an eye on Daisy a time or two.'

'And with the rest of the staff?'

'She did her work.'

Which led Roberts to speculate that Tracy Walsh was not that popular amongst her colleagues.

Roberts tried to think of something more he should be asking or even what he should have gleaned from the interview but his mind had seized up. He simply shook Agostino's hand. 'Well, thanks very much,' he said. 'You've been very helpful.'

Agostino looked a bit puzzled at that but shrugged and smiled. 'It is my duty,' he said.

As he was leaving, Roberts looked around him. 'This is a lovely place,' he said. 'Do you mind me asking how much it costs to stay here a night?'

'It depends on which room you have,' the manager said. 'But around one hundred and twenty pounds is average.'

Roberts nodded. He would love to bring Flora here.

'What sort of people stay here?'

'Well, it is a good base to explore Shropshire from,' Agostino said. 'The hills are great for walkers and explorers. The town is beautiful too. A great antiques centre and lovely individual shops and restaurants. Shrewsbury and Ludlow are not far. There is Acton Scott Farm.' He grinned. 'Plenty to do if you wish to be active. But many people just want to chill.'

Roberts decided Agostino was definitely wearing his hotelier's hat. He was sounding like someone from the Shropshire Tourist Board.

Agostino continued. 'And, of course, we do conferences here too. A month ago we had social workers again. Thirty social workers.' Agostino smiled, showing one stained incisor. 'Imagine thirty social workers.'

Roberts decided he'd rather not.

As he was leaving Agostino put his hand on his arm. 'I hope you find the little girl,' he said. 'She was such a sweet little thing. A real hit with some of the guests.'

Roberts left then, turning back as he drove back down towards the town of Church Stretton.

Just as Randall and DS Talith were heading for the airport, events took an unexpected turn.

NINETEEN

Thursday, 25 April, 9.45 a.m.

I t began with that most innocuous event of all, yet another phone call from a member of the public. The investigating team was getting more than a hundred a day, usually from people who *thought* they'd seen Daisy. It was impossible to look into them all. The team did what they could, looked into the most likely sightings and relied on local police forces to help them out. Already the numbers of officers assigned to the case was over a hundred. There were literally yards of computer printouts, megabytes of information stored and hundreds of statements and forensic results. As was usual in cases like this, the information gathering had been wide and extensive, proliferating as though it had a life of its own, which in a way it did. Information appeared to generate information. The phrase *no stone unturned* was perfectly appropriate.

But this phone call was different from the others. For a start it originated from an alert octogenarian who kept fit by trotting up and down Carding Mill Valley. Daily, come rain or shine, snow, frost or heat wave. He timed himself rigorously and stuck to *exactly* the same route every day so the search for Daisy Walsh had been an inconvenience, messing up his lifestyle of extreme regularity. But that was the point. 'Exactly the same route,' he barked down the phone. 'No deviation whatsoever. I could do it blindfolded.' Only he hadn't. He'd kept his eyes wide open.

Added to that this interesting and unique situation the octogenarian's eyesight was as sharp as an eagle's and he also had the observation powers of a secret agent. These were the points to consider and to remember. And Desk Sergeant Sandy Mucklow did. The life of a desk sergeant could be sadly mundane – plenty of drunks, arguing motorists, stroppy druggies and so on, but as he listened to the content of the call his toes began their familiar twitching. There was something about Freddy Ribbler's voice, born to command, which made perfect sense as he had served his country proudly in the Second World War alongside General Montgomery. Incidentally it was 'Monty' who had handed him his first cigarette, a habit he had struggled to conquer for the next fifteen years.

'It wasn't there yesterday,' Ribble insisted. No one would have argued with him.

Mucklow frowned. 'What wasn't there?'

'Well, it's a bit sodden but it looks like a child's dressing gown, if you ask me.' There was a moment of bluster before Ribbler continued. 'Not that I'm in any way an expert. My wife and I were not blessed with little sprogs but I rather think it might be the one that the little girl— The child who's missing. It could be the very one she was wearing. It's pink with a little motif on the front. And I'm afraid . . .'

Mucklow listened with dread.

'I'm afraid there's a stain on it. It looks very much like blood.'

Desk Sergeant Mucklow was instantly alert. 'We'll send somebody out. I don't suppose you'd mind waiting with the garment?'

'We-ell. It's freezing cold, you know, now I've stopped running.'

'We'll be no longer than half an hour, sir. We'd be very grateful.'

'All right, if it helps to find the poor child. Wherever she is,' he added gruffly.

'And please try not to touch it.'

The request provoked a harrumph in response.

So at the very time that Talith and Alex Randall were airborne, mobiles off, heading up to Scotland, PC Sean Dart was heading south down the A49 back towards Church Stretton. Knowing it wasn't really justified, he didn't dare put the blue light on but broke the speed limit anyway, straightening out the corners in his anxiety to arrive.

What the hell was going on? Was this it? Was it a deliberate plant by someone with a warped interest in the case? Would the next thing they discovered be her body? Was this trail of clues leading them to that, or something else?

Thursday, 25 April, 10 a.m.
Scotland.

A car had been provided to take Randall and Talith to a small cottage, just outside a village ten miles from Inverness, where Allistair Donaldson lived – with his mother, they'd imagined.

When they reached the cottage they saw two cars outside, a four-wheel drive Toyota and a small Hyundai. But when they knocked on the door it was pulled open by a very pretty, young girl with waist-length poker straight blonde hair, patently not Mrs Donaldson. Talith simply stared. The girl was a vision, bright red lipstick, sprayed-on tight black leggings on long, long legs and a loose white shirt unbuttoned at the top to show . . . Talith cleared his throat noisily and the girl stepped forward, a warm smile sweetening her face even more. 'You must be the police,' she said, not a trace of anxiety. 'Sorry you've had to come all this way for nothing. Come in,' she continued and they followed the swinging blonde hair into the inside.

The up-to-date look of the girl was at odds with the interior of the cottage, which was quite rough and old fashioned. She led them into a sitting room where a tall young man was just easing himself out of a deep chintzy sofa. 'Hello there,' he said, with only the faintest of Scottish brogues. 'I'm Allistair. And I think you've already met Arlene.'

The blonde girl gave the two police a wide smile. 'We've met,' she said with the confidence of the beautiful.

Thursday, 25 April, 10.10 a.m.

Lara Tinsley had finally got through to passport control and had some answers. Charity Ignatio had left the UK on 3 April and returned on 24 April. She was out of the picture. With iris recognition, she was assured, by a rather snotty immigration official, no, Ms Ignatio could *not* possibly have slipped back into the country. She scored her own back by responding in an equally aloof tone that she was one of the officers assigned to investigate a fatal car accident and the abduction of a four-year-old girl. That shut his pompous mouth. She banged the phone down.

Thursday, 25 April, 10.20 a.m.

WPC Delia Shaw had hit lucky. When she pulled up outside Lucy Stanstead's house she could see only one car in the drive and a pale face staring out of the window. Lucy Stanstead opened the door before she'd even had time to knock. 'He's had to report back to his boat,' she said breathlessly. 'Sorry – his ship,' she corrected with a grin.

WPC Shaw could imagine she used the word *boat* simply to annoy her husband, and she responded with a grin of her own.

'Only for some checks,' Lucy added, 'but he'll be away all day.'

Delia Shaw had been a good choice to tease out any facts from Lucy Stanstead. She put the general public at their ease. They liked her friendly, rather mumsy manner, her scrubbed, wholesome face, and were reassured by her wide smile. WPC Shaw would be regarded by some as plain and by others as beautiful. She had that sort of face. You saw what you wanted to see. But no one, male or female, ever felt threatened by the PC.

The first thing that struck her about Mrs Stanstead was that she appeared to live in a permanently nervous state, her eyes frequently focusing back towards the window and the front drive, flinching every time a car went past.

The woman lives on her nerves, she thought.

She let her make her a cup of tea and settled down on the cream-coloured sofa which was soft with duck down and soporifically comfortable.

'Mrs Stanstead,' she began, leaning forward, an open, earnest, inviting expression on her face, 'nothing you say will go any further unless it has a bearing on the investigation, you understand.'

The woman's returning smile was both cynical and sad. She wafted her hands up. 'It doesn't matter now,' she said. 'Not now that Tracy's dead and Daisy . . .' A spasm crossed her face. She twisted her eyes up but the action failed to prevent a tear squeezing out of her eye.

'It's all . . .'

'What is?'

'Nothing is as it was.'

'Sorry?'

'I can't have children of my own,' she said bluntly.

Delia Shaw felt a frisson of embarrassment. Sometimes it was hard to separate one's personal life from work. 'There's things they can do,' she said awkwardly. 'Treatments.'

And have you tried them?

'Not in my case,' Lucy Stanstead said sadly. 'I can't have children,' she said, even more firmly.

'So Daisy . . .?' Shaw felt she was punching holes in the dark. But beyond that was a bright light so dazzling she felt her eyes start to screw up in an involuntary squint.

'Tracy didn't *want* her,' Lucy Stanstead said, her voice hard with accusation. 'Daisy was just a *nuisance* to her. Neil told me that Tracy's attitude to the child was that Daisy stopped her "*having a life*".' She scribbled the quote with her fingers. The way she spoke the words Delia Shaw could almost see them spewing out of Tracy Walsh's mouth as a sneer, bitter and angry of the life she *could* have had without a child to hamper her style.

'Whereas Neil . . .' She licked her lips, her voice smug now. 'Neil and I – we simply adored her. She was a lovely little girl.'

Shaw picked up quickly on the tense. 'Was?'

'She can't still be alive, can she? It's been more than two weeks. And no sign of her.'

'So where do you think she is?'

Again Lucy looked evasive, cunning.

'Mrs Stanstead,' Coleman said, 'if you know where Daisy is you must tell me.'

The blue eyes looked panicked.

'Mrs Stanstead?'

'I have nothing more to say,' she said. 'Except I don't know what's happened to Daisy. I wish I did.'

WPC Shaw wasn't sure whether this was the truth. But she reverted to the conventional questions. 'The Saturday night of the accident – where were you?'

'Here.'

'Alone?'

'Yes – alone.'

'Mrs Stanstead, what plans did you have for Neil and Daisy?'

The woman stonewalled her. 'I'm sorry,' she said politely, 'I don't know what you mean.'

Oh yes you do, Shaw thought. 'Let me put it this way, Mrs Stanstead: were you planning to leave your husband for Neil Mansfield?'

The woman's shoulders drooped. 'It doesn't matter now.'

It was not an answer.

'But Daisy was not his daughter. She wasn't even legally adopted. He would have had no rights.'

And suddenly the claws were out. 'He wouldn't have needed it.' The words burst out of her like an erupting boil. 'If Tracy hadn't made such a fuss we could have brought her up.'

'But . . .?' Shaw asked the question gently.

But . . . Lucy Stanstead had clammed up.

Shaw tried another tack. 'Are you able to shed any light on the accident and the possible whereabouts of Daisy?'

Lucy Stanstead simply shook her head.

Shaw gave her one more chance. 'Is there anything *more* you want to tell me at this point?'

She kept her eyes trained on the woman's face, studied her expression, tried to penetrate the mask of studious blankness, the eyes emptied of emotion and truth, and Shaw wondered. She waited, hoping that Lucy Stanstead would drop something into the silence. But there was nothing. She simply gave a long, slow blink. 'I'm afraid, Constable Shaw, that you've had a wasted journey.'

Delia couldn't resist throwing one last pebble into the pond. 'I wonder,' she said. And this time it was she who looked smug and Lucy Stanstead who looked concerned.

Thursday, 25 April, 10.30 a.m.

Had it not been for the gravity of the situation PC Sean Dart would have burst out laughing at the sight.

Freddy Ribbler, tall, skinny, silver haired and wearing shorts, was bouncing up and down on the spot, elbows stiffly held at an angle.

And he looked cold. He actually looked relieved when Dart's car skidded to a halt right by him.

'Morning!' he shouted out, still bouncing but less energetically now, as though he knew his ordeal was coming to an end.

'Hello, sir.' Dart held his hand out and was rewarded with a knuckle-crushing grip that brought tears to his eyes.

Ribble stopped bouncing. 'Over there,' he said, pointing.

Where the stream flowed over rocks, in the middle of the white spray, something pink lay on the bottom. 'Didn't touch it, of course,' Ribbler said gruffly.

Dart simply stared.

It was a small garment with a Barbie doll motif on the front and it was weighed down with a large, smooth stone which had kept it beneath the water. And yet the colour was so bright, so foreign that it stood out like a beacon. All around was green, the stream silver and blue, the stones grey. The pink stood out as a sickly bright colour. Nothing in nature is quite so garish as Barbie-doll pink and Ribble was quite right: it had not been there when the police search had been ongoing. Someone had put it there since yesterday's run. And Ribble, pale, goose-pimply focusing on the sodden garment, echoed his observation.

'It's been placed there,' he barked. 'Some time since yesterday. I do my run every single morning. Military training,' he said proudly, chest puffed out, 'means you keep your eyes and ears open. Know what I mean, Constable?' He was still in some sort of running rhythm. Even his words were spoken in time.

Dart nodded. He glanced superstitiously around him. It was still early. Few people were here. Those that were watched him curiously. Was the person who had placed the child's dressing gown oh-so-carefully at the bottom of the stream, with equal care weighted it down with the rock, watched and waited for someone to see it and make the connection? Were they watching him now? Had they known about Ribble's daily runs, regular as clockwork, observant and passing within feet of the gaudy pink? Dart groaned. They were going to have to seal off the immediate area – again. And for the life of him he couldn't see where this case was heading. The SIO was up in Scotland. For the moment they were a ship without a captain. No one in charge. He put the now shivering Freddy Ribble in his car with, despite his protestations, the heater full on, and made his way to the National Trust shop and a telephone.

Thursday, 25 April, 11.15 a.m.

Arlene and Allistair seemed the perfect couple – amicable, friendly, and Talith couldn't take his eyes off the swinging blonde hair and the beautifully applied lipstick on her mouth.

Arlene did quite a bit of the talking, using her sexual charm to wind DS Paul Talith right round her little finger.

Randall could have kicked him.

'Of course, I knew that Allistair had been married before,' she said with a smiling flash of white teeth. 'I knew he had a daughter. And I wouldn't have minded if he'd wanted to keep contact with her.' She actually batted her eyelashes at Talith, instinctively knowing that she would have cut no ice with his superior.

'But things had been so acrimonious with Tracy.' She sighed. 'In the beginning Allistair tried,' she turned her head, 'didn't you?'

He nodded, as mesmerized by Arlene as Talith was.

'But every contact provoked rows and shouting, misunderstandings, didn't they, darl.'

Donaldson nodded. He was patently a man of few words.

Arlene fixed her blue eyes on Talith. 'We plan to get married in the summer,' she said softly, her tone practically seducing Talith. 'We don't want any trouble.'

Randall interrupted the soliloquy. 'Did you ever meet Daisy, Arlene?'

Wonderingly, she shook her head. 'No.'

Randall ignored her then and turned to Tracy's ex. 'And when did you last see her, sir?'

'When she was about six months old,' he said with a hint of shame.

'You haven't seen her since?'

'No.' He patently felt some explanation was called for. 'In the beginning things were acrimonious between me and Tracy. And then later – well, it seemed too late. From all accounts Neil had a good relationship with her. She had a new dad. She didn't need me. I was only going to muddy the waters.'

Arlene nodded her agreement and suddenly Randall felt he would explode. A child doesn't have a new father just as a father cannot ever replace a child. He felt a momentary pain in his chest.

'What about your mother, Daisy's grandmother?'

Allistair looked a little evasive at the question. He gave a swift, checking glance at his fiancée and reluctantly dragged out an answer. 'I think she did ring her up once or twice,' he said.

'Did she ever go south and visit her?'

Allistair stared at the carpet. 'Not that I know of.'

'And did Daisy ever come up here to stay with her grandmother?'

'No.'

'But you did send your daughter money for birthdays and Christmas?'

'I sent it to Tracy, thinking she could buy Daisy something. Whether she'd say it was from me or not I never knew. It didn't really matter one way or the other.'

'You realize that now Tracy's dead you're Daisy's next of kin?'

'Yeah.'

Randall felt the anger rise like an insurrection. 'So aren't you at least concerned at your daughter's disappearance?'

And at last he'd provoked a response. 'Of course I am,' Donaldson burst out. 'But . . .' Here he hesitated. 'She doesn't feel like my daughter. We'd never . . .' He was searching in his mind for a suitable phrase and came up with, 'bonded.'

Randall blinked.

'What Allistair's trying to explain,' Arlene put in silkily, 'is that he only felt the same as if *any* four-year-old had gone missing. Understand?'

Randall ignored her. She was beginning to annoy him. He addressed his next question to Donaldson and him alone. 'Can you shed any light on your daughter's disappearance?'

He shook his head.

'We're going to have a word with your mother. Can you give us her address?'

Donaldson obliged and the two officers left, Randall feeling dissatisfied and as for Talith . . . He'd had a glimpse of a goddess and now he had to come right back down to earth again.

Thursday, 25 April, 12.35 p.m.

Mrs Donaldson didn't live in anything like as salubrious an area as her son and his partner. In fact, she lived in a rather unpleasant block of flats in a rundown area of Inverness, on the seventh floor of an ugly, communist-looking gulag of a place, a square concrete block with little to relieve it apart from a few colourful sheets and towels placed out, in the vain and highly optimistic hope that they would dry on the miniscule balconies.

She looked older than she should have been with a thirty-year-old son, but that was partly due to very poor dentition and witch-like pointed features. She even cackled as she opened the door. 'So you'll be the policemen,' she said in a strong Scottish brogue. 'You found me all right, then?'

They both smiled their responses and flashed their ID. She didn't bother to look at the cards but showed them into a tiny lounge which smelt of chip fat. But the views, to the north, over the city and beyond towards the Moray Firth, were astonishing.

The witchy woman spoke. 'So you've met the wee Arlene then?'

They both nodded.

'Had me out of ma own house,' she said, her mouth tightening as though in preparation for sucking a particularly bitter lemon. 'Aye, that girl,' she said in disgust. 'He shouldna allowed it. But there we are. Men's always a fool when it comes to a sweet-lookin' thing like oor Arlene.'

Talith looked embarrassed and felt he wanted to go home. Back to his good, familiar, pleasant life. Domestication. *Get me out of here.*

Randall took over. 'You know we're investigating the disappearance of your granddaughter.'

Mairie Donaldson cackled again disconcertingly. 'Oh, ma granddaughter now, is it,' she mocked. 'Well, there's a turn up for the books.'

The officers waited.

'Look,' Mairie said, more reasonably now. 'I went to the weddin' when he married Tracy though I didna like her. Right? I played my part. I sent down a Mothercare voucher after wee Daisy was born. That's as much as I know. I never was invited down to Shropshire. Not for a visit or to take a wee peek at the little girl. For a year after Tracy and my son broke up I sent Christmas and birthday presents but Tracy never acknowledged them. I rang my granddaughter but there was not a word not a phone call or a letter back so I stopped and that, Inspector, is as much I know about ma own granddaughter. That is sum total. You understand?'

In an effort to connect with them, she added, 'I know it's tradition for a woman not to like the girl or in this case girls her son marries but that isna it at all. My son, not unlike others of his sex . . .' This provoked a severe stare at each of the male policeman in turn, holding her stare twice as long on Talith, which seemed to see right through to his inner thoughts, 'is very susceptible to the charms of a pretty female. And it makes him ignore other, less pleasant aspects of their character, you understand? So he ends up with complete bitches.' This time there was no cackle, no irregularly toothed smile. Just a nod of the head and a general acceptance of the status quo.

Thursday, 25 April, 1 p.m.

They had sealed off the area, created a corridor of access and carefully pulled the dressing gown out of the running water. But even the cool, fast flow of the stream had failed to rinse away the crusted bloodstain. Dart looked at it and his heart sank.

Thursday, 25 April, 2 p.m.

PC Gary Coleman had found Mansfield's house empty and abandoned, so had returned to the office to hack into his computer. And what he found was very interesting indeed. Well, maybe not so much interesting as odd. Certainly odd. Not quite what he had expected.

TWENTY

R andall got the call about the dressing gown just as they were driving back to the airport and the news gave him the bad feeling of having been in the wrong place at the wrong time. *Well done, Randall,* he thought. Backed the wrong horse – again. He should have been there instead of leaving it all behind to the junior officers. He needed to regain control. Talith, he noticed, wisely kept mum on the subject when he voiced this point of view. But even his silence was a sort of tacit agreement.

During the brief flight Randall was fidgety. His mind was posing questions. How did the garment get there? If, as it appeared, it had been put there in the last twenty-four hours, why? Why hold back a vital piece of evidence only to plant it weeks later? What could the motive be except to keep taunting the police and prove that he or she was smarter than they were? So what was the game? Hide and seek? Or was the abductor after money? In which case why not simply come forward with a demand? Had they asked for a ransom it would likely be paid by public subscription anyway. He could well imagine a couple of the tabloids running a Save Daisy campaign. For such a cute child money would pour in but it was a very risky strategy. Ransom money and the swap-over frequently led straight back to the kidnapper who would be unable to benefit from his ill-gotten gains. And there was always a risk to the child. No, he could not think of this as a kidnapping. It didn't fit right. This could hardly have been a planned kidnapping. It was, surely, a chance encounter?

Randall gritted his teeth. 'Ask a bloody ransom if you like,' he growled under his breath, 'but don't play tease me, squeeze me.'

Being drip-fed clues left them wondering whether every minute, every hour that they failed to find Daisy was costing the little girl her life? It was cruel. Worse, it was pointless.

His impatience and frustration lasted all the way from Manchester airport to the outskirts of Shrewsbury. He wanted to reach the police station as quickly as possible and speak to Sean Dart himself. He wanted to see the garment. Touch it. Randall gave a twisted smile. If one could divine the fate of the child from a bright pink dressing gown it would be helpful. As it was he contented himself with summoning the lead officers to a briefing as soon as he touched the station door.

As he was talking Talith was aiming a look of sympathy his way. He wouldn't have liked to be the SIO on this case. Oh no, thank you. He'd stick to sergeant. For now.

Randall saw the look out of the corner of his eye and appreciated it while thinking up another scenario. It was possible that someone, not even the abductor, but someone else, someone unconnected with the crime, could have bought a similar dressing gown and planted it themselves in the Carding Mill brook. Bloodstained?

Well, people were strange.

He rejected the idea. No. This was a tease from their abductor, all right. He was beginning to get a feel for this person. Martha had hit the nail on the head. Someone with a mystical sense of superiority. Someone superstitious and obscure. Someone who thought up ideas like the twisted clues of a crossword puzzle; someone who liked to make their clues none too easy. Someone who . . . He could have gone on and on. And all of it bad. He was learning not to trust this adversary. Her clues were not always what they seemed. A gift could be a Trojan horse guaranteed to hide some obscure evil.

On his return to Monkmoor Police Station he was presented with the evidence bag and its sad, still sodden contents. His four leading officers were waiting for him in one of the briefing rooms.

PC Sean Dart spoke out first. 'We've cordoned off the area, sir, and asked Neil Mansfield to come in.'

Randall looked up. 'Good. And this, er, Freddy Ribble, the chap who found it?'

'He's a reliable witness, sir. Runs that route every morning, sometime between eight and ten a.m. He's ex-military, very observant and absolutely certain it wasn't there yesterday.'

Dart's face was anxious, his voice taut with tension. He was aware this was a test. Had he followed the correct protocol with such a significant piece of evidence in a major case? Had he got anything wrong? He waited, holding his breath. He had the feeling that while Inspector Randall could be indulgent with junior officers who tried hard, if he had mishandled this event Randall would be blistering. But for now the inspector was neither. He was appraising the evidence. And came to his conclusion. 'So we're looking at a twenty-four-hour slot,' he observed, 'sometime between, say, ten on Wednesday morning and nine forty-five this morning.' He couldn't resist tacking on the proviso, 'If he's to be believed.'

Dart did not reply immediately but shifted uncomfortably on his feet. While it had initially occurred to him to doubt the gentleman's word, once he had met Freddy Ribble he had been convinced. He was a perfect witness. And when his inspector met him he would agree.

He said so and Randall smiled at him indulgently, a friendly hand on his shoulder. 'Well done, Dart, he said. 'You're proving an asset to the Shrewsbury police.'

Dart let out his breath with relief. He was going to fit in here all right. It was all going to be OK.

After the nightmare comes the dream.

'We'd better get this . . .' Randall patted the bag, '. . . to forensics.' The words were accompanied by a sinking feeling. In his heart of hearts he had never lost hope that Daisy Walsh was alive somewhere. Not that she was well. That would be too much to hope for after such a serious accident. But as his eyes scanned the pink towelling with its ominous stain, his brain was assessing it. Even for her age Daisy had been a very small child, a dainty little girl and this was a sizeable patch of blood. He closed his eyes for a minute and knew this signified a change in the investigation. After nearly three weeks it was becoming increasingly likely that the little girl who had played her own game of peekaboo, peeping so endearingly around a doorway, was dead, her body concealed somewhere, and the person who had torn her from the accident site was now playing another cruel game of cat and mouse with the police. Randall felt suddenly weary.

'We might hit lucky,' he said, fingering the evidence bag, but without hope in his voice, 'and find some trace evidence of where Daisy is now but . . .' He fell quiet and looked around the room. Anything else?'

Gary Coleman spoke up, handing him a sheet of paper.

'This is a list of the websites I've printed off Mansfield's computer.'

Randall read through them then looked up, confused. 'What are they?'

'Officially child model websites,' Coleman said, 'most of them in the States. But if you look at them the little girls are very tarted up. It looks as though Mansfield was trying to get Daisy some modelling work in America.'

The rest of the officers clustered round, a few exclaiming at the fees promised.

'A thousand pounds a job?' Randall looked at Coleman who nodded.

'It's big business, sir.'

'So that's why those professional photographs were taken of Daisy. Did she get any work?'

'I couldn't tell, sir. I found plenty of photographs. Daisy's never been out of the country but a passport was issued to her back in November.' He left it at that.

'Right. Anything else?'

'Some sites about fertility treatment.'

'They were planning on having another child?'

Coleman shrugged.

Delia Shaw spoke up. 'Maybe I can help here,' she said. 'I spoke to Lucy Stanstead. I managed to catch her alone. The captain was away with his ship – checking it over before he sails.'

'And?'

'She's apparently unable to have children herself. I wonder – perhaps

Neil has been searching the internet for some fertility treatment not for Tracy but for Lucy Stanstead.' She frowned. 'She seemed to have some half-hatched idea that Neil would leave Tracy and that they would bring up Daisy as their own. Only it seems that Tracy didn't want to play ball. In fact, she was absolutely furious. Maybe it was that row that led to her grabbing Daisy and belting from the house.'

Randall looked up. 'So far from Daisy Walsh being an unwanted child,' he observed, 'she was a little girl very much in demand. With a value,' he added thoughtfully, realizing they'd thought along traditional lines, of a four-year-old child being small and vulnerable. They would never have believed she could have a market value all of her own which her mother was planning to exploit. He felt slightly sick. To him a child was a child.

'Tinsley?'

Lara Tinsley shook her head. 'Charity Ignatio's off the hook,' she said. 'She didn't come back to UK in early April. In fact, from the eighth to the tenth she was on some sort of trip to one of the resorts over in Dubai – Jumeirah.'

'Nothing in this case is working out neat.' Randall sighed.

Mansfield arrived at six o'clock, just as the poor light of the day was fading into evening and the last of the sun dropping behind the skyline. He looked truly awful, Randall thought: pale and pasty, as though he lived below ground and never saw the light of day any more. But he looked worried rather than upset.

He dropped his thick form heavily into a chair opposite. 'Inspector,' he said wearily, then, turning to Gethin Roberts, 'Constable? What can I do for you?'

'This isn't a formal interview, Neil,' Randall said, trying to put the poor man at his ease. 'We know all this has been difficult for you.'

Mansfield was not mollified but remained wary.

'And we know that you are genuinely fond of Daisy.' Then, without warning, Randall put the evidence bag on the desk. 'As far as you can tell, Neil, is this Daisy's dressing gown?'

Mansfield's started back as though repulsed by the bloody garment. His eyes fixed on the rusty stain his fingers could feel was stiff with the dried blood, even through the evidence bag, and the water seemed to seep through, cold as the grave. No sign of the lively child any more. It was simply a garment.

Mansfield looked at each of them in turn as though wondering which one was responsible for this. His eyes narrowed; his face grew even more wary. 'Where . . .' He cleared his throat. 'Where . . .' He swallowed. 'Where did you find this?'

'In Carding Mill Valley,' Randall said gently. 'Not far from the crash site.' He gave Roberts a swift, warning glance.

Don't tell him it was put there in the last twenty-four hours.

But Mansfield was no fool. His face hardened and he confronted the detectives with a hostile, guarded look and spoke with accusation ripening his voice. 'So why didn't you find it before?'

Randall gave in. 'Because it wasn't there, Neil.'

'How can you know that?'

Randall wasn't going to tell him. 'We just know,' he said, without inflection, without emotion.

Mansfield licked his plump lips, slumped his shoulders and dropped his gaze back to the contents of the evidence bag. 'And this,' he said, his finger almost making a rasping sound over the crust of blood. 'Is this blood?'

'We'll have to get it tested to be certain.'

'Is it *her* blood?'

The answer was the same but Randall had to be sure. 'I take it then, just for the record, Neil, that this is similar to Daisy's dressing gown?' He was trying to heal the rift that had opened between them.

'Yes.'

Now it was time to divert Mansfield's attention away from the garment.

'There is another issue,' he said. Mansfield looked up. Not concerned or worried, just curious.

'The photographs of Daisy,' he began. 'PC Coleman here has taken a look at some of the websites you've visited.' Randall frowned. 'Child models and such like. Did you have aspirations for Daisy to be a child model?'

Mansfield looked a bit confused. 'Not exactly,' he said very carefully. 'The friend who took the photograph you've used in your publicity stuff said that she was pretty enough to *use* as a child model.' Mansfield suddenly looked alarmed. 'Nothing tacky,' he protested.

'Sure about that?'

Mansfield simply stared. 'What are you getting at?'

'Some of the sites, Neil, the little girls were wearing make-up. A lot of make-up. High heels and stuff to make them look – well, tarty. Adult.'

Mansfield still looked confused. 'What are you saying?'

'We're just trying to get to the truth.'

Mansfield scowled.

'Does anyone else have access to your computer?'

'No.' Mansfield swallowed. 'Except . . .'

And Randall clicked. 'Did Tracy know your password?'

''Course.' Mansfield looked confused for only one moment longer. Then it hit him with a sledgehammer. 'She were up to summat, weren't she?'

'We don't know yet.'

It quietened him and made Neil reflective. Both officers could see that his mind was burrowing into things. Randall revised the situation in his mind. Shared passwords, like PIN numbers, had a big problem. You never could tell who was pressing the keys. And certainly it could be difficult to prove in a court of law.

He decided to appeal. 'Help us, Neil, please.'

Oddly enough, the appeal had quite an effect on Neil. He looked distressed. 'And you think I'm not?' His face twisted like a child's. 'You think I'm just pissing around? I want to find her just as much as you do. She was *my* little girl.' Then he looked wary. '*Our* little girl,' he corrected, which gave Randall the perfect opening. 'Our being . . .' he asked innocently.

But Mansfield was on his guard now.

'Mine and Tracy's,' he said smoothly.

'Right. And were you and Tracy planning another child?'

Mansfield looked positively bovine. 'No,' he said. 'No.' His face screwed up. 'What are you on about?'

'Nothing,' Randall said sweetly.

PC Coleman was continuing with his scrutiny of recently visited websites. He was frowning into the screen, not liking what he saw. There was something inherently wrong about the poses of the child models. He tried to find out who had been visiting the sites but there was no chance. With the same password there was no clue. Except . . . Coleman looked a bit more carefully. Most of these tacky little sites had been visited during the working day. Tracy herself worked evenings, mainly, leaving Neil to keep an eye on Daisy. Daisy, the lively little four-year-old who didn't like going to bed so had to be read stories until even Neil himself fell asleep. So one p.m., two p.m. internet visits were unlikely to be him.

Computers do leave footprints after all. It must have been Tracy who'd been visiting the child modelling sites.

He sat back, frowning. Coleman was a conventional man. He had a long-term partner, Patty, and he had, for the last six months, been trying to pluck up courage to ask her to marry him. The trouble was firstly that he needed the right time and the right place and secondly, Patty had told him on more than one occasion (six, actually – he'd been counting) that she didn't believe in marriage. When they'd been shopping in Chester last summer he'd observed her very carefully as they'd passed two or three bridal shops with the most fantastic displays of dresses – meringues, elegant, sexy, huge trains, glinting crystals fit to blind a man. And this was the vision Coleman had of his nuptials. He wanted the bloody lot. Church, giggling bridesmaids, dreadful speeches, sparkling wine masquerading as champagne. The lot. Unusually for a man, he loved weddings and dreamed of Patty walking towards him up the aisle, train billowing out behind her, with at least six bridesmaids in bright dresses and huge smiles, to the cheering of the few friends he had confided this particular ambition to. It would make him so happy. And then Coleman wanted the next stage of life: 2.4 children. That was what he wanted.

But he was terrified that Patty would simply say *no* in that uncompromising way she had. And then he would be left with nothing. No great hopes for the future. No visions of everlasting romance and dreamy weddings. No one boy, one girl and one other. Just a great, big, wide, black, horrible tunnel of a life.

And he didn't like looking at these images on the computer screen. What did they say about Tracy as a mother? That she was driven by greed, rather than Daisy's best interests? Did she even care about her child?

Now the interview with Mansfield was over PC Roberts was following his own hunch. One phrase that the manager of the Long Mynd Hotel had used was lying untidily in his mind. *Tracy was a hit with the men – and occasionally some of the women.* For some reason the words were coiling around in his mind, its head wickedly peeping up, like a snake coming out of its basket in time to piped music. It wheeled and twisted, now up, now down and then looking directly at him with bold black eyes.

And then he felt a jolt. He knew what it was. A room full of social workers. Roberts smiled. He could just imagine them. All National

Health glasses and tweedy skirts, slightly offensive armpits, hair where it shouldn't be on a woman like on the upper lip, and hugging trees for a hobby. Oh, yes. He could imagine them, glowing with goodness. Idly he wondered what the collective term for a load of social workers was: a goodness of social workers? A meddling of social workers? A kindness of social workers? An inactivity of social workers? An ineffectiveness of social workers. Social workers who drowned in their own jargon and had every excuse for doing zilch.

It depended on your point of view, he supposed. Even his reflections thought in a Welsh lilt.

And for some reason his next thought was to do a little snooping. After all – that is what policeman are famous for.

A snoopery of policemen.

I'll just take a peek, he thought, at the guest list of the Long Mynd Hotel for the whole of last year because a silly little idea was worming its way into his brain. More a worm than a snake, then? Silly idea? Was it so silly? They had supposed from the first that the drunken argument, the accident, the missing child, Charity Ignatio being away, they had surmised that it was all coincidence. But what if it wasn't? What if it had all been planned? But already Roberts could see a problem with this. Tracy would hardly have planned her own death, would she, silly? But what if something had been planned but it had all gone wrong? What?

The accident.

Roberts sat and thought. He had a feeling, silly and inconsequential as his musings might be, that he was stumbling, like a blind man over rocks, over something of significance. What he couldn't say was what, except that he felt warm and good because he believed he was on to something.

DI Alex Randall was pacing his office. He was on a tightrope and he knew it. If he charged Mansfield (and he didn't even know what with) the PACE clock would start ticking. *Tick-tock* and he would have to let him go. Could Mansfield have been involved in the fate of his partner and her daughter? For the life of him Randall couldn't work it out. He had to let him go. It was a painful but necessary step. He carried on pacing his small office for a few more minutes then he gave in, put his jacket on.

He was going home.

TWENTY-ONE

Friday, 26 April, 9.30 a.m.

He couldn't face trying to justify an appointment through Jericho Palfreyman, so he simply turned up. As he'd anticipated Jericho demurred, but seeing the complete lack of compromise on the detective's face, for once he didn't pursue the objection; instead he knocked on Martha's door, stood back and let DI Randall in.

But coming without warning or an appointment was a mistake. It was as though he had walked in on her private self and caught her with her guard down. He was seeing Martha unprepared and it gave him a shock. He instantly realized he'd barged in on her and she wasn't looking too happy as she pored over some sheets on her desk, peering up into the computer screen and frowning.

'Nursing homes,' she said in explanation, without looking up. It struck him that she was evading his eyes, fixing her gaze on her work and she made no comment on the unexpectedness of his visit. 'Clusters of deaths.' Then she looked up and he saw her face was sad. 'I can't look into all of them, Alex,' she said, 'but there does seem to be one particular nursing home where the life expectancy in there is significantly lower than the others.' Then his presence must have registered and she morphed into the coroner he knew so well, with a bright smile and a happy look. But he had seen beneath the surface and read vulnerability and sadness. Sadness she was so good at disguising. After all, she was widowed. The job was always connected with death. Her children were growing up. Perhaps her life wasn't as full as . . .

Stop it, he lectured himself.

She must have caught his expression and half rose from her chair. 'Alex,' she said, concerned, 'what is it? I heard something yesterday on the lunchtime news. Have you found her?'

It was like finding a port in a storm. He sank down into the chair; put his hand over his face. 'Just her blood-stained dressing gown,' he said, his fingers trying to erase the creases from his forehead. 'We haven't found her or her body.'

'And you think it was planted there in the last twenty-four hours?'

'I *know* it was,' he said. 'There is absolutely no way we would have missed it on our search, quite besides the evidence of the very observant man who found it. He runs the same route every single day and the dressing gown, weighted down with a stone, is bright pink and lay at the bottom of the brook. If you want to know what I think,' he continued, his voice angry, 'I think it's all a big tease. Someone out there is enjoying themselves playing games.'

'You think she's dead?'

Reluctantly, Alex Randall nodded. 'She probably died in the accident or soon after it.'

Martha was still. It had been a terrible case from the start. Could it get any worse?

'And there is always the chance that she was badly injured in the accident and is dying right now. Martha,' he appealed, 'what sort of person would do this? Why not give up either the child or her body? What can they possibly hope to *gain* by this concealment? Is she dead and part of some bizarre and horrible ritual?' He wished the phrase did not resonate quite so loudly around his head. He wished that the accident hadn't happened in a place with such a bad and sinister reputation.

She leaned towards him, extending her hands across the desk, and Randall continued.

'The nightmare is not that she's dead but that she's alive, frightened, hurt and in danger, a four-year-old in the hands of a sadist. A sadist who wants to extract the maximum pleasure from it all, a person who is not only callous and sadistic towards a child but also wants the police to be publicly humiliated. And . . .' The hazel eyes searched hers as you would search for a hand in the dark. She was so tempted to console him, to reach out and stroke his cheek.

Martha exerted an iron resolve. It wasn't going to happen.

She read pain in his eyes. Pain she had seen even before this case had wrapped its chilly fingers around his neck. He was in a truly awful place. Silently, she waited.

Back at the station, Coleman's assiduity was paying off. Now he'd cracked the pattern of computer use he was finding out more and more. Looked at from this different angle it was interesting, intriguing and thoroughly puzzling. Now why on earth would *Tracy* have been searching this particular site set up for people who desperately wanted a family but were unable to conceive? She must have been a little bit web-wise because all her emails prior to 6 April had been deleted. There was nothing that predated the accident. The whole lot had been scrubbed out. *She'd covered her tracks.* And that, in itself, was unusual, not to say *very* unusual, not to say strange, not to say thoroughly bloody suspicious. Coleman blinked, his brain working overtime. There was not one single email left in the box that was dated before 6 p.m. on 6 April. Nothing in Draft. Nothing even in Spam or Trash that predated the accident. Tracy had dumped the lot, clever girl. Well, Coleman reasoned, Tracy or Neil had something they wished to bury very deeply. And he was pretty sure it was Tracy.

She had been cute. Everything on email post-dated the accident. He went through them methodically but, like many other people, most were advertising something – tooth whitener, holiday bargains, cruises. Tracy had lived a life of wishful thinking. There were plenty of online shopping sites, some of them for perfumes and fancy goods, others for the big supermarkets. Coleman went through them all and came up with . . . nothing.

Now then.

Coleman decided that Tracy was either one of those very tidy people who clear up their emails on a daily basis, which he very much doubted or, much more likely, she had something to hide. But she couldn't delete *all* her clues. The first email in the box was for 6.30 p.m. on the evening of Saturday, 6 April, so her deletion had happened sometime on the Saturday evening, before she'd left the house with Daisy. Clue one.

He took a swig of lukewarm coffee and leaned back in his chair. So no emails, only the browsing history. Well, well, well. This was interesting. But what on earth was she doing, looking at these sorts of sites? Coleman scratched his head. This didn't make any sense.

He called up Neil Mansfield. 'Hello,' he said. 'It's PC Coleman here. I wonder . . . You and Tracy only have Daisy, don't you?'

'Yeah.' Mansfield's answer was suitably truculent and defensive.

'She didn't have any other children?'

'Not as far as I know.' Mansfield paused. 'Mind you,' he said, 'I'm not sure I ever really knew her. Know what I mean?'

Yes and no, Coleman thought, and pursued his point. 'She'd never had a child adopted?'

Mansfield sounded bemused. 'Not as far as I know.'

'Did you *want* more children?'

'No.' Mansfield's patience was running out. 'I'd had enough of her. We were going to be splittin' up, no doubt about it. If she hadn't had the accident we probably wouldn't still be together.' He paused. 'We'd have split up before the accident if it hadn't been for Daisy.' Another pause. 'The last thing I'd have wanted is more kids – with her.'

'But you were fond of Daisy.'

'Yeah. Daisy was a little darling. Unlike her mother.'

Coleman persisted. 'But you say you weren't trying for a baby?'

'No.' Said emphatically.

'Was *Tracy* trying for a baby?'

'Not that I know of, though I wouldn't have put anything past that conniving little . . .' Then he remembered. Tracy was dead. 'Look,' he said suddenly, 'the inspector's had me up the nick for ages. What is all this about?'

'I don't know,' Coleman answered honestly. 'I've been going through the sites that were visited on your computer. A lot of them are to do with women who can't have children.'

'Well, that wasn't Trace, I can assure you. She got pregnant with Daisy really easily, or so she told me. And she was on the Pill. To be honest she wasn't that maternal. If she'd found out she couldn't have had children her attitude would have been, "Oh, goody, now I don't have to bother with the Pill."'

Coleman frowned at the screen, trying to make sense between what his ears were hearing and what his eyes were seeing.

'Look, mate,' Mansfield said into the silence, 'I don't want to be rude but at the moment I'm a bit tied up trying to organize her funeral, which is proving surprisingly difficult. I had to wait for the coroner to release the body for burial and all of a sudden bloody Tracy's mum and sister seem to want to get involved. Call me cynical but I get the feeling they just want to be part of the media attention. Sad, isn't it? We've had so many arguments – just about a funeral.' He sounded incredulous. 'But I'm the one who knows what Tracy's wishes were. They don't.'

Coleman was listening with less than half an ear.

'I know she didn't want no flowers – or so she said – but they seem to want the damned lot. Horse and carriage, half a florist's. I told 'em she didn't want no flowers. She wanted money to go to her chosen charity, not a load of flowers that are dead two days after the funeral.'

And all of a sudden Coleman's ears pricked right up. 'What was Tracy's charity?'

'Something about woman who can't have children,' he scoffed. 'Don't know why she'd be interested in that sort of thing. But sometimes she did have a kind heart,' he conceded.

It wasn't much of a tribute.

TWENTY-TWO

Saturday, 27 April, 3 p.m.

Sam was at a match. This time she had not gone with him. He'd had a lift with a Shrewsbury friend who also played for Stoke. It was a lovely day, warm and sunny and very tempting to sit and read in the garden once Martha had finished her chores. She leafed through the paper. It had consigned Daisy Walsh to page four and the fairly predictable headline of:

WHERE IS SHE?

She looked at the now familiar picture. Papers usually stuck with the one image and used it over and over again. She closed her eyes for a moment but could still see the outline of the child, curly hair and small, round chin. Much as she'd tried to push the case to the back of her mind and focus on other things it still lay there, an amorphic unhappiness. She read on.

There had been various spurious sightings from Glasgow to Bournemouth, Anglesey to Norwich, but none had turned out to have any connection with Daisy. One little girl had subsequently turned out to be ten years old and her mother had been affronted at the confusion with a missing four-year-old. There was a note of indignation from mother and daughter. No regrets. She read on, realizing that there was nothing new. The child had simply vanished as though she had followed Alice's fate and fallen down the rabbit hole.

Would they ever know the child's fate or would her story prove to be another Madeline McCann: her fate a subject of endless conjecture with no facts and no explanation? Just stories? Would she be relegated into folklore? A threat to naughty children, that they too could vanish like Daisy Walsh?

She closed the paper, feeling unhappy and anxious in spite of the beautiful and welcome sunshine that beamed in through windows, freshly polished by a vigorous and suddenly extra house-proud Vera, her daily, or more precisely *twice weekly* cleaner.

But Bobby was wagging his tail optimistically and dogs do have to be walked. Maybe her daughter would like to join her so she called up the stairs. 'Sukey – fancy a walk?'

A face appeared at the top of the stairs. 'With Bobby?'

'I thought we'd just go through the woods, towards Haughmond Abbey. It's such a lovely day,' she coaxed, hoping her daughter would join her. She loved her chatter and besides, with these morbid thoughts about Daisy Walsh going round in her head she wanted to keep her own child close, though Sukey was more woman than child and Martha had the feeling she would be able to look after herself.

Other parents have made that same mistake.

Sukey appeared at the top of the stairs, thought for a minute then said, 'OK. Yeah. Why not? Just wait a minute, Mum. I'll be down.'

For a slim young woman Sukey made an awful lot of noise as she galloped down the stairs moments later in tiny denim shorts and a loose cotton top under which Martha suspected she was wearing nothing at all.

She sighed. Women of a certain age, particularly when they'd breast fed twins for six months, needed what her mother coyly called *support*. Ah, well, that was the price of motherhood. But there were compensations too. She pocketed her mobile phone and the dog lead, Bobby now thumping the floor with his tail as though it was a bongo drum. And how could a mongrel manage such an expressively hopeful look? He was just a dog.

Haughmond Abbey was the ruin of a twelfth-century Augustinian monastery. It was a spectacularly beautiful sight on the east side of Shrewsbury, slightly elevated so it provided a perfect view over the town's skyline and the beginnings of the Welsh hills beyond. It was surrounded by a wood and a network of footpaths and was a popular site for dog-walkers. Added to that list of recommendations it was only a short walk from The White House, Martha's embarrassingly pretentiously named home. When she and Martin had moved there fifteen years ago they had tried to think of a new name that would not sound as though they were mimicking a connection to the home of the president of the United States. The trouble was that the house was well named, being large and white, even with a bowed veranda at its front. It sat like an iceberg with a nose and on balance they had decided that they would sooner live in The White House than the Iceberg with its unpleasant connotations of sinking ships. And so, she suspected, the name would stay. She looked back at the house and remembered. Those had been the happy days – before Martin fell ill.

Sukey's long legs ending in Reeboks strode out along the path slightly ahead of her, Bobby keeping a watchful eye on the two women. He had a tendency to herd them like two dippy sheep. But they'd only gone a couple of hundred yards when Martha's mobile buzzed in her pocket. She recognized the caller ID: Simon. Simon Pendlebury, who had once been married to her dear friend, Evelyn. But, like Martin, Martha's husband, Evie had died and since then an uneasy friendship had sprung up between the two bereaved people. Uneasy? How so? First of all, uneasy because Martha didn't quite trust Simon. From humble beginnings he had become one of the super wealthy and she didn't quite know how except to trust that her friend, Evie, would never have condoned anything dishonest or underhand. Evie had been one of the most decent people Martha had ever known and she would not have married Simon unless she knew the answer to this puzzle.

Secondly Simon (and necessarily Evie too, although it was hard to believe) had somehow bred two of the most insufferable, selfish, ghastly daughters, Jocasta and Armenia. It would be a very brave woman who took on the chore of being stepmother to those two particular vipers: spoiled, demanding, determined to keep their father and their lifestyle to themselves. Martha suspected Simon would not marry again until both his daughters were also wed.

Her last reason for having reservations about him was that only a year ago Simon who was, like her, in his early forties, had 'fallen in love' in the most clichéd and ridiculous way with a twenty-three-year-old girl called, just to complete the idiotic picture, Christabel. It had been a brief and passionate affair, predictably scuppered by the daughters, who had exposed a deprived and murky past for the poor girl and she'd taken off in a flood of tears. Since then Martha had felt even more that she wanted to distance herself from him. However, recently they had fallen back into an easy habit of meeting for dinner or just for a drink every few weeks. It was a casual and undemanding arrangement which suited them both. For all her reservations about him Simon was good company, intelligent, well read, charming and polite. But she could never quite relax in his company.

And now here he was, back on the line again.

He must have sensed that she was out of doors, perhaps from the echo of her voice, or maybe the ambient rustle of trees and twittering birdsong. 'Where are you?'

'Walking Bobby,' she said. 'Why?'

He didn't answer straight away. 'Wish I was with you,' he said. 'Are you on your own?'

Martha glanced along the path. Though still in earshot Sukey had considerately moved fifty yards away and was playing throw the stick, catch the stick, bring the stick back, with an enthusiastic hound. She was pointedly *not* listening.

'Where are *you?*' she asked, more out of politeness than curiosity.

'In the hot office,' he said, 'up to my eyeballs and looking out enviously at the bluest sky I've ever seen.' He gave a tight, humourless laugh. 'I can't believe I still have to work so hard. Surely I should have some minions to do the dirty work?'

She caught her breath. *Dirty work?*

He continued, 'But I should be finished in a couple of hours. Are you busy tonight?'

She wished she was but the truth was, 'No.'

'Let me buy you dinner?'

Sukey was still eyeing her. Martha frowned. She didn't want to go out tonight. Not with Simon, not with anybody. Well, perhaps not with *anybody* – a certain pair of humour-filled hazel eyes seemed to blink, disembodied, right in front of her, but she certainly couldn't be bothered to make the effort with Simon. She heaved a great mental sigh and tried to inject some enthusiasm into her voice. 'OK.'

'Dress casual,' he said, sounding pleased. 'I'll pick you up from your house. Seven o'clock.'

This was unusual. They usually met at the venue, both driving themselves as though neither wanted to risk extending the evening beyond dinner. Simon had almost *never* picked her up. Besides, seven was early for him. And he had never rung her in the afternoon to suggest a meeting that very night. Normally she had a couple of days' notice. The other thing that struck her was that he usually liked to eat at formal hotels. She couldn't remember a night when he had said 'dress casual'. So what did this set of unusual circumstances signify? She just hoped he hadn't *fallen in love* again. She didn't think she could bear the toe-curling, cringingly embarrassing confessions. While there had been nothing wrong with poor Christabel there had been the undoubted disparity in their ages. And once the poor child had met Armenia and Jocasta it hadn't been long before she'd wisely taken to her heels and fled – even from the charming and urbane, expensively suited Simon, his beautiful house perfectly run by a German housekeeper, his top-of-the-range cars and flashy wealth. But once the two daughters had unearthed Christabel's *terrible* secret that her father was a jail bird, she had not stood a chance. And Simon's love had flown straight out of the window. He had never mentioned her since. Such is *lurve*.

Sukey was watching her with an adult perception in her bright eyes. 'You don't really like him much, do you?'

Martha defended herself. 'I don't not like him, Sukes,' she said, awkwardly defending herself. 'I wouldn't have dinner with him if I didn't like him.' She was speaking the truth. It really wasn't that she didn't like him. Apart from the little objections she had just raised in her mind there was something else. She sensed a coldness around his heart. An icicle that she believed only Evelyn, with her soft ways and gentle voice, could have melted. The worst was that when they ate dinner together, sometimes laughing about events, she would look deep into his eyes and sense the same fear and knowledge inside him, however hard he tried to conceal it. Only Evie had held the key to his heart and anyone else would only ever come second best.

Martha knew that she herself had never known the core of the man. Like many charming and sophisticated men he kept his true self well hidden. Tightly wrapped up.

'Yes, you *like* him,' Sukey persisted, frowning with adult perspicuity. 'But why nothing more? He's good looking,' cheeky smile, 'for an older man. He's got *pots* of money.'

'I can't explain,' Martha said, wincing at her daughter's avarice. 'I just know he's not . . .'

'*Nobody's* going to be like Dad,' Sukey said with heavy, resigned firmness. It was obviously a well-worn phrase, dog-eared as an old book.

Then suddenly Martha laughed, throwing back her head and laughing loudly to the bright blue sky which seemed to laugh with her with her mouth wide open. Sukey watched, puzzled. 'What?'

Mischievously, Martha chuckled. 'And I'm sure you'd *really* like Armenia and Jocasta as your stepsisters.' Her chuckle grew even louder as she watched Sukey's expression of doubt as she absorbed the question. The next minute they were both running through the woods, Bobby snapping at their heels, barking joyfully. They ran until they were both breathless and stopped, still laughing in gasps of humour, Sukey bending over, hands on her knees. Martha felt like Christian at the end of *Pilgrim's Progress*, her burden rolling from her as she realized that she didn't have to love Simon. She didn't have to love anyone. She didn't have to fall in love again. There was no law that dictated she must marry again. And suddenly she was intoxicated with the pure expansive freedom of it. She was as free as a butterfly or a bird or any other of God's unfettered creatures. She could travel the world if she so wanted. And the word *alone* held no fear for her any more.

Sukey put her arms around her and pressed her cheek to her mother's. 'Oh, Mum,' she said. 'What am I going to do with you?'

And they ran again.

I read the papers too. I see what they make of the story. Nothing, actually. They have no perception, no insight. But my job is almost done. What job is that, you ask. Wait and see. You must be patient. The time must be right. So I study my fingers. I see the power that gleams from them; the ability to control is better than drinking the blood of infants. Even unbaptized infants. I can convert order into disorder. I am the destroyer as well as the creator; the healer as well as the cause of injury. I am both virus and bacteria. I am everything. I deliver a message so mystical only the blessed can read them and I am the blunt instrument of information, the knife that cuts through ties and slices through knots. I am Shiva and Parvati, both love and destruction. For isn't one simply the other in deceitful form?

Saturday, 27 April, 5 p.m.

Alex Randall was not allowing himself Saturday off in such a major and so far fruitless investigation. Besides, weekends at home were to be avoided as much as possible. Why stay, Alex? he asked himself frequently. Why stay? Why not go? Be free? There was no logical answer to this particular poser.

But for now he must leave behind his own private problems and focus on the missing child. Feeling that the answer had to lie somewhere in the vicinity of the Stretton Hills, he had driven down to Carding Mill Valley himself, parked and headed up the slope towards Hope Cottage.

Signs had been left all over the place appealing for any help tracing Daisy but they were rain-stained now, dog-eared and torn in spite of being laminated, and some had dropped to the floor, trampled into the mud. If anything signified the depressing lack of progress in this case, these were the tangible evidence. An area around the stream was marked with Police Do Not Cross tape and two personnel were searching the ground, but Randall could have told them that they would find nothing there. He was beginning to understand the subtlety of their adversary. She was not careless.

On the warm, weekend day, plenty of people were around; more than usual, Randall sensed. Some of them, he guessed, were not pleasure-seekers but thrill-seekers hoping to find a trace of Daisy and maybe claim the £20,000 reward that had been put up by Shrewsbury Police. In the absence of anything but the false trail of clues which was leading nowhere it was to be hoped that the money would flush out some of the secrets surrounding Daisy's disappearance.

He could see Charity's four-by-four parked outside so it was reasonable to assume that she was at home.

He was right.

She opened the door, her smile fading when she realized who her visitor was. She looked questioningly at him, vaguely hostile.

'I'm sorry to bother you, Ms Ignatio,' he began, 'but we're still curious as to the connection between the accident, the disappearance of the little girl and the mystery call.' He opened his eyes wide. 'Why your cottage?' he asked bluntly.

'Oh, come on, Inspector,' she responded, her eyes hard. 'Look around you. It's not exactly a housing estate here, is it? It's practically the only house in the vicinity.'

'I know,' he said awkwardly, 'but there are others just down the track. If this person was local they would have known that. Besides, if you climb only a little way up the hill you get a perfectly good mobile signal so they needn't have broken into your cottage to use the phone. I would have thought they would have known that too.'

'The caller may not have had a mobile phone.'

'Practically everybody does these days,' Alex Randall pointed out gently. 'And whatever the facts of the case, why leave the scene? Why not wait for the emergency services to arrive? Why take the child? For what purpose?'

Charity simply shrugged as though it was nothing to do with her, implying that she didn't care either.

But Randall didn't want to leave it at this. He hesitated on the doorstep, anxious not to leave. He felt instinctively that either Charity or her home held some sort of clue. There were these fragile and tenuous connections. The bunch of herbs, the Death Cap left on the doorstep, the use of her home which surely pointed to something? And he still had the card of her old maybe-crime hidden up his sleeve ready to flourish when it would produce the biggest reaction. Aware that he was still grasping at straws he prompted her, conversationally, 'Tell me a bit about Hope Cottage.'

She looked a bit embarrassed. Then she smiled. The smile transformed her face into something almost open, almost happy. But only almost. 'All right,' she said. 'I'm not doing anything else today. The weather's so lovely, why don't we sit in the garden and I'll make us a cup of tea.'

Randall practically rubbed his hands together. What an attractive proposition. He sat at the small wooden table and chairs and surveyed the valley, waited for the rattle of tea cups. Then a sliver of unease trickled down his back like cold sweat.

A cup of tea? Mushroom soup? Hell – was she going to try to poison him?

It gave him some insight into people who have been acquitted of a crime. They may be acquitted but are they ever really free? Is it possible that the human mind never really forgets? That some small doubt always creaks in through the cracks underneath the door?

He pasted a deliberately bland expression on his face.

Charity reappeared with a tea tray, sat down and poured, not asking him whether he wanted milk or sugar, simply pouring it with milk and pushing the sugar bowl across.

'You ask me about Hope Cottage,' she began. 'There was a family tragedy when I was a teenager and so I came into money when I was twenty-one. That enabled me to buy here.'

She had pre-empted him. Her dark eyes mocked him, her mouth curving into a smile.

Randall nodded to show that he was listening and made no comment about the *family tragedy*. Charity took a lady-like sip of tea, and continued. 'When I bought it,' she said in her pleasantly husky voice, 'seven years ago, it was in a very bad condition. It had been derelict for a number of years and needed a lot of renovation. Bringing up to date,' she expanded, waving her hands in apology.

The question about the cottage had simply been preamble. Randall really wanted to question her about the old poisoning case but he suddenly sensed a secret. He focused his eyes down as he stirred sugar into his tea. Then he looked up. Charity's face was flushed, her pupils dilated, her mouth open and the hand that held the dainty china cup shook as she lifted it from her saucer.

'Who lived here before you?'

'An old lady in her nineties who was taken eventually into a nursing home. Her name was Eva Taylor.' She flushed slightly. 'She was a bit batty.'

'Is she still alive?'

'I don't know. It was seven years ago. She would be about a hundred by now so probably not.'

She looked at him expectantly as though she fully expected him to pursue the subject.

'Which nursing home?'

'I don't know the name. I'm sorry. It's probably somewhere near here. Why?'

Randall made a mental note to trace her. Why? He didn't know.

'Did she have any family?'

'I did speak to a daughter once or twice but I never met her.'

'In what way was Mrs Taylor batty?'

Charity looked slightly bored. 'Oh, the usual – forgetful, full of old stories, wandered around the Long Mynd in all weathers, at all times apparently, day and night, collecting herbs and fungi and such like for her spells.'

Randall realized this was just the sort of person he had imagined had planted the bouquet of herbs. He frowned. 'Spells?'

Charity looked bored with the subject. 'Oh, the usual,' she repeated. 'She had a reputation for being a witch.' She laughed, putting her hand in front of her mouth as though it was impolite to giggle. 'She did have a few hairs sprouting on her chin and she was bent up with arthritis. She walked with a stick, not flew on a broomstick.' She smiled. 'And she did have a black cat too. I only met her a couple of times. She just seemed like a typical old woman to me but people in Church Stretton told me they'd come to Hope Cottage to sort out life's little problems.'

DI Randall lifted his eyebrows.

'Oh, yes. She claimed to be able to make love potions and things to make people lose a baby or . . .' Her voice trailed away. 'I suppose if she wasn't so aged and almost certainly dead by now she's just the sort of person that it's rumoured has spirited little Daisy away.' She giggled. 'Probably needed a little girl who hadn't been christened for one of her black magic spells.'

Randall frowned. He did not like supernatural explanations for what was patently not a supernatural abduction of a little girl and there was nothing funny about any of this.

'That's right,' he said, suppressing his disapproval. He deliberately did not mention the flower message. There were always facts the police held back.

'In fact,' Charity said with another embarrassed laugh, volunteering information now, 'it seems I'm the first non-witch to live here. The entire area . . .' She looked across the valley, 'is full of folklore, all of it evil and connected with the Devil. But . . .' She put her elbows on the table, her chin cupped in her palm and looked up into Randall's face with a small hint of a smile. 'I just love it here. It's so raw and wild.' She smiled. 'The very opposite of my work environment, the manufactured world of the Middle East. Everything there is . . . so,' she frowned, 'false. Everything.'

And yet that was the world she chose to work in. But then it would be a well-paid job and give her financial freedom. He met her eyes and saw a determined, ambitious and professional woman.

What was he missing? What else?

'Have you ever had the feeling before that someone's been in your cottage while you were away?'

'Well . . . Shirley usually comes in just before I'm due back and gives the place a tidy over, puts the heating and hot water on. That sort of thing, you know?'

'You've never had the feeling that somebody other than Shirley has been in?'

'No-o-o.' But she was frowning and her tone was dubious. She added quietly, 'At least, sometimes I've thought things have been moved but I've always decided it's probably Shirley.' She sounded less sure of herself now and was frowning. 'It's a horrible thought,' she said softly, 'someone invading your home, your private space, your inner self.'

'Yes,' Randall agreed.

Why did she live out here? Why in such a lonely and wild place? She had given an explanation of sorts but it didn't satisfy Randall. Charity Ignatio was keeping something from him. And it wasn't the old tragedy. She had flaunted that in front of him, waving it as audaciously as a national flag.

But she was hiding something else. What he wanted to ask her was *What?*

'More tea?' she asked sweetly. Randall shook his head. 'No, thanks,' he said, 'one's enough.'

Not too many, he thought.

TWENTY-THREE

Saturday, 27 April, 6.55 p.m.

Randall tracked Eva Taylor down in an old folks' home just outside Church Stretton – easily done if you're in the police. She was not gaga by any means but a sharp-eyed, sharp-nosed lady with sparkling blue eyes and an intelligent manner. He shook her hand.

'Now why have you come to see me?'

He had the feeling she knew perfectly well why he was here. But she was calling the shots.

'The little girl,' she said. 'Oh, my, there's evil there all right.'

'What do you know?'

The old lady sat back and regarded him. 'Where do I start?' she said, perfectly at ease.

'I don't know,' he said.

'Hope Cottage. She's there now, isn't she?'

'You mean Charity.'

She nodded. 'That's a name I wouldn't have chosen for her.'

Randall decided to play her game. 'So what name would you have chosen for her?'

She whispered something in his ear.

Randall made one more phone call before he clocked off for the evening.

'Mansfield,' he said, 'DI Randall here. Just one small question. Was Daisy christened?'

Mansfield spluttered. 'What the fuck's that got to do with anything?'

'Something someone said,' Randall replied. 'So was she?'

'No. Neither of us believed in it,' Neil said.

Randall thanked him and put down the phone.

Saturday, 27 April, 7 p.m.

In the end, uncertain what the instruction 'casual dress' meant, she'd chosen a pair of snug-fitting jeans teamed with a black T-shirt and high-heeled black leather boots, with the result that she felt under-dressed to be going out for dinner with Simon Pendlebury.

Right up until he arrived in similar garb of jeans and a check shirt. She gaped at him. His hair was tousled and he looked comfortable, relaxed compared to the habitually tense person usually turned out to immaculate perfection.

She regarded him without saying a word, simply looking curious and intrigued.

'I meant what I said,' he said, smiling. Not grinning. 'Casual dress and you'll need something for your hair.'

Still bemused, she fished out a headscarf, tied it under her chin Audrey Hepburn style, and followed him outside to a gleaming white Mercedes E Class with red leather seats, the hood down. He held the door open with a little bow. 'My lady.'

Still feeling a little more like Audrey Hepburn than Martha Gunn, coroner of Shrewsbury and its environs, she slid into the seat and sat back, wondering where this was heading and she didn't just mean which pub.

Simon eased the car out on to the bypass.

Martha had always believed that you could judge a man by his driving. But if this was true she'd been wrong about Simon. She would have imagined he would have driven furiously, recklessly and fast. *Taking no prisoners*, as her father would have said.

In fact, he drove rather sedately with a lot more patience than she would have imagined, sizing up the road and the opportunities before pulling out to overtake. After half an hour they drew up outside an unpretentious country pub. Simon opened her door and she stepped out, shaking her hair free. She looked at him, puzzled. 'Whatever are you up to, Simon?' she asked, half laughing.

'I just wanted you to see a different side of me,' he said seriously. 'I feel . . .' He steered her towards the pub door. 'Oh, let's get a couple of drinks in and chat across a table,' he said.

Martha was bemused. She really didn't get this.

He returned with a glass of red wine and a beer, his face still cheerful and friendly. There was none of the tight-lipped stare he had adopted since Evie had died. He looked happy – happier than she had seen him for years.

'I've been busy,' he said.

'Yes, you said.'

'I'm finally putting my house in order.'

'Ri-ight?'

He leaned in. There was nothing threatening about his proximity. He simply looked like a very good friend who had something to say.

'When I said to you about working so hard,' he said, 'I realized.'

She didn't even prompt him with a *go on*. She knew this was a significant moment in their relationship.

'The trouble is,' he said, 'that with a successful business . . .'

What is your business?

'You're all too aware how easily it can all go under.'

'But you have . . .' she grasped for the word. 'You have managers?'

'It sounds like a cliché, Martha,' he said, 'but they don't do the job as well as I do.'

She nodded. 'So you have no one to delegate to.'

'Exactly. And . . .' again he hesitated, 'I'm not looking for sympathy,' he said, 'but what's the point of pretending you want to lotus eat alone?'

She snorted. 'I've never been a great one for lotus eating,' she said. 'It sounds great but, well, I'm happier working.'

And suddenly he was like the older brother she didn't have, looking at her slyly from narrowed eyes. 'And what if you meet someone special?'

She flushed. What she wanted to say was, *I have. But he's not for me.*

What she actually said was, 'I'll cross that bridge when I reach it.'

The evening passed pleasantly. They had reached a new and happy place in their relationship and any awkwardness between them had melted. She felt the parameters had been set. He dropped her off a little before eleven p.m. with a chaste kiss on her cheek and a very chummy hug. Again, nothing threatening. The car roared off as she closed the front door behind her.

To an empty house.

Sukey had gone out with friends and Sam had left a message to say he was staying overnight with his buddy. She was alone. It was a taste of the future.

Sunday, 28 April, 7.30 a.m.

This is as risky as it is necessary. I need to keep the child's disappearance in the public eye.
And this is a sure way to do it.
I smile.

Sunday, 28 April, 9.50 a.m.

She always did this: arrived at the supermarket early, forgetting that it didn't open until ten on a Sunday morning. So now she had ten minutes to kill. She glanced around her car. Full of rubbish as usual: old half-read newspapers, sweet wrappers, a couple of empty Coke bottles. She'd fill the time by tidying it out. And so it was Maria Shelling who found them. She had tied her rubbish into a plastic carrier bag and was about to drop it into the bin when she saw, folded neatly, right on the top of the other trash, a pair of child's pyjamas. She stared at them. The papers had been full of the clothes little Daisy Walsh had been wearing when she had vanished. White pyjamas with a pattern of yellow teddy bears, available from Tesco's stores up and down the country. Without touching them Maria continued to stare. The way the clothes were arranged deliberately, exposing the torn and blood-stained pyjama bottoms there was no doubt in her mind that these clothes were Daisy's. Not only that but they were the very clothes she had been wearing when the accident had happened. They must have been taken off her and put here ostentatiously and deliberately by the person who had abducted her from the accident site, and it must have been done fairly recently by that same person. That person might still be here, watching her. Maria looked around her, suddenly on her guard. Who was it? All around her cars were pulling in now the shop was open. People were coming and going, threading into the store. Families. Couples. Lone men, lone women, young and old. Was it any of them? A few were gossiping at the shop's entrance. Was it one of them? That shifty-looking man. Did he have Daisy? That thin, cross-looking woman using the ATM. Was it her? That couple just getting out of that car. Was it them? Did they have Daisy secreted away somewhere?

Knowing she shouldn't she fingered the small garments, felt the stiffness of the dried blood. She couldn't rid herself of the conviction that she was being watched. Was she?

Yes. Oh, yes.

This is a valuable lead. If someone careless had simply dumped their rubbish on the top without noticing them the clue would be wasted. And, regretfully, people can be so unobservant. What a tragedy if this most precious item is not appreciated to its full extent. But as I watch my prayers are answered. The tall, thin woman, bare ankles exposed by too-short jeans, is holding them up. Her focus and immobility tell me all.

I can leave now.

Slowly, slowly, practically causing not a ripple of air around her to be disturbed by the surreptitious gesture, Maria pulled her mobile phone from her bag, took a couple of photos then phoned the police.

There wasn't usually a heavy police presence around Church Stretton but since the Burway mystery (as it was currently being called) there were a few more squad cars marauding the town centre. As though by magic they arrived seconds after the phone call, sirens blaring, shattering the sleepy peace of a rural Shropshire town on a Sunday morning. Maria Shelling stepped back in awe as a tall, skinny cop in uniform stepped towards her. 'Was it you who made the call, ma'am?'

She nodded. 'I haven't touched anything or disturbed the . . .'

Their eyes followed the same trajectory.

The bin was simply a tub fixed to a lamppost. High enough off the ground so rats, dogs, children and cats could not forage.

PC Gethin Roberts' eyes took in, as Maria's had done, the pyjamas neatly folded, the pretty pattern designed to appeal to children and their doting parents, then he too took in the long tear in the fabric and the blood.

His mouth dropped open and without thinking he called up DI Randall's mobile and connected with his answerphone. But while he was leaving his message, like Maria he scanned the car park and the growing crowd of curious people who watched, in excitement. *They need to be kept back*, was his first thought. His second was, *Is Daisy near?* Was her abductor, male or female, amongst them?

Don't worry. I've gone.

Then all hell broke loose.

Squad cars poured in. The officers quickly did the necessary, taped off the area, made the phone calls, started looking for evidence and conducting a half-hearted fingertip search. Of a car park?

Randall arrived half an hour later and took over directing the search. Finally they bagged up the depressing little bundle. Randall's heart sank as he carried out the task. The stain of blood was large and the tear on the pyjama leg surely indicated a life-*threatening* wound? A life-*costing* wound?

In contrast to the trousers the pyjama jacket was relatively undamaged and less grubby, protected, as it would have been, by the dressing gown. 'Oh, Daisy,' Randall said and handed the package to Roddie Hughes. Like Roberts he too looked around him and then upwards. At least the supermarket had installed CCTV cameras and for once they looked to be in the right place and angled properly. Maybe their person wasn't so smart after all.

Oh, yes I am, Inspector. So much smarter than you, actually. Just look. I am ready. I am waiting for you.

DI Alex Randall began to take stock. Like the slippers these pyjamas were tangible evidence and could well provide forensic information. *They* were on top of this case now. The police. This person, whoever he or she was, might be playing cat and mouse but he and his team were inching ever closer, flushing out the truth.

You can play games but you leave clues.

He felt optimistic yet at the same time apprehensive. Where would this latest piece of evidence take them? What horrible truth lay behind the trail of breadcrumbs that seemed to be leading them straight to the gingerbread house? Randall knew better than anyone that if they found out that Daisy had died between the time of the crash and her discovery the force might well be held responsible. And as SIO he would ultimately carry the can. He had watched investigations being conducted before. The entire case would be picked apart like a knitted pullover destined to be reduced to balls of wool.

But every trick this person played revealed a little more about themselves. He or she couldn't help but leave stray clues around. The crumbs would lead to the witch's house. He started instructing his officers.

At eight that night Neil Mansfield arrived at Monkmoor Police Station and nodded when he saw the pyjamas, then sobbed when he saw the blood and the tear in the trouser leg. He left a broken man. His shoulders bowed, all hope gone.

Monday, 29 April, 8.30 a.m.

Randall began the briefing with the initial findings on the pyjamas. Testing for blood might be quick but it had also been obvious from the start that the pyjama trousers were Daisy's. It had told them nothing they hadn't already known.

'Right, obviously we don't have all the results yet.' He risked a glance around the room, took in the expectant faces and continued. 'But we are pretty certain . . .' he indicated the photograph, the child's pyjamas spread out as though waiting for a child to put them on, kiss goodnight and climb into bed, 'that these are the pyjamas that Daisy Walsh was wearing on the night of the accident.' Most of the officers looked at the photograph, their faces becoming glum. 'It also appears,' he said, 'that as the garments were found yesterday, neatly folded on the top of the rubbish bin in the Co-op car park, that they were placed there relatively recently, probably early yesterday morning as the bins are emptied weekly on a Thursday and there was little rubbish in it. We are taking this as deliberate provocation.' He frowned for a minute. What was the best way to interpret this? Provocation or that little trail of breadcrumbs meant to lead them to the child?

He leaned forward and met each officer's eyes in turn. 'We're initially focusing on the CCTV footage starting at daybreak yesterday in the hope that we might be able identify the person who planted these. Talith, perhaps you'll take charge of that?'

DS Paul Talith nodded.

'Needless to say, we don't know whether the child is alive.' He hesitated. 'Looking at the bloodstain . . .' all eyes turned to the second photograph, top right, close up the blood stain, then back at Randall, '. . . it seems certain that Daisy sustained a severe injury or injuries during the accident. Initial examination of the right leg of the pyjama trousers suggests she may have had a broken leg, probably a tibia. There was a fragment of bone halfway down the tear.'

The faces of the surrounding officers were grim. Some of them were imagining their own children, badly hurt, away from a hospital or their mothers and fathers.

Randall read their faces and knew he needed to focus their attention on the hard investigation rather than on the suffering of a child. 'Let's face facts,' he said gently, 'and not get too distracted by folklore, by . . .' he tried to laugh it off, 'the reputation of the Long Mynd and by its awesome geography. Let's act as though it all happened somewhere else. If it had happened elsewhere we would be concentrating less on the causes of the accident and more on the fact that a little girl, four years old, has been missing for nearly a month.'

The officers were wary now.

'Church Stretton is a largely rural town with a small resident population but a large influx of visitors – hikers and bikers mainly.' He stopped, his thoughts snagged by the words he had just used so flippantly. *Large influx of visitors*. People came and they went. His eyes met those of young PC Gethin Roberts and something seemed to pass between them, recognized only by them and not picked up by anyone else in the room.

To buy time and gather his thoughts, Randall recapped.

'Daisy hasn't been seen since the night of the accident. At first we wondered whether she was even in the car but finding the slipper and her little toy appeared to indicate that she was there and so suffered the accident. Later we find that her mother's partner, Neil Mansfield, was having a relationship with another woman, Lucy Stanstead, who is unable to have her own children. She appears to have formed an attachment to the little girl. It is not impossible, even, that Lucy Stanstead was our mystery caller. Her husband was away at sea at the time. But in light of Daisy's clothing being planted in various places,' again Randall stopped, testing each statement as carefully as a foot tentatively testing thin ice, 'the appearance,' he continued slowly, 'of the damaged and bloodstained pyjama trousers yesterday *appears* to discredit that theory. Daisy is not at the

Stanstead home and our caller appears to be leading us towards her wherever she is.' Again he stopped. What assumptions was he making that would lead them all up the garden path?

The room was not only silent but still. He had all their attention.

He continued, 'Let's look a little closer at what we know. Drunk, Tracy leaves the house with Daisy. She drives up a narrow, dangerous and lonely road at two a.m. on a Sunday morning.'

Still no one either moved or spoke.

'She does an emergency stop. We know that from the tyre marks. She then reverses, loses her track and tumbles down into Carding Mill Valley. Again, we know that. The accident is reported at six a.m. by an unknown person. We have never traced that person; neither have they come forward in spite of numerous appeals.'

All eyes were on him.

'Tracy ends up in hospital and dies and the child has vanished. One slipper was found immediately after the crash at the crash site; the other was left in the loft of Hope Cottage some time later. Her dressing gown has also been planted near the crash site. And now her pyjamas have appeared in town, put there some time since Thursday. I think we can assume by the way they were placed that they were meant to be found and were probably put there only a few hours before Mrs Shelling found them. The pyjama trousers seem to indicate that Daisy, at the very least, has a broken leg. And that, I'm afraid, is the sum total of what we know.'

'Not quite.' Gary Coleman had finally got his chance to speak.

TWENTY-FOUR

As they left the interview room, PC Gethin Roberts caught up with Gary Coleman and tried to persuade him to focus at least some of their interest on the Long Mynd Hotel.

'There's something there,' he said. 'I can feel it in my bones.'

Coleman rolled his eyes then looked at him, puzzled. 'What?' he asked bluntly.

'Well,' Roberts began, 'from what you got on the computer, it looks like Tracy was looking on the internet to profit out of her little girl. Child modelling, didn't you say?'

'So?'

Coleman tried to ignore his colleague but there was something about the earnestness of Roberts that had always endeared the younger copper to him.

'I don't know what it is, Gary,' Roberts insisted as they strode down the corridor towards their cars. 'But it's something to do with the place. Why don't we pay it a visit?' he suggested hopefully.

Although Coleman's instinct was to scoff at Roberts' idea, it struck him that only Gethin Roberts had been there already. Perhaps he had seen something.

But he didn't want to appear too enthusiastic. 'I suppose it's an idea,' he conceded. 'Maybe it would explain some of what's been going on. Perhaps someone there does know a bit more than they're saying.' He speared his colleague with a stare. 'It's a worth a little bit of digging.'

'Now?'

'OK. But first, why revisit the hotel, Gethin?'

'It was that one social worker,' Roberts said with deliberation. 'The one Tracy was closeted up with for ages. Sheila Weston; the one that kept an eye on the little girl when Tracy was busy at work. I did some checking. She worked for a while out in Dubai as a teacher. Now, I'm not saying there's a connection,' he put in quickly. 'I mean, lots of people have worked in Dubai.' He grinned. 'I'd work out there for the pay and the tax situation but it *is* a connection. And there *is* a lot of money out there. And . . .'

His voice trailed off.

He'd run out of ideas but Coleman pressed his key tag and the car responded with a flash of its hazards and the click of doors opening. 'So what are we waiting for?'

Roberts grinned. 'The Long Mynd Hotel?'

WPC Lara Tinsley, in the meantime, was following up a hunch of her own.

Randall was sitting in the briefing room, staring at the pictures which lined the boards, Daisy peeping out from behind the door, Tracy on a night out looking drunk, but happy. The wrecked car, Tracy's facial injuries. Tracy in intensive care, tubes sticking out of her nose and mouth, huge machines in the background.

Randall swivelled around in his chair to look at photos of other people involved in the case. Neil Mansfield, his face a mixture of powerful emotion: bewilderment at the situation he found himself in, grief at the loss of his partner and the child he had so obviously loved, worry at the charges that he feared might be made against him. And overlying all that, a huge swamp of unhappiness that blurred and bloated his features. Randall peered along the wall, towards the other people less affected by the Long Mynd tragedy: Tracy's mother and sister and her ex-husband, father of the missing child. Then there were people whose connection was more difficult to place. Charity Ignatio. What part was she playing in this drama? Was she a killer? Had it been an accident or had she liquidated her family by poisoning them all those years ago? He was irritated that he couldn't get a handle on the girl.

And then there was the puzzle. Who had left the fungi on Charity's doorstep all those years ago, and why? To point the police in the right direction? If so, why be so obscure about it? Why not simply say what they knew? Indeed, why was their mystery woman being so obscure with them now? Were they one and the same person – the old woman in a nursing home? If she knew something about the whereabouts of the little girl why not simply bring her forward? Why not produce her?

Save us all time and worry.

Above all, what was the connection?

Randall closed his eyes in a long and tired blink. He needed air. He needed Martha.

Martha was, as usual, in her office, working through piles of papers and computer records. She made a face as she tried to read some facsimiles of hospital notes. When would doctors learn to write? Medical records were so unsatisfactory. Pages missing, sometimes out of order, results of tests scratchily filled in, sometimes patently obviously not correct. When were alarm bells raised that something was not right?

She too felt she needed air that morning. What she really fancied, to wake her up, instead of yet another cup of coffee, was a walk in the crisp spring air through Haughmond Woods.

She smiled to herself, crossed the room and lifted the sash window. Just an inch but the scent of lilac carried in on the breeze and tempted her even more.

She looked around her.

Her room looked different today. Prettier, brighter. And she *felt* different too. Oh for goodness' sake, Martha, she lectured herself. You can't fall for bloody Simon. It would be a disaster. One: he's a total worm. Two: he was married to your very best friend in the world bar one – Evie. Three: whatever he says you can't trust him and you never will. Four: there's that pathetic Christabel business. She had a sudden vision of Simon Pendlebury's sheep-like face as he confessed to her he'd *fallen in love*.

She would never get that image out of her mind. Never. He had looked so completely and utterly and pathetically foolish. And five: last but not least there's Jocasta and Armenia. So forget it.

But still . . . she had really enjoyed last night. Not having to drive for once, she'd relaxed her one glass of wine rule and had had two glasses of some very good Rioja which had had the result that she'd drunk a third glass of wine which had made her mellow, relaxed and happy in Simon's company like never before. They'd fallen into easy conversation, ragging each other about past events and mishaps. But then . . . she suddenly remembered venturing a negative comment about his daughters and how he'd laughed and agreed with her. 'The trouble was,' he'd said, his hand touching hers in a gentle, non-sexual gesture of friendship, 'that Evie, as you know, was ill for a while and she just didn't have the energy to stop them. And besides, she didn't want the girls to remember her as someone who nagged so they just got worse and worse.' He'd laughed then screwed up his face. 'What they need is a strict stepmother.'

She'd put a hand further up his arm and giggled. 'A *wicked* step-mother,' she'd said and he had put his face very close to hers and said nothing, but his brown eyes had been warm and friendly.

Now, next morning, stone cold sober, she was wincing at the memories.

She was tugged out of her reverie by a *rat-a-tat-tat* on the door. Jericho Palfreyman, coroner's assistant, stuck his head round, shaking his grey locks disapprovingly and looking distinctly out of sorts. 'That inspector,' he said. 'He's here again.'

'I'm sorry, Martha.' Alex's head appeared over Jericho's. 'I wanted to keep you up to date on developments.' He had a large brown envelope under his arm. 'And show you these.'

'It's OK, Jericho,' she said, smiling at her disgruntled assistant, yet she felt awkward. She was going to find it difficult to fit in her workload if Alex was going to make a frequent habit of these visits. But she smiled. 'There's been a development?'

He filled her in on the planting of the pyjamas and pulled the photographs out of the envelope. As Martha looked down her face changed, became careworn and sad. She looked up. 'What sort of person would do this to a four-year-old, Alex?'

'Someone who . . .' But his ideas didn't make any more sense in the coroner's office than they had in front of the assembled officers earlier in the day.

Martha watched his struggle for a moment and realized it was better not to ask him direct questions that he was patently finding difficulty with and instead asked him what evidence had been unearthed yesterday morning. 'Tell me about the pyjamas,' she said. 'What can you glean from them so far? And most importantly, are they Daisy's?'

'It appears so,' he said very carefully, his hazel eyes meeting hers with sudden pain and frankness. He fingered the photographs one by one, close-ups of the blood staining, another very close up of the jagged tear in the pyjama leg, blood-stained and large, the way they had been folded so neatly and placed in the mouth of the litter bin.

'So far all we know is that there is this bloodstaining and damage to the pyjamas consistent with a leg injury. A small fragment of bone has been found embedded in the material and initial DNA analysis indicates that the bone is – was – Daisy's. It leads us to think she probably had a broken leg.'

Martha winced, feeling the shooting agony of a broken limb. 'Untreated she could easily have died from that alone, combined with the blood loss,' she said. Her eyes dropped back to the sheaf of photos scattered across the surface of her desk. 'Infection, shock.'

'There was no chest wound, apparently,' Alex put in quickly. 'Or at least, what I mean to say,' he corrected with a quick, connecting flash of a smile, 'is that there is no blood and no sign of damage to the pyjama top.' He paused before adding quietly, 'But of course the dressing gown was bloodstained low down. It could have come from the same wound.'

He looked down at the floor, not at the face across the desk. It took Martha's soft question to persuade him to lift his gaze.

'And is there any clue as to how or when the pyjamas were planted?'

'Well, there we've been a bit lucky,' Randall said, feeling the glow he often felt in the coroner's presence. 'It's nothing definite yet, but the CCTV footage shows a car driving right up to the small bin.' He gave a regretful but resigned smile. 'The car being between the camera and the person you don't see as much as we would hope. But we see enough. There is a small delay while the person presumably folds the pyjamas and places them on the top of the bin. And this is the breakthrough. The car has been identified as a ten-year-old Toyota four-wheel drive. The number is too mud spattered to read but we have a list of models in a thirty-mile perimeter and will be working through their owners. There aren't too many,' he said encouragingly. 'Just forty.' He paused. 'No one really obvious springs to mind.' He allowed himself a warm smile aimed in her direction. 'By that I mean no one with a criminal record or a conviction for witchcraft.' Her eyes warmed and for a split second they were again connected by a bridge of . . . friendship? Martha gave a little shake of her head. No – this was something else. Something much more intimate.

There was the briefest of pauses then Randall hurried on with his story. 'We'll initially focus on women as the caller was a woman. Then if we've had no joy we'll move on to men.' He stopped. What he wasn't saying was that in his heart of hearts he believed this would be a futile search, its end result a mound of earth and underneath that mound of earth a little girl's body.

Coleman and Roberts had reached the Long Mynd Hotel and as before PC Gethin Roberts allowed himself a brief daydream that was currently slipping away from him: that he was bringing Flora here post-wedding for two nights before they set off to the Caribbean for their honeymoon. Coleman watched him indulgently.

Roberto Agostino had practically crossed himself as Coleman and Roberts' squad car pulled on to the forecourt of the Long Mynd Hotel. A police presence was the very last thing they needed after the expensive refurbishment of the large hotel.

'Oh, God,' he said, crossing himself. 'Now what has happened?'

'Nothing to worry about, sir.'

Agostino didn't look at all reassured by Coleman's bluff sentence.

They ushered him into his office and filled him in on the finding of some *'garments of clothing'*.

He looked bemused. 'But how can I help you in this?'

'You said that Tracy seemed to get on well with one particular social worker at your convention in November – Sheila Weston.'

Agostino looked wary. He held his palms out wide in the well-known gesture of disclosure. 'So what?'

Roberts glanced down at his notepad. 'And did you also say that Tracy brought Daisy in a day or two during November?'

'She said she had no one to leave her with.'

'What about her partner, Neil Mansfield?'

Agostino shrugged.

Roberts had a flash of inspiration. 'The social worker who kept an eye on Daisy.'

Agostino still looked bemused. He shrugged again. 'So?'

'Can you give us her name and address?'

He caved in. 'But of course. Just a minute.'

He vanished from the room and they heard a swift chatter of instructions. Then Agostino returned and with a flourish worthy of Valentino he produced a neatly written card. Pink, the size of a postcard. 'Here.'

Written neatly in thin-tipped black felt pen was an address in Slough, Bucks, for Sheila Weston.

For the first time that day Gary Coleman looked a bit uncomfortable. 'Slough,' he said, glancing at his colleague. 'It'll take us most of the day to get there and back and speak to her. We'd better clear it with the inspector. It could be a wasted journey, Geth,' he said, trying to wipe the disappointed look from his pal's face. 'We might not get anything from her.'

But DI Randall, now he had a positive lead to work on, was more than happy for his two officers to interview someone they thought might be able to help them find the child and give them a reason why these events had happened.

As Coleman and Roberts were heading south down the M40 scores of police, specials and regulars, were engaged in house-to-house enquiries around Church Stretton, conducting interviews around the town, cross-checking vehicle numbers on the police computer and following up leads on the Toyota. And Lara Tinsley was wondering how her new information fitted in with the case.

Still more personnel were peering down microscopes in the laboratory, searching for something in the fibres of the teddy bear pyjamas, hoping to find a thread of material or a strand of hair, a tiny fragment of paint or soil, dog or cat hair or traces of flora or fauna; anything that would bind their perpetrator to this little girl's clothes and convict her of her crime. To the more fanciful of them Daisy Walsh was the princess imprisoned in a castle, sleeping in the centre of a forest of thorns. They would set her free with science.

Coleman and Roberts were on the M6 toll, forking out the £6.50 for safe passage. 'And what do we do when we get there?'

Roberts' Adam's apple bobbed up and down in his throat. The truth was he wasn't sure.

Coleman chewed back a grin. 'You don't know, do you, Geth?'
Roberts sulked.

Coleman pushed on. 'You're a bloody idiot, you know.'

'Yeah. Flora thinks so too.'

'You haven't had a row?'

'Not exactly, but just . . . Put it like this.' Roberts turned a pair
of anxious dark eyes on his colleague. 'Now is not exactly the
moment to ask her to marry me.'

'Oh.' Coleman shut up then asked curiously in a mockney accent,
'What 'ave you done to upset the adoring girlfriend?'

'Well, she thought we were idiots not to find the little girl's
slipper in the first place. I said to her we didn't find it because it
wasn't there, stating the obvious. And she just laughed and said,
'"Course it was." I saw red then, Gary,' he said. 'Saw red. And we
haven't exactly made it up either.' He waited for his colleague to
support him and when he ventured no words of consolation Roberts
added, piqued, 'I'm waiting for *her* to apologize.'

Slowly Gary Coleman turned his head. 'Haven't you learned
anything in that short, eventful life you've had so far, Roberts?
Waiting for her to apologize? You'll wait for ever, my mate. *You*
apologize.'

Roberts protested. 'But I haven't done anything wrong. She
shouldn't have said it.'

'You don't have to have done anything wrong,' Coleman advised.
'Just apologize anyway.'

Roberts sat back grumpily, folded his arms then glanced across
at his colleague curiously. 'You mean it?'

'Yeah. Life's too short Gezza, my old sport.'

Roberts sat back and folded his arms. Apologize? When he'd done
nothing wrong, only stated the truth? He needed to work this one out.

TWENTY-FIVE

They were silent until their satnav led them to a small, semi-
detached house on the outskirts of Slough. It was neat and
tidy, a small red Ford Ka sitting in the drive. It was in the
middle of a long, straight row of almost identical houses, lawns and

drives identical too; the only item that distinguished each house from its other was the make of the car that sat in the drive.

The woman who opened the door to them looked pale, tired and very worried. She was wearing a loose top over denim jeans that looked pale and tired as well. Over-washed and sun bleached, the pair of them. She didn't look in the least bit surprised to see them even when they flashed their ID cards in front of her weary eyes. 'Come in,' she said resignedly.

The two officers glanced at each other. They hadn't even said why they'd come. And she hadn't asked . . . Interesting considering the conference at the Long Mynd Hotel had been six months ago and she had been there for a brief weekend course – hardly a powerful connection.

Roberts blew out through his teeth while Coleman began the questions.

'Mrs Weston, I don't know if you've been following the case of the little girl who disappeared after a car accident?'

She blinked.

'It happened at the Long Mynd just outside Church Stretton?'

She blinked again and looked as wary as a cat.

'We understand you were at a conference at the hotel there last November.'

It drew another blank look, which was then replaced by one of incredulity and a protestation. 'What on earth can that possibly have to do with me?'

'I believe you met the little girl's mother there.'

She put her head on one side in puzzlement. The two officers exchanged glances, lifted their eyebrows and wondered if this was a wild goose chase after all.

Ms Weston cleared her throat and finally spoke. 'I really don't understand why you've come here,' she said.

'We understand you struck up a friendship with Tracy Walsh?'

It drew another blank look.

'She was one of the waitresses at the hotel where the conference was held,' Coleman filled in, feeling some sympathy with Roberts who must, he was thinking, be feeling a bit foolish.

Sheila Weston gave her head an imperceptible twitch. 'I still don't understand what you're doing here,' she said. 'I might well have talked to . . .' she hesitated, '. . . one of the waitresses six months ago. How can this possibly connect me with her daughter's disappearance?'

'So you *have* followed the case through the papers and the internet?' Coleman put only gentle emphasis on the word.

'As has probably the entire nation,' Ms Weston said with a twitch of her lips.

'Do you remember Daisy?'

'Sorry?'

'The little girl. Apparently Tracy brought her in . . .' Roberts improvised, '. . . on the weekend of the conference.'

Coleman gave him a swift look.

It threw Sheila Weston. 'Oh,' she said. '*That* little girl.'

Roberts couldn't resist a swift grin. 'Yes,' he said, mimicking her tone. '*That* little girl.'

'I, um, kept an eye on her,' she said.

PC Gethin Roberts gave it one last push, which was his downfall. 'We understand you once worked in Dubai.'

At this Ms Weston threw back her head and burst out laughing. 'You mean you've come all the way from Shropshire to ask me that?'

Please don't add the comment: *No wonder the police are over-stretched and under resourced.*

Roberts had never felt so humiliated. PC Gary Coleman took pity on him. 'You understand,' he said with dignity, 'that this is a *major* investigation.'

Ms Weston fixed a stare on him.

'And that means we follow up some very tenuous leads, Ms Weston.' He'd noted the absence of a wedding ring. 'Did you ever meet a lady called Charity Ignatio in Dubai?'

Ms Weston looked bored. 'I may have done,' she said, shrugging. 'I meet lots of people out there.'

'She lives in Church Stretton,' Coleman said.

She practically yawned. 'What a small world we live in.'

'Indeed. Anyway.' Coleman gave a bland smile as he stood up. 'Thank you for your time. If we think of anything else to ask you we may well come again.'

She returned a confident glance. 'Next time you might try using the phone first,' she said haughtily.

'Oh, we will, Ms Weston. We will be in touch.'

TWENTY-SIX

Coleman kindly waited until they were safely back on the M40 before making his comment to Gethin Roberts. 'Well, that was a fat lot of good.'

'I don't know,' Roberts said defensively. 'Considering she went on a weekend course six months ago and had a couple of chats with one of the waitresses, how come she never asked us what we were really doing there? How come we didn't even have to remind her who Tracy Walsh was? Or Daisy,' he added meaningfully.

'It's been in the papers.'

'Yeah, but it's nothing to do with *her*, is it?'

'I see what you mean.'

'Besides, I thought there was definitely something there. We've rattled her all right.'

'If you say so.'

'Anyway,' Roberts continued, 'I do feel a bit guilty dragging you all the way down here on a wild goose . . .'

'I thought you said it wasn't a wild goose chase.'

'Well, anyway, I'm buying lunch.'

Coleman grinned and patted his stomach. 'I won't argue with that, Gethin, my boy.'

WPC Lara Tinsley was on the telephone to Charity Ignatio's employers in Dubai. And they were being very helpful indeed.

They confirmed the dates she had been at the resort. 'Poor girl,' the secretary said. 'She spends such a lot of time out there setting up businesses and helping with supply chains. It must be awfully lonely, staying in the hotel all on her own. I'm always pleased when she takes a bit of a break.'

'Perhaps she makes friends out there.' Tinsley was floundering.

'I think she does.' The girl responded brightly. 'Probably meets people in the hotel. She usually takes some time off when she's there, goes down to the Palm Jumeirah for a couple of days or something.'

'Oh.'

'And she took practically the whole week off in April.' The girl was still trying to be helpful. 'That's unusual for her.'

Tinsley's ears pricked up. 'How so?'

'Well, she rang in from her two-day leave and said she didn't feel very well. I've never known her to do that before. Had to reschedule her meetings.'

Tinsley frowned. 'I don't suppose you can remember the dates?'

'Oh, yes I can.' The girl rose to the challenge. 'It was my boyfriend's grandma's ninetieth at the beginning of the week. The week of Monday the eighth.'

The week following the accident.

Somehow it seemed significant. But for the life of her Lara Tinsley couldn't work out how or why.

Tuesday, 30 April, 3.30 p.m.
Church Stretton Antiques Centre.

The child stood quite still, as she'd been told to do and for a while no one noticed her. Everyone assumed her parents were just around the corner, on the other floor, looking at some other piece of furniture or ornament or picture – if they thought about her at all. Most people didn't. They were wrapped up in their own lives, their own search for a bargain or something that would transform their homes.

The child clutched the bunch of herbs as tightly as she'd been told to do, the letter in the other hand. And she waited, again as she'd been told to do.

At some point someone will notice you and then you must tell them the words I said and hand them the letter. Do you understand, child?

She had nodded solemnly, risked a sneaky smile.

You're going to be all right now.

The child's eyes had locked into hers, one set trusting and innocent, the other neither.

Finally at 3.50 p.m., the teenage girl who helped serve behind the counter addressed the child, who stood as still as a garden statue.

'You all right there, love?'

Kelly Simms had been texting her boyfriend for the last twenty minutes, giggling at his suggestive responses and only now had she become aware of her surroundings. She eyed the little girl in the sprigged dress. The girl nodded gravely but said nothing.

Kelly came around to the front of the counter and bent over. 'Your mum upstairs, is she?'

The little girl shook her head solemnly.

'You with your dad then?'

Again the little girl shook her head with the same mute solemnity.

'Who *are* you with?' Kelly's voice had grown sharp. Instinctively she felt that something here was unusual.

And at last the child spoke. 'I'm not with anyone,' she said. 'I'm on my own.'

Kelly hunkered down to meet the little girl's eyes. They were wide open. 'You must be with *someone*,' she prompted.

'No, I'm not.' The little girl shook her head, dimples in her cheeks, golden curls feathering out. 'I am on my own.'

'Well, how did you get here?'

'She brought me.'

'Who brought you?'

'The lady.'

'What lady?' Kelly scouted around for someone to lay claim to this one.

'She's gone now.' The little girl put her hand on her arm. 'She said she was going so there's no use you lookin' for her. She's gone back.'

'Gone back where?'

The child looked at her as though she was stupid. 'To her house,' she said, stating the obvious.

Kelly was taken aback.

The little girl spoke with growing confidence. 'She told me you was to get the plees.'

'Sorry? Oh, the police.'

'And to give this letter and the bunch of flowers to the lady.'

'What lady?'

The child pointed to the name on the front of the envelope.

Written clearly in large bold letters, she read:

A message to Martha.

TWENTY-SEVEN

A message to Martha. The phrase brought back memories.
Martha glanced up at the mantelpiece. There was a postcard there. Where it had come from was unmistakable. Lady Liberty held her lamp up high.

It had been sent by Finton Cley, one-time accused stalker through a misunderstanding about his family and the coroner's verdict of suicide which had impacted them all so hard. Now, hatchets buried, he was running a successful antiques business in the Big Apple. The message on the back of the card was jaunty. *Best thing I ever did, moving here. Sister engaged!!!*

She smiled. Sometimes things turned out well after all. She turned her attention back to the white envelope. 'And you say this was with her?' Gloves on, she fingered the envelope.

Randall was pale and looked exhausted. He nodded and handed her the bunch of plants. 'Together with this. She was clutching it like her life depended on it.'

Martha eyed the sprigs and thoughts began to tumble through her mind. Helter-skelter.

Oblivious to this, Randall continued apologetically, 'I wasn't sure if both were meant for you.'

'I think they were.' Martha slid a paperknife along the top of the envelope, preserving the glue, although no one licked envelopes these days. They either trusted the pathetically weak adhesive on both envelope flaps or they stuck on a strip of Sellotape. Still, you never knew your luck. Perhaps this once their perpetrator might have been careless, though she doubted it. The person behind all this didn't strike her as someone who was careless.

She pulled out a blank sheet of paper. 'I see,' she said, unsurprised. The child had been the clue. That and the bouquet of plants.

Randall nodded wearily and Martha took her eyes off the sheet of paper and focused on him instead. 'Alex,' she said with concern, 'are you all right?'

DI Randall shook his head.

'But surely . . .' She reached across and touched his hand. 'The child is safe.' This is wonderful. A success story – surely?'

He met her eyes briefly. 'Of course,' he said, not moving his hand away. 'Of course. It's wonderful. I can't believe that Daisy is all right. It is fantastic.'

'But . . .?'

He gave a deep sigh. And Martha decided it was time to jump the next big step.

'Alex,' she said tentatively, 'we've been colleagues. No – friends – for a few years now. I've offered before . . . if ever you want to confide in me . . .' she felt compelled to add, '. . . as a friend.'

For what more can a married man be?

Alex Randall hesitated, then lifted his eyes. 'Thank you,' he said simply. 'You don't know how very comforting I find that.' He smiled at her and her heart began to sing.

There was a moment's pause, which was broken by the detective just before it became embarrassing. He indicated the blank sheet of paper, the envelope and the sprig of herbs which the child had delivered so conscientiously. 'So what on earth is the significance of this?'

Martha was silent, thinking and working out before speaking. 'Where is Daisy now?'

'With social services at a foster home.'

'Has she said anything?'

'Not much – mainly that she hurt her leg and a lady looked after her.'

'Has a doctor examined her leg?'

'It looks fine. There's a wound that looks as though it came from the accident. It's quite nasty and would account for the blood found in the car.'

Martha dropped her gaze to the sprig of plants and began to understand. She fingered the hairy leaves, the bell-shaped blue flowers. 'And the X-rays?'

'Show a recent fracture of the right tibia, now healed.' He screwed up his face. 'I think they called it callus formation and . . .' he was less sure of himself now, '. . . greenstick?'

Martha nodded. 'Aligned?'

In spite of his weariness, Randall smothered a smile. He often forgot that Martha was a qualified doctor.

'Perfect alignment,' he said.

'Has Daisy said anything else?'

'Very little so far. We've had some of the experts in child psychology interview her but it's very difficult. It's almost as though she's been warned not to speak.'

'Maybe she has.'

Randall nodded, watching her. 'This woman is dangerous,' he said.

'But she kept Daisy safe. You have no evidence she's dangerous.'

'We might have, soon,' he said.

Martha lifted her eyebrows in enquiry.

'We've subjected Daisy's dress to forensic analysis,' he said. 'It was bought in Tesco's and only stocked there since last week. It was probably bought in Shrewsbury so we can look at their CCTV. And . . .' His pause was significant. 'We've come up with some dog hairs. Short and gingery. We're thinking a terrier.' His eyes gleamed. 'The field is narrowing.'

She met his eyes fearlessly. 'I want to see Daisy,' she said. 'I want to talk to her.'

The child who had been the focus of so much attention was smaller than Martha had imagined. She was tiny – even for a four-year-old, and entrancing, mainly due to her very beautiful bright blue eyes, which gazed back at Martha with the transparency that only a small child can give. She was sitting on the floor, surrounded by Lego bricks and small plastic farm animals. She was being watched by a stocky woman in a tweed skirt, presumably one of the team of social workers assigned to her care.

Alex nodded the woman a greeting while Martha sat down next to the little girl on the floor. 'Hello, Daisy,' she said softly and picked up one of the large Lego bricks. The child put her head on one side and regarded her solemnly, saying nothing. Martha clicked the brick on to its partner and reached out for another one while the child continued to watch her warily.

'Is your leg better?' Martha asked, still playing with the bricks, forming them now into a bridge. The child's attention was split between Martha and Martha's building activity.

'Yes,' she said.

'Well, that's good,' Martha said, reaching out for one of the Lego people to stand on the bridge. 'It must have hurt.'

The child nodded. 'A lot,' she said.

'It's a good job the lady made it better.'

The mention of the lady increased the child's tension. Her shoulders stiffened but she handed Martha one of the Lego people, a little girl. Now she was making a face, considering.

Considering what?

Whether to speak? Whom to trust? She licked her lips and Martha reached out for a red Lego car. Daisy Walsh drew in a deep breath.

Martha changed the subject. 'That's a pretty dress,' she said.

The child's attention was focused now on her frock and she stroked the flowered material and looked up at Martha. 'She bought it for me,' she said.

'Well, I think that was very kind of her.' Martha hesitated before pushing on. 'And she was very kind to look after you too.'

Daisy nodded. And then she smiled, the sun coming out from behind a cloud. 'She made me better,' she said firmly. 'Like she *promised* she would.'

Martha took a chance. 'I think her house is nice too.'

Randall was watching from the doorway, his expression softer than usual as he watched Martha with the child.

The child looked up. 'It's *quite* pretty,' she said. Then added, 'Yellow.'

Martha picked up a yellow brick. 'Like this?'

'Not the same yellow,' Daisy said.

'Paler?'

Daisy nodded and picked up the red car. She looked at it thoughtfully, then back at Martha. Tracy's car. Red VW.

'It's a pity it fell off the mountain,' Martha said, deliberately vague.

Daisy nodded, then threw the car right across the room. It hit the wall with a soft smash then landed on the floor. The social worker's head flew up. Alex put a hand on her arm.

'Did you like the dog, though?'

Daisy started giggling, putting her hand over her mouth. 'He had a funny name,' she said. 'Sick something.'

Martha giggled too. 'Was it really sick?'

The child was still frowning. 'No,' she said, puzzled. 'Not sick. His *nam*e. Seck *something*.'

Martha did not want to prompt her. She bunched her shoulders up in a silent query. 'Oh, I'd really like to know,' she said.

Daisy was frowning fiercely. 'Seck Met,' she said.

Martha could hardly conceal her triumph. She blazed a smile at Alex.

Oh, what a neat little puzzle this was turning out to be.

TWENTY-EIGHT

'Quite extraordinary,' Alex said, handing Martha a cup of coffee. They had left the little girl still playing with her Lego. Instead of returning to their respective offices they had elected for neutral ground – Costa Coffee on the High Street, near Grope Lane and Waterstones.

'The whole thing is quite extraordinary,' he repeated.

'So what do we actually know, Alex?'

Alex paused, put his cup down on the saucer deliberately. 'We know that our person is a lady,' he said, 'who has looked after Daisy and then given her up. We know she lives in a yellow house and has a dog called . . .' He eyed Martha suspiciously.

'Sekhmet,' she supplied innocently.

Randall raised his eyebrows. 'And the significance of that is?'

'You'd like to hear a story?' Martha asked teasingly.

Randall smiled, knowing he was playing her game, and enjoying it. He nodded, picked up his cup of coffee and eyed her over the rim.

'Right then.' Her eyes were merry. 'You asked for it. Sekhmet is an ancient Egyptian goddess usually associated with war and destruction, but also with both plagues and healing. Her name means "The Powerful One". She is usually depicted as a woman with the head of a lioness, sometimes also with the sun disc and the Egyptian cobra on her headdress.'

'Go on. This is more interesting than I thought,' Alex prompted, 'though exactly what it's got to do with our abductor I'm not sure.'

'Yet,' Martha said. 'It's a pretty nasty tale,' she said, 'typical of the Egyptians. The story is that Ra, the old king of the gods, became angry with wayward humans and in his wrath ripped out his eye and threw it down to Earth. This divine eye became the Goddess Sekhmet, who in the form of a lioness, set about slaughtering humans, butchering them and drinking their blood.' She made a face at Alex, who was watching her, a tilt of amusement lifting his normally straight mouth.

'Ra, seeing the appalling habits of Sekhmet and realizing that at the rate she was going no one would be left alive on Earth, tried to calm her. But she refused to listen. She was enjoying her killing far too much. So Ra filled a lake with a mixture of beer and pomegranate juice, and Sekhmet, thinking it was blood, drank the lot then fell asleep. When she woke the next morning, she was much calmer but had a terrible headache!'

Alex was puzzled. 'I can't work out what this has to do with Daisy's abductor.'

'Patience,' Martha said. 'Though Sekhmet was known primarily as a violent goddess, she was also known as a healer who set and cured broken bones.'

Alex was thinking about this. He was silent, then looked up and asked quietly, 'What was the plant, Martha?'

'Comfrey,' she said. 'Sometimes known as knitbone. Daisy had a broken leg. This woman, whoever she was, healed it using traditional remedies.'

Randall drank his coffee thoughtfully before speaking again. 'But it still doesn't tell us what happened that night, why Tracy took her car out, why she tried to reverse and how or why Daisy was removed from the scene.'

'And I don't know either. We'll have to ask her.'

TWENTY-NINE

Thursday, 2 May, 10 a.m.

In the end, it was surprisingly easy. It had taken less than twenty-four hours to find Primrose Cottage, partly through the recall of some of the team who had conducted the house-to-house searches and remembered its yellow exterior, the only yellow-painted house in the area, and partly through the unusual name of the dog. Vets proved very helpful and in this case led them straight to the cottage, which was owned by a woman called Violet Taylor, daughter of Eva, the woman who had once lived in Hope Cottage.

Things were turning full circle.

Alex was left in a quandary over whether to take Martha along with him. As coroner this was nothing to do with her but Martha, yet again, had proved pivotal in this case. Besides which, it appeared that Violet Taylor, whatever her connection, wanted the coroner to come along. The letter had been addressed to her. It had been an invitation. There was a backstory, which the police didn't know. It was something to do with Charity Ignatio but Randall couldn't make a connection. Charity had checked out. So he needed not only Ms Taylor's help here but Martha's too. His instincts might scream that there was something strange, something sinister about the events on that night, of 6 and 7 April, but he wasn't going to be able to piece together the inexplicable fragments without help. He was only too aware that he was still missing many of the pieces. And so, after a great deal of thought, when he was sure that the remote cottage near Snailbeach was the one, he decided he would take Martha with him.

They both knew it was irregular but Randall believed that Violet Taylor, daughter of Eva, wanted to speak more to the coroner – for whatever reason – than to him.

Snailbeach was an old lead mining area on the edge of their search zone to the north-west of Church Stretton. It was a rural village with a few mine workers' cottages and little else.

As the car drew up on that Thursday morning the first thing they heard was the staccato barks of Sekhmet. Martha couldn't resist giving Alex a grin which he acknowledged, cocking his head. The cottage door opened and the dog came flying out. A ginger-coated terrier. In the doorway stood a woman.

Randall stared. His mind had been unable to produce any sort of picture before. If anything Violet Taylor looked just like the popular image of a witch. Long grey hair, a floor-length skirt, piercing black eyes. But looked at with more realistic eyes, she was less intimidating. Mid-fifties, an ageing hippy rather than someone with magical powers.

She was unsmiling and looked wary, but her face warmed a little when she saw Martha Gunn climbing out of the squad car.

There was no verbal greeting. She simply regarded them.

It was Martha who spoke first. 'Hello,' she said. 'I'm pleased to meet you. It is Miss Taylor, isn't it?'

Violet nodded. 'I'm glad you came too,' she said, adding, 'at last,' in a dry tone which robbed the words of any warmth. Her accent was just as they had imagined it: a rich, Shropshire burr.

The butter-coloured walls of the cottage seemed to absorb the spring sunlight so it looked as though the walls generated some of the glow themselves. Violet Taylor turned her back on them and went inside, the dog, quiet now, following warily. The interior of the cottage, in contrast, was dingy and dull, with heavy black beams criss-crossing the ceiling. Like many old houses the windows were too small to let in sufficient light, but there was a pleasant scent of lavender and a few early roses cut from the climber which had grown so thick it practically blocked the front door, its thorns meant to catch the unwary.

Randall followed the two women in, feeling strangely out of control. Whoever was pulling the strings in this case now, it certainly wasn't the senior investigating officer.

Martha found herself staring up at the painting which hung over the fireplace. She turned and confronted its owner. 'Horrible,' she commented. 'It's horrible. A really nightmarish subject.'

'To some, maybe,' Violet said, her words thick. 'Not to me. Everyone needs a source of inspiration.'

Randall shifted uncomfortably on his feet, unsure what revelations were about to pour from this person. He couldn't cope with the supernatural and disliked images of the Devil and his minions. He cleared his throat noisily and fingered his mobile phone, keeping his mind aware of the fact that this really was the twenty-first century. He only had to call and officers would come from all directions.

Violet's beady eyes were small and suspicious, hard enough to drill holes right through Martha. But Martha was unfazed. She knew she was here by invitation. She eyed Violet Taylor right back without flinching.

'I think you'd better tell me the full story, Miss Taylor,' she said, 'before the police press charges of abduction.'

It broke the spell. Violet gestured for them to sink into the chintzy sofa which faced the fireplace square on so they had no option but to look up at the painting. 'You're right,' she said, heaving a big sigh and dropping into the armchair. 'You're right.'

She looked from one to the other. 'I don't know how much you know,' she said. 'So I don't know where to start.'

'Assume we know nothing,' Randall said, speaking with difficulty.

'It all starts with Charity,' Violet said and Martha nodded. She had suspected as much.

Violet pointed an accusing knobbly finger at Martha. '*You* should remember the case.'

Martha nodded. 'I do,' she said. 'But I have the feeling that you know more than I did – or do.'

Violet nodded. 'That girl murdered her family.'

Randall cut in tersely. 'How can you know that?'

Violet's face was firm. 'I know.'

Martha waited. This woman would not be hurried. She would take her time. Like a cheese with a vein of blue mould running through it, this story had been a long time maturing. Let them wait.

'My mother and I used to live in Hope Cottage,' Violet said, her eyes skimming first the picture, then the room and its occupants. 'People thought of us as witches but that just wasn't so. We simply understood our plants and fungi. We knew the medicinal values of what grows around us. Some of these herbs and fungi need to be collected at strange times. In the dark. With dew on them. On certain days of the year. And so it was on that day. I was collecting fungi when I saw Charity. You have to realize that we not only understand plants but people too. We sense good and evil by the aura which surrounds a person. Charity grabbed my attention because the aura around her was anger and violence and resentment too. Pure hatred. Black as blood, and it's never left her. Bitter to the end. A hateful girl who grew into a hateful woman.'

Randall and Martha waited.

'I was searching the woods at the bottom of the Long Mynd and I saw her. She had a basket with her and she had some Death Cap in the basket.' She drew in a long, sucking breath.

'I told her,' she said. 'I told her it was poisonous. Yes, I told her. I warned her what happened to people who ate them. *By mistake*,' she added mockingly.

Martha was still. Then she leaned forward. 'Why didn't you come forward at the inquest?'

Violet stuck her pointy chin out. 'You think I don't regret it?'

Alex Randall was becoming impatient. 'What does this have to do with Daisy's abduction?'

Violet gave him a withering look, as though he was of no account. 'Wait,' she said. 'If you don't know all the facts you're not going to understand. Believe me.'

Martha tried to silence Alex with a brief look and whether it was that or Violet's request, he was quiet.

'I knew Charity was bad.'

Randall wanted to hurry her along but he kept silent. He wanted to know.

'And Tracy, well, she was weak and greedy. She had a greeny, yellowy aura around her, nasty as vomit, it was.'

Martha listened. She couldn't see where this was going either but was blessed with more patience than the detective.

'And then there's that other woman.'

Martha couldn't even guess who that other woman was and shook her head, but Randall had a stab at it.

'Sheila Weston? How did you know about her?'

Violet simply tapped her nose. 'She's different. A sort of . . .' Her eyes flicked up to the painting with its sinister implication. 'Sheila thinks she can dance through the world doing nothing but good. She's that stupid. Thinks she can right all the wrongs. Of course, she does it for money but she pretends to herself that she's some sort of saint. Then put the two together . . . Daisy is such a pretty child. I knew when I saw Tracy talking to Charity in the coffee bar a few months ago that they were up to something. I knew it would be about money. And when the pair of them turned to look at the child I felt my blood run cold. People have auras, you know, and around that child was the cloak of pure innocence. She didn't know the two women were plotting. Small and pretty, she was, and all they could see was how to profit out of her.'

'How?' Martha couldn't stop herself.

'Women who can't have children will pay a lot for a pretty little girl like Daisy.'

Violet's eyes swivelled up again towards the picture. *Harvesting the unbaptized*. 'There's different ways of doing that,' she said, nodding her head at it. 'And different reasons too. No one notices an old crone sitting bent over her cup of tea, of course. I listened in.

'The deal was this: Tracy was to hand the child over to that Weston woman. It was to take place at night. But Neil was protective of the little girl. He would want to know where she was. So she would deliberately cause an argument and leave. Then Tracy would say she'd gone to stay with her mother or some such nonsense. Even that she'd lost her. Children aren't always found.'

'No,' Alex commented drily.

'Obviously, I'm not sure which story Tracy was planning on telling, only that she was planning on letting another woman have Daisy and she would make a deal of money out of it. I couldn't know what or when she was going to carry out her evil plan, but that night I just couldn't settle. There'd been strange lights over the Long Mynd, dancing will-o'-the-wisp sort of lights, and I knew something was afoot so I went for a walk. And I saw the car lights.

'Weston was waiting in a big black car. Tracy drove up in that little red thing of hers. Actually hit Weston's car, she was that drunk. And then I like to think it knocked some sense into her and she thought the better of her idea. Maybe she wasn't all bad. Maybe she did have some feeling for the child after all. Or maybe she didn't quite trust that lady Weston and was worried that she wouldn't get her money after all. And she could hardly go to the police, could she?' Violet cackled. Neither Alex nor Martha joined her. They were both thinking the same thing: *Would a woman really sell her own daughter?*

Violet continued: 'Anyway, I showed myself.' She grinned. 'That shocked her all right. I could see the terror in her eyes. Then Tracy started to back down the Burway in a bit of a state and a panic. Next thing I knew the car's careered over the side. Over and over and over. Metal jangling. Her screaming, little Daisy screaming too. The noise was enough to wake the Devil. I've never been so frightened for a child as at that moment. As soon as the car was still I got Daisy out. Her leg was broken – badly. The bone was stickin' through her skin. She was crying. I knew I could heal her without further suffering. I knew I could keep her safe. I took her back to my cottage and gave her something to make her sleep before I set the bone. Then I had a conscience about Tracy and I went to Hope Cottage. Charity's cottage. I wanted to implicate her.'

'But how can she possibly have had anything to do with it?' Alex asked, exasperated. 'She was in bloody Dubai.'

'And where to do you think the handover was to take place? She was out of the compound, Inspector, wasn't she? In a holiday resort where there are plenty of tourists. I suggest you go through some of the guest lists of the hotels there, Inspector. She'd gone there to receive the little girl that Weston the meddler was bringing over. An American lady was to buy her, I wouldn't be surprised, though I can't be sure.'

DI Randall's jaw dropped open.

'I kept Daisy here. I didn't want her moved. The bone was in alignment. It was just a greenstick. I gave her comfrey – or knitbone. Tell me,' she finished with a touch of pride, 'perfect alignment?'

They both nodded.

'And the wound's clean and healed?'

Again he nodded. 'But the garments left around?' Alex persisted.

'I left clues so you'd keep looking around here for her and keep trying to find her. I was hoping that by the time she had healed, you'd have almost worked it out. I knew that at some point I would have to return her. She couldn't just stay here with me for ever, never found. In the end, once Daisy got better, I couldn't keep waiting. I thought it best to let her go.' She paused for a second. 'Neil and Lucy love her as if she's their own, you know.'

Martha glanced across at DI Randall.

'Incredible,' he said, and Violet challenged him with a look and a triumphant smile. *What would they charge her with?*

'Abduction,' he out loud, but even then looking doubtful. 'Though God only knows whether we'll make it stick,' he said, standing up.

'You think God knows?' Violet glanced upwards at the picture again and jerked her head towards it. 'Or him? Maybe the Devil has more idea than God.'

But for all her professed supernatural wisdom, Violet couldn't resist asking the question, 'What'll happen to Daisy now?'

And Alex gave her the straight answer. 'The way the child courts tend to work these days is to give the child the main say in it. Daisy has said that she wants to be with Neil, and he wants her.' He couldn't resist a smirk, which he aimed at Martha. 'Lucy Stanstead wants her too. She's walked out on her bully of a husband and moved in with Neil. They'll stay in Church Stretton and couldn't be happier.'

'So something good might have come out of this.'

Randall nodded. Something good. He fixed his eyes on Martha Gunn. Possibly something very good.

He turned to go. Violet had the last word, following them to the door. 'Just remember,' she said, looking at each of them in turn, 'there's white magic as well as black.'

THIRTY

Two weeks later.

In Martha's office, Randall was filling her in on the results of the investigations. She had shut the door firmly in Jericho's face so this time there wasn't even any coffee.

'So?' she queried.

'Well, we have a passport and plane tickets in Daisy's real name plus a letter from Tracy saying the child was visiting Dubai with her grandmother.'

Martha waited.

Naturally Sheila Weston was the 'grandmother'.

'Why? What was in it for her?'

'She says doing good, helping to "place" a child in a better home.' Randall frowned. 'The truth is she was making thirty thousand pounds out of the deal – more even than the mother.'

Randall gave a cynical smile. 'The only charge we have any chance of making stick against her is the intended abduction of a child.'

'Oh?'

'There was only one return ticket.' He sighed. 'But the CPS can be very tricky and there is precious little evidence.'

'How did Tracy and Sheila cook this up on such a slight acquaintance?'

'I don't know,' he said. 'And Sheila isn't being exactly forthcoming. They obviously kept in touch and in that first weekend they must have recognized something in each other. Perhaps Sheila, being a social worker, had met enough greedy dysfunctional mothers to recognize one. I don't know. Something must have been said that gave a clue that Tracy was more anxious to make a bit of money than to be a mother, and Sheila must have proffered a solution. To both problems,' he finished.

'But how was Tracy going to explain Daisy's disappearance?'

'Wanda Stefano gave us the answer to that one. She said that, according to Tracy, Allistair had been expressing an interest in his daughter.' Randall screwed up his face. 'Tracy said he was getting married and his soon-to-be wife was anxious to meet the little girl.'

'A half-truth,' Martha said.

'But not the whole truth. In reality Allistair couldn't give a damn about Daisy, but he is getting married. Tracy said that Daisy was going to stay with her father and that if things worked out she might just be staying.'

'And Charity,' Martha said. 'How did she know Tracy?'

Randall leaned back in his chair. 'I find it hard to get the real truth out of that woman,' he said. 'I think some of what she says is true and other bits pure fantasy, but from what we can gather it appears that Charity noticed her bawling the child out in the supermarket. What she actually said was that she could see Tracy hated and resented her daughter. Very quietly she said to me that she knew what it was like to be hated by your mother. She spoke to Tracy. I have the feeling that money, probably a substantial amount of money, was involved, but we're having trouble getting any information out of the Emirates where her account is. We're still working on that one. One of Charity's colleagues said that Charity had been looking at a property on the Palm Jumeirah. I think even a flat there would set you back over a million.'

'So they both thought they were putting the world to rights, but being greedy at the same time. How did Charity know Sheila?'

Randall crossed his legs. 'Well, that's an interesting one. You remember the deaths of Charity's family?'

'Yes.'

'Well, it turns out that Sheila gave her some bereavement counselling. I don't know how close they became, but it's possible that Charity confided in Sheila about her childhood at the time – we don't know what was going on in that cottage leading up to the deaths. I think that Charity probably mentioned how she was an unhappy child, which touched a nerve in Sheila. When the two met up in Dubai, they renewed their acquaintance. Sheila, after seeing Tracy at the hotel with Daisy, probably remembered what Charity had told her about her own childhood. And then, when Charity came across Tracy and Daisy in the supermarket, she would have been upset by what she saw and gone straight to Sheila. Being someone who felt she could put the world to rights, Sheila set about finding a family whom she believed would love little Daisy and bring her up in a wealthy and secure environment. False papers, a new identity. All so much simpler when an American family repatriate after working abroad, having adopted a little girl while away. It would all have worked out if Violet hadn't interfered.'

'Have you found the woman who was trying to buy a child?'

'We're trying but it might be very difficult to prove. There are hundreds of Americans in the two Palm resorts. Plenty of childless ones or women who might like a pretty little daughter as they might want a Hermes bag.'

In spite of the grim tone of the conversation Martha smiled. 'I didn't know you were in to expensive handbags, Alex.'

The look he gave was very straight and honest. 'There's a lot you don't know about me, Martha.'

And she had no response to this except to watch as he left, the door swinging behind him.

Lightning Source UK Ltd.
Milton Keynes UK
UKOW04f2313231017
311521UK00001B/15/P